After graduating from Durham University, Colin Reed spent some time in the Navy before embarking on a career in teaching. After a variety of teaching positions in the Middle East and East Africa, he returned to the UK, where he taught English at a comprehensive school. Married with children and grandchildren, he now resides in Whitby, on the North Yorkshire coast.

ALL MANNER OF THINGS

The sequel to
TO REASON WHY and TIES OF BLOOD

Just before his departure for the desert
campaign, newly commissioned John
Wright marries his college sweetheart,
Jenny. Their already fragile union, daily
threatened by the London Blitz, is shaken
by his long absence, leaving Jenny
vulnerable as she enters the exciting
world of Bletchley Park. John's brother,
Teddy, becomes a POW after Dunkirk.
His estranged but loyal wife, Marian, left
at home with their little daughter, must
also confront a lonely future. These
enforced absences take their toll on both
Jenny and Marian and their fidelity is
cruelly tested. The boys' mother, May,
widowed in the First World War, prays
that tragedy will not rob her of those she
loves for a second time.

Books by C. W. Reed
Published by The House of Ulverscroft:

TO REASON WHY
TIES OF BLOOD

C. W. REED

ALL MANNER OF THINGS

Complete and Unabridged

ULVERSCROFT
Leicester

First published in Great Britain in 2001 by
Robert Hale Limited
London

First Large Print Edition
published 2002
by arrangement with
Robert Hale Limited
London

British Library CIP Data

Reed, C.W. (Colin W.)
All manner of things.—Large print ed.—
Ulverscroft large print series: family saga
1. World War. *1939 – 1945*—Social aspects—England
—London—Fiction 2. Mothers and sons—Fiction
3. Domestic fiction 4. Large type books
I. Title
823.9′14 [F]

ISBN 0–7089–4758–1

Published by
F. A. Thorpe (Publishing)
Anstey, Leicestershire

Set by Words & Graphics Ltd.
Anstey, Leicestershire
Printed and bound in Great Britain by
T. J. International Ltd., Padstow, Cornwall

This book is printed on acid-free paper

In memory of Margy and Ron Horsley

'Let not man glory in this that he loves his country, but let him rather glory in this, that he loves his kind.'

(Bahá'u'lláh).

Part I

Miles To Go

1

May Wright smiled with relief at the blessed sound of the bell clanging. She pushed herself up from the wooden bench, painted a dingy chocolate brown like all the woodwork in the tiny waiting room, and went out on to the platform. The engine chuffed in fussily. Not one of your streamlined mainline monsters, but a panting little locomotive not much bigger than the colliery tank engines that pulled the pit wagons about. Still, it released an impressive enough cloud of steam as it hissed to a halt, wreathing the already grey platform in a dense and pungent fog, which rolled and cleared slowly.

'Hexham!' Mr Nicholson bellowed, unnecessarily, May thought. There was hardly likely to be anyone on this three-carriage train out of Newcastle who wouldn't know the location. Then, as if to refute her thought, a knot of figures clad in enveloping khaki greatcoats came tumbling out in a tangle of kitbags and knapsacks and rifles, and the war was, as always, unavoidably there, with the reminder that all station names had been removed. Mind you, you didn't have to be a

3

Mata Hari to make out the letters which could still be traced beneath the green paint slapped over them on the wooden seats.

She saw the imposing figure of Iris loom through the disappearing wraiths of smoke from one of the few first class compartments at the front of the first carriage. 'They put them there so that if there's a crash we get rid of a few more toffs first!' The sound of her younger son's voice sounded so suddenly and so clearly inside her head that May felt her mouth corners twitch in an involuntary smile. Had he really said that at some time or other? It was very likely. It was just the sort of remark the young Bolshie would make. Or was this part of the endless reels of fantasy taking place inside her head these days?

She had such vivid moments of conversation. Not only with Teddy, who was a POW in France, or maybe already in, or on his way to, Germany, but with Jack, her long-dead husband, killed in the war before this one. The war to end all wars. Even her mam's voice came through loud and clear at times, and she'd been dead five years now.

They populated her nightly dreams, too, with a clarity she hadn't known for years. Even her darling Jack, whom she hadn't dreamt about no matter how much she'd longed to, since that one night — she still had a mystical, secret feeling after all this time that it was more than just a dream — when he had told her to give up that desperate refusal to accept the fact of his death. She had clung to the hopeless doubt provided in the phrase 'missing presumed killed' for agonizing weeks, burying and shunning that part of her that knew what they told her was the truth. His life had been obliterated, his body fragmented, in a fraction of a second on a day when she was going about her work entirely unaware that the man who was the most important part of her life had already gone from her for good.

Maybe she was a 'receiver', she mocked at herself wryly. That was what Maggy Ray, who had lived two streets away from Sidney Terrace in Gateshead, her girlhood home, had called herself. Chattily passing on messages from the known and unknown dead to all and sundry in the neighbourhood, like an operator at a busy telephone exchange. Or maybe it was something to do with the change, that dreaded milestone which, in her forty-seventh year, must surely lurk round a not too distant corner for her now?

For her dearest friend also, who came striding with her usual dreadnought energy, bearing down on her, arms outstretched and ruddy face wreathed in a loving smile so at odds with the elegant sombreness of the black mourning she was wearing.

'Have you been waiting long, you poor thing? Oh, God! Am I glad to see you, darling!' They hugged, May's face was tickled by the damp fur draped over the bulky shoulders, and scratched by the caught up veil of the chic little hat poised on the crimped, iron-grey curls.

It was the second time in recent months that May had seen her friend in the stylish outfit and again she was struck by the unaccustomed impressiveness of the large figure. Imposing: the severe lines of the clothing, the smart, heeled shoes emphasizing the height which could carry, in this garb, the weight which she had put on over the past two decades. Certainly different from her usual casual wear of baggy slacks and careless jumpers.

'How was it?' May asked, when she had extricated herself from Iris's smothering embrace, and, arm in arm, they made their way to the narrow exit and the cobbled forecourt.

Iris grimaced. 'Rather quiet, really. Small church, so we looked a crowd. Bertie tells me we're going to have to do it all again. They're having a memorial service up at the cathedral in a week or two.' She shook the fur wrapped around her neck. 'Be getting the smell of moth balls well and truly out of this old thing if we keep this up.'

She had just travelled down to the distant south, to attend her father's funeral. Sir Nicholas Mayfield had been one of the industrial barons of the north-east in former times, with a thriving timber business, and shares in both coal mines and shipping. He had retired around twelve years ago, in the late Twenties, after suffering increasing problems with his heart. 'Didn't know he had one,' Iris had quipped ungenerously, when he had used his illness as an excuse not to attend her wedding to May's brother-in-law, Dan Wright, in 1929. Sir Nicholas and his wife, Mary, had lived a comparatively reclusive life for one so deeply involved hitherto in local business and political life. They had settled in a village near Bournemouth, and, in spite of his illness, Sir Nicholas had outlived his wife by four years and more.

'I've got a cab for us,' May said, leading her over to where the solid black Austin was waiting. Frank Leeson, the local owner and now sole driver of the business, nodded in polite friendliness.

'Thank God!' Iris sighed, eyes rolling. 'I couldn't walk another step in these shoes!'

The last time May had seen her in this

sadly distinguished regalia had been for the funeral of Iris's husband, less than four months previously. And what a simmering time of repressed emotions that had been. Poor Dan! May could think that, even then, in the midst of that charged feeling, though she couldn't say it to his widow. Dan had been one of the first fatalities of the night bombing raids which had begun back in September, about the same time that the daily and nightly attacks on the capital had started — the Blitz, as the papers were now referring to it. And it was not only in London, though they had suffered more than most. Two months ago Coventry had been bombed, its beautiful fourteenth-century cathedral destroyed, hundreds killed. Probably far more than the papers let on. 'Like a bombarded French town', was how the *Herald* described it, in a reference to those other years of mad violence which had so devastated May's personal life.

There was a savage irony in the fact that Dan should come through the untold horrors of that war, only to end up a victim of its successor. And in such shoddy, sordid circumstances. Not fighting for king and country, but found in the ruins of a lodging house in Jesmond, naked in bed with a married woman. A woman, it came out later, in whispered family scandal, he had been carrying on with for years, long before he had married Iris.

May still didn't know whether the details of Dan's disgrace were known to his mother, the formidable matriarch of the clan, Sophia. It was almost impossible to believe she could not know, with the shocked, scandalized, sniggering whispers that flew around them. It was never mentioned in her presence, not even by the bitterly distraught Iris, and Sophia never let on, by word or gesture. At the funeral she stood there, at seventy still slim and erect, flanked by her only surviving son, Joe, her daughter, Cissy, and her two daughters-in-law. Surely she must have wondered at its discreetly muted atmosphere, the smallness of the congregation, for Dan had been a bluff, gregarious drinker at his club and other hostelries both fashionable and unfashionable about the district. But she passed no comment, shed no tears either, in public. Even Iris, scourged and humiliated as she was, lacked vengeful spite enough to say anything.

Iris had moved back into the cottage she and May had shared for ten years, the original site of The Tea Cosy, the café they had established together, a business May had built up, and which was still operating successfully in the high street of the market town, despite the increasing exigencies of the war. The cake shop had all but fallen by the wayside, for sugar had been one of the first commodities to be rationed a year ago, when 'the phoney war' was still in existence. But the ladies of the town still liked to congregate in its genteel ambience, and Mr Lord, the dairy farmer who supplied The Tea Cosy's needs, could be carelessly generous for a price.

May felt guilty at the pleasure she took from Iris's moving back in with her. Though she had been an enthusiastic advocate of Iris's marriage to Dan, delighted for both her closest friends, she had missed her more than she cared to admit, especially after John and Teddy had both left home. Of course, Iris did not go far away. Only just down the road to Corbridge, and they still met almost every day, but May had to admit, though only to herself, that it was not the same.

She missed the companionable silences when they lounged, feet up after a hard day, the boys packed off to bed. The nightly mugs of cocoa round the kitchen range, and listening to the nine o'clock news before they went up to bed. The innocent comfort of a warm, snuggling body to share the bed. A loved partner whose steadfastness had helped her to rebuild a life in danger of remaining shattered after Jack's death.

And now it was she who could repay all that love and concern, after the double blow of loss and betrayal which Iris suffered at her husband's demise. Her arms had been open for the wounded tears which no one else had seen.

The help, Ruby, called out an affectionate greeting when they got back to the cottage, and Iris headed gratefully upstairs to climb out of her 'sad rags' and into a hot bath, for she had spent all night and half the previous day travelling from the distant south.

'We didn't even touch London,' she called out to May as she wriggled thankfully out of the restricting corset. 'Stood for hours in a siding near Reading somewhere, in pitch black, of course. They even put the carriage lights out. Not that you can see to do anything with those silly blue pin-point things. Make everyone look like ghastly corpses! And the train crammed with military types. Couldn't even go for a pee without turfing three or four of them out of the lavs!'

'Stay and chat,' Iris urged, slipping off her dressing gown and stepping into the water May had run for her. May saw the red marks on the white skin where the undergarment had dug into the flesh. Substantial flesh, May could not help but observe as Iris climbed into the tub and lowered herself luxuriously. May felt her face pink a little, glanced quickly away, acknowledging the touch of prudery in herself that made her do so. She thought of the portrait of herself hanging on the bedroom wall. Nude. Jack had begun it on their honeymoon, just a pencil sketch, which he had worked on later and framed. 'Never be ashamed, May!' he had said.

It was ridiculous, she knew, that she should feel embarrassed. Especially with Iris, after all the years they had spent together; dressed and undressed, slept together, in each other's arms half the night. Yet she always half turned, pulling on her clothes, hid her body when she could. It was a natural reaction, going back to the earliest days of childhood that she could remember, when the humbleness of her surroundings forced a lack of privacy.

The terraced house in Sidney Terrace had held seven of them. Her ma and pa, and her four siblings and herself. Though she was the oldest, she had at one time shared a bedroom, and a bed, with her sister, Julia, and her two brothers. By the time her youngest brother, Jimmy, was born, she was twelve, and soon afterwards she and Julia were given a room of their own, while the two brothers slept in a long, sloping kind of cupboard under the stairs. Little Jimmy, of course, stayed in with Mam and Dad.

Modesty in such circumstances was strictly enforced. You dressed behind a makeshift screen. On the girls' bath night, the kitchen was strictly out of bounds for the boys, while she wallowed in splendour in the zinc tub before the glowing, blackleaded range, screened off for extra seemliness by the standing, draped clothes-horse.

Now, May perched on the cork-topped stool while Iris lay back, savouring the soothing enfolding of the warm water around her travel-weary limbs. 'I think I'm going to be a fairly wealthy woman. From what Bertie was saying. There's a fair bit left. He's in the process of sorting it out with the solicitors now. Daddy was never what you'd call extravagant. And he lived even quieter after Mummy died. Poor old thing.'

May was well aware that Iris's relationship with her father had been stormy to say the least in the past, especially when she was much younger. The meeting which had led to this abiding friendship was indicative enough of that. The daughter of the industrialist had just heaved a brick through the labour exchange window in Gateshead to further the cause of women's suffrage when May had come across her being harassed by an angry crowd and an embarrassed bobby.

'The gallant chippy's daughter' was the way Sir Nicholas had sarcastically referred to his daughter's rescuer and friend, Iris had told her long afterwards. It had been hard for him to swallow, her alliance with the offspring of a shipyard worker, and he had never digested it properly. He had never been able to decide which was worse: the fact that the two women had chosen to live together and run a tea-shop or that, subsequently, Iris had chosen to marry her partner's brother-in-law, and at an age when, approaching forty, she should at last have begun to know better.

It was with deep private sorrow that May had watched the marriage of the two people she cared most for after her own sons gradually erode, until Dan was drinking far too much, as he had when he had returned badly crippled from the war, and spending far too many nights away from home. It was sad that, close as they were, Iris seemed unable to discuss her marital problems with May, beyond the curt and scathing references to Dan's drinking habits and his frequent absences. 'P'raps he's got a floozy somewhere on the side!' Iris quipped cynically once, as though she couldn't care less. She was devastated when, at his death, this was proved to be true.

Since Iris's return to the cottage, she had occupied what had been known in those happier days of the Twenties as 'Dan's room', for when he came out from Gateshead in his bachelor days to pay one of his regular visits while the boys were growing up. So this unlooked for intimacy in the steamy January chill of the bathroom was even more special. It assumed the air of the confessional as Iris sat up and began the business of washing herself.

'I've been doing a lot of thinking while I've been away,' she said, her eyes not meeting with May's. 'Most of it painful. I know I haven't been very forthcoming, and I know how splendidly you've coped with me since I got here.' She gave a sad little laugh. 'I nearly said came home, then.' Now she did glance up at May, with that shy, tender expression May recognized so well.

She sighed deeply, continued with an effort. 'I've been less than honest really, as far as Dan's concerned. You know, our married life was never that great. I mean — the physical side of things.' She paused, and they both sat, gripped in the sudden embarrassment which held them. 'That wasn't what motivated us, I know,' she resumed quickly, with another ashamed laugh. 'Certainly not for me. Nor for Dan, either. Except, well — it mattered to him, more than I realized. He was — you know, perfectly normal — I mean, in spite of his wound.' She blundered on, red-faced, suffering but determined. 'What I'm saying is, I wasn't — I never — did my wifely duties. Not properly — not enough . . .'

May gazed at her in helpless compassion. 'I'm sure — Dan did love you — what-ever . . .'

Iris shook her head, heaved herself up out of the water, her body now pink and gleaming, little sworls of steam arising from her. May passed her the towel and she wrapped her bulk in it gratefully. 'I'm not saying it was right, what he did,' Iris said, as she swung out of the water to stand dripping on the mat. 'But I know I've been bitchy and hard to live with these past weeks. Old Dan was no saint. But neither am I!'

She sniffed back the choking tears, gave her brave smile. 'There now! I've had my say. Sorry for playing the martyr for so long. You have my permission to kick my backside hard if I ever do it again. Now! Tell me what's been happening? Any more news of Teddy yet? And what about John? Has he got himself on that officers' training course? Have they fixed a date for the wedding?'

May held out her arms and hugged the damp figure to her, their faces pressed close. 'Welcome back, love. It's so good to have you home again!'

2

'For Christ's sake try to look relaxed!' John Wright hissed to his squad sitting tensely under the canvas cover of the light truck. 'If they stop us, just pile out and make a run for it.'

His stomach was tight, his heart thumping, but with excitement rather than fear. It's all just a silly game, he kept telling himself, as he had throughout the weeks of the arduous course. And it was, most of it. Apart from the physical jerks, and the runs through the dim grey blanket of Scottish dawn mists, and the wearying foot slog of the route marches. The discussions and the lectures you had to give — come out the front and pick a piece of folded paper with a topic written on it, and talk for at least three minutes — were just like being back at school. So were these initiative tasks; divided into six-man squads, one of you appointed leader for the day, addressing one another only by numbers. 'Right, Number One and Number Three. Get that barrel over there. Number Four, lash that rope to the end there!' Pretending that the fastflowing, foot-deep Highland stream was a bottomless gorge, or the tussocky slope lethally dotted with mines.

But at least it was different from the mind-numbing bullshit of basic training, with its endless freezing hours on the parade ground, the endless kit and hut and weapon inspections, the endless hours of fag-puffing, beer-swigging sex talk in the bleak NAAFI hut, evening after endless evening. The only escape he had was to settle himself in the corner of the hut they laughingly called the Reading Room, with his writing pad and his snapshots of Jenny.

'Sod me, Schooly! You're not writing to that party of yours again, are you? You'll have sweet FA to say when you see her again if you don't watch it.' Then the look of dripping lechery, the lascivious wink. 'Still, you won't be interested in talking, eh? Not when you can get to grips with it! And she'll be steaming for it all right after all that pash you scribble away to her. Dirty bastard!'

The idea of returning to a duration of such a lifestyle was enough to spur on any waning ambition. At least his fellow entrants on the officers' selection board, or OSB, as the course was familiarly known, didn't have their thought processes permanently linked to their bollocks.

Several of them were not too happy with

him as leader for this final task, though. 'Stealing a bloody truck. Impersonating an officer. We'll be in jankers for the rest of the war!'

'Not our responsibility, chaps.' Number One, Frank Hughes, at twenty-seven the oldest candidate, was a schoolmaster like himself. And quite sanguine about the whole business. 'John's leader. We simply do what he tells us. That's the most important thing about the art of soldiering. Keep your head down, your mouth shut, and obey orders. When the shit hits the fan John will be the sole recipient.'

'Thanks, mate,' John answered dryly. He adjusted the purloined captain's cap, squared his shoulders with the three illicit pips on the blouse. 'Here's the bridge. Get ready.'

He held his breath, tapped Number Two's knee, who slowed down, staring straight ahead like a frightened rabbit. There was a staff car parked at the far end of the hump-backed bridge, two or three OR's lounging against it. The row of figures, with the blue arm-bands of adjudicators, were all leaning over the low stone parapet, staring eagerly downstream. One turned back briefly, glanced at the vehicle, then directed his gaze back at the tumbling water. They eased past the stationary car, Number Two admirably controlling his desire to put his foot down and gun the motor, and they were away.

Next day, up before the four members of the selection board, John was sure he had blown his chances of gaining a commission. 'No one actually told us that we couldn't use the bridge to cross the river,' John argued. He could feel the sweat gathering at his rough collar. 'It seemed like a sensible idea, as it was there.'

The most junior officer of the panel, Captain Ormesby, only half hid his twitch of amusement.

'And stealing army transport. Good God, man! You could have got you and your whole squad shot if you'd been challenged!' John thought of the devious and costly preparations he had made with the driver at the training camp. Two quid for him to sit drinking in the Tigh na Truish and look the other way while they pinched his truck.

'I understood we were supposed to use our initiative, sir,' John risked answering. 'We did succeed in breaking through the cordon and getting back to our lines.'

'By breaking every bloody rule in the book,' the lieutenant colonel muttered sourly. 'You even took your arm bands off.'

'We didn't actually take them off, sir. We were wearing them — under our battledress.'

The blistering look he received in reply convinced John of the futility of further argument. He stood smartly, stomped his foot and stiffened to attention before whirling about and stamping his way out. 'Bags of swank,' as the drill sergeant had said. That was what they wanted. He was sure he had failed.

Never mind. He was disappointed, but nothing could really dismay him, with the thought of a glorious 'forty-eight' before reporting back to the base camp at Catterick. He expected that it would be days if not weeks before he learned the result of the course.

He was already packed, ready for his final night in the bleak highland site, when Captain Ormesby sent for him.

'All strictly on the QT, Wright, but you'll be pleased, and surprised maybe, to learn that you've passed. Well done. It won't come through officially for a while, but I don't see why you lads shouldn't know the score.'

He didn't add that John's success was in large measure due to his personal intervention on his behalf, for the board was divided on this borderline case. 'If you ask me, Wright showed a lot more gumption than most of the others. And more imagination. He bent the rules all right. But war's no longer conducted according to the rules. We're learning that every day. All of us, civilians and all, with this blitzkrieg.' His senior officer didn't like it much, but his eloquence persuaded the others to come down in favour of Private Wright.

Captain Ormesby had informed the other successful candidates, so there were at least four others who were equally delighted as they bounced their way along the narrow roads leading down to Oban in the back of a three-tonner. Even the rest of the intake, failures by inference, following their lack of communication with Ormesby, weren't too despondent as they picked the white shoulder tabs from their shoulders. Not with a forty-eight-hour leave to rejoice in.

★ ★ ★

John sat in the waiting room of Carlisle station, huddling down as far as his nose into his greatcoat, the collar turned up about his ears. A freezing February night had already descended, and the feeble, hooded light of the blackout-curtained room made reading a squinting, irksome task. In contrast with the bitter weather, the news was determinedly cheerful. In North Africa all was going well. The RAF had carried out bombing raids on

Tripoli, and British and Commonwealth forces were poised to capture Benghazi. If the present successes continued, the desert campaign might well be over before he had a chance to be posted.

But thoughts on the war were only a distraction, and not very effective. He felt the well-recognized knotting of his stomach, the butterfly fluttering as the time of meeting drew nearer. He had not seen Jenny for over four months, though he had written at least a paragraph or two almost every day of their separation. They had spoken four times on the telephone, far less satisfying than their communication on paper, though it was wonderful to hear her tinnily distorted voice: sweetness and pain in the crackling, rushing sighs and the choked back tears he could hear, the desperate 'love yous' before he forced himself to put the phone down. It reminded him, again bitter-sweetly, of his final, lonely year at college, after Jenny had left. 'You hang up first.' 'No. You.'

It was strange. Since joining up, the daily letters in which he had poured out his deepest feelings for her, and she to him in the thick, scented bundles he was always overjoyed to receive, brought them closer than ever in tenderness. It shocked him, therefore, to think that in the past two and a half years, almost, he had been with her for only two days, and that, if it hadn't been for that frantic dash across to Keswick back in September, just before he went into the army, she would not be a part of his life again. Not a part, he corrected himself, the linchpin of his existence.

But she had always been that, even after the breaking off of the engagement, and all through the aridity of the two years that followed. He couldn't understand, looking back, how stupidly he had behaved. Why he had allowed that eternity to pass, without making every frantic effort he was capable of to win her back. How could she possibly believe the strength of the love he claimed for her when he had sat back and done absolutely nothing to make the world right again?

The argument that she had done nothing, either, was irrelevant. She claimed that she was no longer worthy of him, but it seemed now to him that his inertia had been a colossal act of folly. If it had not been for the catalyst of his call-up, and, he acknowledged, his mother's encouragement, he would not have made that spontaneous gesture of his innermost feeling and gone unannounced to Jenny's home; would never perhaps have found that she, like him, was still deeply loving, and grieving her loss.

The chewing nervousness he was now experiencing was still connected to that fateful night. Stunned as well as thankful at the dramatic way their lives had come together again, and all too aware of the painful cause of the break-up, they had shied away from it. John had bravely attempted to sweep it aside. 'We're together again. That's all that matters now.' Brave words, and almost true. But the shadow of their infidelity to each other was like a sword. Shyly, tenderly, they had sought to ignore it, and she had wept with gratitude for his determination to do so. And yet it was there, more painfully apparent when, separate again, he had time to reflect upon it, in the almost shy way they had kissed and held each other. Even in the firelit solitude after her welcoming parents had left them, on the sofa where their passion had, in earlier, happier times, been held in check only with difficulty, she sat almost primly while he sat at her feet, leaning back against her knees and holding her palm gently to his cheek. The threat of death seemingly unreal, he planned their future, while turning steadfastly from the swordlike past, which he vowed would never be a threat again.

He was waiting when she stepped from the train, ready to hold her, weeping, in his arms.

She had a small overnight case. A blue beret was pulled down fetchingly over her right eye. Her belted dark winter coat emphasized her slimness, her smart heeled shoes and dark silk stockings gave her a sophisticated look. In his coarse army uniform, the tent-like overcoat that flapped about his gaitered ankles, the ugly forage cap, he felt clumsy and uncouth.

'I have an address,' Jenny said, looking bravely at him but unable to keep the blood from flooding into her face. 'I got it from a girl at the WVS. She says it's all right. In Campion Street. It's not far. I think we can walk. I've got a torch.'

He pulled her close. 'Listen,' he said tensely, 'we don't have to. If you don't want — we can just wait here. In the buffet. And then there's the waiting room. There's a milk train . . . ' He had telephoned his mother, told her that he, and Jenny, would arrive some time on Saturday.

Her eyes held him. He saw the love in them. And the pain, too. 'No. I want to. I want to spend the night — together. I want to belong to you. Properly.'

He kissed her again, saw the tears in her eyes. He swung his kitbag up on his shoulder, and she slipped her hand through his free arm.

There was a terrible moment at the

boarding house when the landlady, who had smiled kindly at them, asked to see Jenny's identity card. Jenny blushed. 'It's not in my married name,' she faltered.

The landlady's lips compressed. John swept up his pay book, blundered desperately into the fraught silence. 'Look. We're engaged. I swear — we're going to get married. As soon as we can. We're trying to fix it up.' The landlady blushed a little herself, but she pushed a key across at them.

John saw that look of misery, and uncertainty, again in Jenny's eyes when she turned to come into his arms in the chill loneliness of the clean bedroom. For a brief instant he felt a pure, knifing hate for the German, Horst Zettel, their former friend and mutual betrayer, for the cruel harm he had done them, and he was savagely glad that war had come to give a legitimacy to his hatred. Then compassion, and love, over-whelmed him as he saw Jenny's huge, tear-filled eyes. His fingers fumbled with the cloth-covered buttons at the back of her neck.

'It's all right,' he whispered hoarsely, and his mouth came down to claim her, and he believed with all his heart that what he said was true.

3

'It'll be all right.' He squeezed Jenny's hand. Her face did not lose its tension as she smiled brightly back at him. There were faint smudges of tiredness under her eyes, slightly darkened little patches which, he thought, only heightened her beauty. A subtle hint of decadence. It made his heart leap as he vividly recalled her unguarded nakedness against his, the unreserved way she had moved, coming up from sleep, already spreading, offering herself in the still dark early morning. He had tried to hold back his urgency, remembering her clenched pain the night before. He had felt it, heard it in her suppressed gasps. But this time, in the dawning, she was the one who had not held back, and afterwards, when he returned dizzily to awareness, with that unsure, wondering feeling, she had kept him to her, cried softly against him, and told him how completely happy she was.

The light from the rain-spotted window fell full on her. He had seen the tension etched more and more strongly on her the closer they got to their destination.

'It's going to be fine,' he repeated, keeping hold of her hand. He knew what she was going through. Sick with anxiety at the thought of meeting his mother again, after all this time. Over three years. 'Don't forget. It was Mam who pushed me into coming over to see you again.'

Another brave smile as she tried to match his mood. 'So. You can blame her for all the trouble you've landed in.' She returned the pressure of his interlaced fingers. The smile left her, she gazed solemnly at him. 'I'll always be grateful to her for that,' she all but whispered. 'I do love you, Johnny. I never stopped. I never will.'

★　★　★

May and Iris were waiting for them at the cottage, lunch already laid in the splendour of the dining room, instead of the homeliness of the kitchen. Ruby stood there, too, pinafored and proud of the substantial spread they had managed to put on, in spite of the fact that by this new year of 1941 most goods were rationed, or limited by the new points system.

'I hope you're not into this black market everyone's talking about,' John teased them, as much to help dispel the tension as anything. But May had come quickly

30

forward, closely followed by Iris, and both had embraced Jenny in an enveloping hug that nearly took the breath out of her. It was a declaration of their faith in her future with John far more eloquent than any words, and she found herself wet-eyed with gratitude.

'It's so good to see you again,' she said, and found, right from that first unexpected minute, that she meant it.

They had already got the news of John's success on the OSB, so there was a doubly celebratory air about the reunion. After the leisurely meal, John and Jenny were planning to take a walk, but the sky closed in, with heavy, slate-grey cloud, and soon volleys of thick sleet were rattling and sliding down the windows, and it was so dark they had to light the lamps in the drawing room. 'We'll not draw the curtains. It's not blackout time yet.'

Iris lumbered up to pour more coffee. 'Never mind. Perhaps it means the siren won't go tonight.'

'They've been going every night,' May answered to John's query. He had already noted the bucket of water and the coiled stirrup-pump beside it by the kitchen door. 'I'm almost wishing we'd get a fire-bomb Fritz just to try it out. We're dab hands at the drill, aren't we, Iris?'

'We don't usually bother going to the

shelter,' Iris told them. There was a microsecond of awkwardness, which John picked up on, before Iris's hearty tones flowed on. Her husband, his Uncle Dan, would still be alive today if he had heeded the siren's warning and gone down to the cellar to join the other residents of the large house in Jesmond, instead of remaining in bed in his rented room with his inamorata.

Out here in the country, it was different. 'It always sounds a lot worse than it is. It's mostly our guns going off. They're putting up so many of these anti-aircraft batteries now, especially at the coast. You can hardly get to the sea at all now, unless you go way up north. They've had a few goes at the yards, and Armstrong's. But it's mostly just Jerries flying inland, then coming out again before dawn. Regular as clockwork, usually. Ten, half ten at night, then the all-clear round three a.m. What's it like over in Keswick?'

'Pretty quiet,' Jenny offered.

The talk drifted round to a more personal angle, as both the young people knew it would. 'Will you be able to stay in your job?' May asked Jenny. Everyone was anticipating that Ernest Bevin, the minister for labour, would be announcing some form of conscription for women any day now. 'Surely teaching's too important to take people out of? Especially now, with so many of the men called up,' she added feelingly, and John gave an embarrassed little laugh, for he knew how badly she had felt about his being taken away from schoolmastering, into the army.

'Well, I dunno,' Jenny answered diffidently. 'I really wouldn't mind going into one of the services. Doing my bit.'

There was another awkward pause, then May said bravely, 'They won't take married women, surely?'

John knew he had to speak into the silence. 'We are going to get married. As soon as we can. Probably when I finish the training course. It's sixteen weeks, I think.'

'The sooner the better,' May declared, so decisively that he was moved with love and thankfulness. He flashed Jenny a quick, conspiratorial smile.

'With you having such a short time, I didn't make any plans,' his mother continued. 'I mean, I thought you'd just want to stay here. Marian sends her love, of course.' Marian was his sister-in-law, the girl his brother, Teddy, had reluctantly married after getting her pregnant. Their little girl was four now. 'She's coping really well. We try to get over to see her at least once a week. We've been on at her to move in with us for a bit, haven't we, Iris? But she says Low Fell's just as quiet. It's far enough out of town. And she's that bit nearer her mam. And there's our Julia's lot, of course,' she added even more grudgingly, referring to her younger sister. 'Dora still stays over with her a lot of the time.' Dora was Julia's oldest child. 'She'll be eighteen in July. She's working in the ordnance factory at Birtley now.' She shook her head. 'I wouldn't let a daughter of mine do that. Far too dangerous, even if it is good money.'

'Mam!' John laughingly protested. 'You did exactly the same, at Armstrong's. And you were already married! Teddy and me were already on the scene!'

A suddenly vivid picture of the huge shed, with the row on row of pointed missiles standing like monoliths, came into May's mind. The incessant noise, the pulleys and the chains, on which the overalled women clung and went whizzing over the upended cones of the lethal projectiles. The odious Harry Turnbull's face — the realization that he was Marian's father always gave her something of a shock — as he came towards her through the racket on the shop-floor. Cissy's tear-streaked face awaiting her in the manager's office, that froze her heart in her belated recognition of its terrible import.

The clarity of her recall startled her.

Twenty-four years ago. She smiled tenderly. 'That was different. Anyway, you're a teacher. You know the old saying. 'Do as I say, not as I do'. I didn't stick it very long,' she added softly.

The winter evening closed in early, before they had tea, which they took balanced on their knees, in front of the blazing log fire, with the blackout curtains secured, and the inner, flowered drapes pulled across. The frequent spatter of sleet on the panes added to the insulated comfort they shared.

'I've put Jenny in your room,' May said, when, shortly after ten, she stretched and yawned elaborately. 'You can go in the front.' She still had to make a conscious effort not to call it Dan's room. 'Iris is moving in with me.'

Iris took her cue and followed suit, beginning to collect the cups. 'Unless she kicks me out for my snoring. She can still hear me even across the landing, she reckons!' She beamed fondly at the couple sitting closely together on the sofa. 'And what did I tell you? Even Jerry's behaving himself and staying indoors on such a foul night!' So far the rise and fall of the siren had not materialized.

'Build the fire up if you like,' May told them after she had given them both a last hug. 'You'll sit up half the night anyway, I'm sure. Even though you'll regret it in the morning.' She turned in the doorway, with a shy, vulnerable look. 'It is good to see you two together again. Goodnight and God bless. And don't worry about us disturbing you. Once we're up those stairs that's it.'

'Night, Mam. Aunt I.' He put another log on the red fire, then held out his arms, and they sank down together on to the cushions on the sofa. He let his hand run up over the silk of her stocking, under the hem of her skirt, until he could feel the cool skin of her thigh and the elastic suspender strap. He nuzzled into her thick hair. 'I don't know if it's just my dirty mind, but I have the distinct feeling Mam was more or less giving us carte blanche just then, don't you?'

She lifted her head from his chest, twisting her neck round to look directly at him. Her expression was solemn, almost anxious. 'Do you want to make love?' she asked. He was taken aback, and before he could answer, she went on, 'I'll have to go and kit up,' she said, nodding towards the door. 'I haven't got it in. I wasn't — I'm quite sore . . . ' She blushed, faltered, and he hugged her into him again.

He knew she was referring to the diaphragm she had worn the previous night, during their first sexual intercourse. Their first together. But not their first ever. He tried valiantly to banish that thought, with its deep and abiding sadness. Horst Zettel had seduced her. John accepted that, had forgiven her, if that was the right word, more easily than she had forgiven herself. She never had, really. Just as he would never forgive himself for his own loss of virginity, also engineered by the young German, who had virtually placed him in bed with a German girl, Inge, during their drunken Berlin spree. A girl from whose bed he arose next morning, a polite, ashamed stranger, and whom he had never set eyes on again.

It was not the way either he or Jenny had always envisaged for their first consummation of their love, that fleshly union in the chill Carlisle boarding house. But they had come through the fire and ice of stark experience since the romantic rosiness of their student days at Durham. They were both still awed, and humbly grateful, that they were reunited after all that had happened.

Jenny had told him, embarrassed but bravely determined, of the mechanics of her contraception, and how she had made use of her knowledgeable friend in the WVS to be shown the technique of fitting the diaphragm, and the application of the spermicidal jelly. A severe blow for the romantic poet in John's nature. But he, too, had sacrificed sensibility and gone along to the sick-bay to acquire the prophylactic devices, as they called the rubber sheaths the orderly handed over with a knowing grin.

He had known their first time together would be tense, fraught with all the unspoken trauma of what each had suffered. But they were together again. This was what they had to keep telling themselves, and each other, through any embarrassment or shame, even. And love, as the truism confirmed, had indeed conquered.

He kissed her now. 'Don't go anywhere,' he whispered. He let his hands move, over skin and silk, exploring, sensual. 'Just let me love you . . . '

Again, she raised herself, and stared intently at him. 'Listen. The only thing I want — have ever wanted — is to belong to you. I do, now, truly. You know that.' As he was about to speak, she made a small, pleading sound, her hand moved towards his mouth as though asking for him to let her continue. 'I love you. But I really do want you to feel absolutely sure of me. After all that's happened. There's nothing I want more than to have your children — our children. But I don't want you ever to regret. Ever to feel you were trapped. Not like Teddy.'

'But I — '

She pressed against him, sought his mouth, stilled his protest, this time with her own lips. 'That's why I want you to have time,' she said, after they had kissed. She lay against him, settled herself with her head on his chest once more, so he felt the movement, the vibration of her words through him. 'That's why I got the diaphragm. Why I've been so clinical. Besides, we've got all our life together.'

There was another, longer pause, but he knew she was not finished, that she had something of equal import to add. 'I want to share my life with you. Everything with you.' Her voice was so small he had to strain almost to pick up her words clearly. 'I couldn't bear it — if anything happened — to keep us apart. What happened to your mother — being left alone — with you and Teddy. I couldn't bear that, Johnny. Our children are a part of you and me — we've got to be together. Do you understand?'

He felt her shaking, then she squirmed into him, as though she could never get close enough, and they clung to each other as she wept against him.

4

'Hiya. You're not off out anywhere, are ye? Alf's on back shift, and it's turned out such a nice day, I'd thought I'd have a walk along. Mebbes we're shot of winter at last, eh?' Julia Dale unknotted her headscarf and shook out her brown curls. She slipped off her winter coat, then bent and eased off her muddy ankle boots while she was still standing on the front door mat.

Marian Wright took the coat and scarf from her and hung them on the hallstand. 'No, I'm glad you called. I was just going to put the kettle on. Teddie's out the back. It's so nice I thought I'd let her play in the garden for a bit. She'll be up to the eyes by now, I expect.' She went through into the square kitchen, and Julia followed her, padding in a pair of her husband's grey socks whose toes flopped comically like flippers ahead of her. They ended at mid-calf where the dark brown lisle stockings showed below the thick, serviceable dark skirt.

'I didn't bother getting dressed up,' Julia said, gesturing at the old red jumper she wore. She groped in her handbag, pulled out a paper five-packet of Wild Woodbine, offered a cigarette to Marian, who took it with a guilty smile.

'Thanks. I shouldn't, really. I've been trying to cut down, but these days, what with the air raids and all that. And worry about Teddy. You know.' She lit the gas under the kettle then sat down opposite Julia at the small table where, unless there was company, they had all their meals.

Julia screwed up her face as she put a match to the thin cigarette, then offered it across to the younger woman. 'Have you heard any more from him? Have they moved them yet?' The cigarette bobbed at her lips as she spoke.

Marian shook her head. The blonde strands escaping from the thin green scarf bound in a narrow turban about her head looked dark and lank. 'Nothing for nearly a month now. Not from the army either. Or the Red Cross. Nobody seems to know anything.'

Julia grimaced in sympathy. 'Never mind, Kidder. You'll be hearing summat soon, I bet. How's our Dora? D'ye know, I haven't seen her at all this week? I presume the young madam is staying here, is she?'

Marian nodded apologetically. 'Oh aye. Of course. She's putting in a lot of overtime. She didn't get in till after eight last night. They're long shifts. Over twelve hours. I don't know how they do it.'

'Aye, well.' Julia frowned, blew out a plume of smoke which hung in the sunlight over their heads. 'There's more than munitions making goes on there, I reckon! I hope she doesn't get herself into trouble.'

Marian felt her face grow hot. She was still deeply sensitive about her own history, especially where her in-laws were concerned. She was sure they still believed she had deliberately set out to get herself pregnant to entrap Teddy. And, what hurt her even more, that it was somehow her fault that Teddy had deserted her immediately after the honeymoon to go off and fight in Spain. Their daughter, Edwina, little Teddie, was almost six months old before he ever saw her. After hardly a year at home with her, he had left again, this time to join the regular army, as though he were eager to embrace the conflict which so many people already believed was inevitable. They had been proved right soon enough. Teddy had been posted to France with the BEF, and captured during the rout that led to the 'miracle' of Dunkirk. She had wept with relief and happiness when she learnt that he was a POW, for she was convinced she had lost him forever.

She had to admit, though, that his mam,

May, had stuck by her right from the beginning, taking her side even against her own son when necessary. Marian had been so scared of her. Of the lot of them, but especially May, who had done so well for herself, running her own business, making a beautiful home for her and her two boys out at Hexham. She looked, and sounded, so nice, almost as posh as her closest friend, Teddy's Aunt I, who really was a toff, her parents a Sir and Lady, no less! No wonder Marian had been terrified. She still squirmed with inner embarrassment when she pictured herself in those early days, leading to the wedding, and afterwards, when Teddy had run off and left her pregnant and alone. His mam must have thought her practically a mental case, for Marian had scarcely been able to string two words together, she was so petrified. She turned beetroot red every time she opened her mouth.

But May Wright had been marvellous. It was she who had got them into this brand new house, which Marian loved and which she had thought would be heaven with her and Teddy and little Teddie living in it. Garden front and back, right on the edge of the town, with fields and cows at the end of the street. It was May who had kept Marian and the baby in it, after Teddy's desertion of them, for the irregular money he sent during his absence was not enough to keep up the mortgage repayments, never mind feed them.

Marian felt doubly guilty about her friendship with Julia Dale, May's younger sister, for Julia was rarely anything but scathing about May's achievements. Marian was even embarrassed to refer to her in Julia's presence. Normally, Marian called May 'mam', at May's insistence, and Marian had felt gratefully happy to do so. When talking to Julia, Marian always said, 'Teddy's mam', but it still never failed to bring that bitter sneering look on Julia's face. She said it now, with the same result.

'Teddy's mam was here yesterday.' Much to Marian's relief, May and Iris usually managed to avoid meeting up with Julia during their weekly visits over to Low Fell.

Julia sniffed expressively. 'Oh aye? I suppose Lady Muck was with her?'

Marian, knowing full well the derogatory term for Iris, nodded. 'They were asking after you,' she said uncomfortably.

'That's nice!' The sarcasm was unmistakable. 'They'll be happy as laddy, the pair of them now that they're back together again. Ye cannot blame that husband of hers for going elsewhere for his bit of what-you-call-it. Poor bugger didn't stand a chance with them two. I

44

tell ye, sometimes I wonder how they've got the brass neck for it, eh? Those toffs have some funny ways on them! Mind you, our May's just as bad, when ye think. She was always a deep one, even as a lass. I'm amazed her Jack ever got near enough to give her two bairns. It's no wonder she never let another feller near her after he was killed. Not with that lah-di-dah bitch getting her claws into her!'

'Oh, there's not — I'm sure they're not . . . ' Marian blushed deeply, her words petering out in the shocking face of the older woman's blatant hint of sexual deviation.

Julia grinned with mean delight at her embarrassment. 'Like I say, the upper crust, my dear! Rife with it, they are!' She changed the subject, with the happy feeling that she had scored a point. 'Well, ye can tell our Dora she can get her bloody self home this weekend, all right? It's my birthday on Monday.' She shook her cap of brown hair. 'Forty-two!' She let out an explosive sigh of disgust. 'I can't believe it. Where did it all go, eh?'

'You don't look anywhere near forty!' Marian said convincingly. It was true that, on the infrequent occasions when Julia got dressed up, she was still a smart woman. Considering that she'd had five children, three of whom, all girls, had survived, she still had a trim figure. But the years, most of them hard, for she was married to a pitman, had left their mark on her sharp face. Whether it was because of a superior lifestyle or no, Marian readily conceded that May, five years older, looked if anything younger than her sister.

Through the window, they saw the bundled figure of a little girl climb unsteadily up the steps of the Anderson shelter and emerge into the sunshine. The woollen pixy hood was askew, the pinned scarf trailing, the leggings under the tight coat spattered with mud. Twin gleaming trails of mucus showed at the nostrils. 'Oh, my God! Will you look at that?' Marian rose and hurried out, scooping Teddie up in her arms and going to work with a handkerchief.

Julia stood on the concrete path, in the doorway of the wooden extension to the side of the house through which you entered the garden. The cold struck up through the material of socks and stockings. 'By, you've got the garden looking grand. How long have you been in here now?'

'Four years. It was just after Teddie was born, wasn't it, pet lamb?' She rubbed her daughter's cold nose against her own. 'Come on, let's go in and get warm, eh? Do you want a wee-wee? Say hello to your Aunty Julia, look. She's come to see you.'

'Your great aunt!' Julia grimaced as they turned back inside. They passed through the kitchen and the small hallway, into the large, sun-filled living room. It ran the length of the house, with wide windows at both front and back. 'You've done a smashing job, I'll give ye that!' Julia said, looking about her at the neat room. 'The place is nipping clean.' Marian smiled and blushed at the compliment, shrugging modestly. 'Specially as you've had to manage on your own so much,' Julia added meaningfully. This time, Marian's colour was not from pleasure.

'Oh, it's not so bad,' she countered quickly. 'That's why — I've always enjoyed having Dora about. Teddie thinks she's like a second mam, don't you, sweetheart? And Mam's been good — May,' Marian amended hastily.

Once again, the eloquent sniff. 'Ye don't want to let them two ride roughshod over you, lass. They think they're the bee's knees, with their motor cars and their posh houses. Mind you,' she smiled mischievously, an arch look on her face, 'you're a bit that way yourself, aren't ye?' She gestured around her. 'This is posh enough. Laa Fell's snooty enough for most!' She gave the broad dialect a drawling exaggeration.

Marian laughed, still a little embarrassed. 'Not with this mucky little tyke. We can't be posh with you around, can we, eh?' She took a packet of cigarettes from the mantelpiece, offered one to Julia. 'Would you like another cup of tea?'

'Aye, go on then. Our Rosie'll let herself in from school. And Alice doesn't get back from work till six o'clock most nights. So, what's our May got to say for herself then? Have they made Master Johnny a general yet? I dunno, eh? Bloody officers in the family now! What are we coming to? And he's back with that posh lass again, isn't he? The one from the Lakes. He'll have to get in there quick if he wants to keep her this time.' She laughed coarsely. 'Get her up the spout, eh? Not that he'll know where to put it, poor lad. Not with our May bringing him up, that's for sure!'

Marian strove desperately to change the subject again. She felt somehow disloyal at hearing John disparaged thus by his aunt. She remembered how he, too, had so terrified her at first. A college student, with letters after his name, and then a schoolmaster at that private school in Corbridge. And such a quiet, gentleman's voice, even nicer spoken than her Teddy, who she knew often deliberately broadened his Tyneside accent, as though he was ashamed of his privileged upbringing. He made such a lot of his Grandad Raynor, and the solid working-class background of his mother's family.

John had seemed distant towards her, at first, though she came to realize that it was more his own shyness that made him seem reserved. Besides, she had scarcely opened her mouth at all during the time she had stayed with them at Hexham, while she was waiting for Teddie to be born. But since her marriage, and especially in the last two years since Teddy had gone into the army, and war had been declared, she had got to know John much better, and to feel more at ease with him. He had been so kind to her, driving over whenever he could, helping with any problems about the house — problems that would have been Teddy's responsibility, had he been here to see to them. Though she was still somewhat in awe of his pretty fiancée, Jenny, she felt quite relaxed in John's presence nowadays. She included him in her nightly prayers, along with her husband, and felt doubly sorry for May's anxiety now that he, like his brother, was in uniform.

She steered Julia on to a litany of complaint about her own household, and the shortcomings of her husband, Alf. 'Working all the hours God sends. And when he's not in-bye he's in the club or pub! Mind you, it makes a change to have a few coppers in me purse and he doesn't keep us short, thank God!' She chuckled with grim satisfaction. 'He wouldn't dare, the bugger! Not with the money he's making!'

★   ★   ★

It was dark, the heavy blackout curtains securely in place, and Julia long gone, before her eldest child, Dora, came in from her shift at the armaments factory in the neighbouring town of Birtley. Dora spent far more time at Low Fell than she did at her parents' house, one of a double row of miners' dwellings across from the colliery less than two miles away. Marian didn't mind having the extra, healthy mouth to feed, even though Dora's ration book remained at home with her mother. Julia was generous — she rarely failed to bring a carrier bag with some extra bits of foodstuff when she called — and so was her mother-in-law, who always came laden on her trips from Hexham in Iris's small car.

Dora, who would be eighteen in less than two months, had the almost elfin good looks that had characterized both her mother and her Aunt May, though, at the moment, they were not seen to best advantage. Her brown eyes showed a flashing white against the grime which stained her face like a chimney sweep, and her hair, when she released it with a shudder of distaste from the confines of the grubby headscarf, straggled in limp, sweat-soaked tangles. The small hands were black, too, the nails short and ingrained.

Marian gave the fire in the low, modern grate a vigorous prodding with the iron poker. 'Come on, ye mucky pup! Away up for your bath. There's loads of hot water. The boiler's been rumbling away like thunder. I was just thinking of running some off, if you were any later. I'll light the oven. Your dinner's in. Just needs warming up.'

'You're an angel!' Dora declared. She moved out into the kitchen, already shedding the long overall, hauling the jumper up over her head. Marian saw the contrasting white of the thin arms, and the grime that ended at the wrists like a pair of black gloves. The girl shrugged down the brown slacks, sat and pulled off the thick woollen stockings which came just above her knees. She sat on the edge of the hard chair, knees spread in an ungainly posture. Her underwear of vest and baggy cotton knickers was pink and substantially serviceable. Even its ugliness could not entirely hide her slender attractiveness.

She looked appealingly at Marian, who

scooped up the work clothes and hung them on their peg on the back door. 'Listen. I said I'd pop out with Meg Reynolds and one or two more. Just for a drink. We won't be late.'

Marian frowned. 'That's twice this week. You hardly get any sleep as it is. Why don't you save it for the weekend?' She went on, over Dora's wheedling protest. 'Your mam was here this afternoon. She was on about never seeing you. She wants you home this weekend. It's her birthday next week. So don't you forget it!' She paused significantly. 'You seeing that lad again? What's his name? Ray?'

It was impossible to tell under the coating of dirt whether Dora was blushing. 'Yeah. He'll be there, I expect. Why?' There was more than a hint of challenge in the question.

'Nowt. Have ye said anything to your mam about him yet?'

'No. Why should I? I've only been out with him a couple of times.'

'You spent the whole weekend with him, practically. You should take him home — you know. If you're keen.'

The white teeth showed against the blackness in a cheeky grin. 'Don't fret yourself. I'll not get myself into any trouble. I know what's what. You're as bad as me mam, you!'

Marian acknowledged she was rather thin-skinned when it came to talk of this intimate nature, but she was almost certain Dora was mockingly hinting at her own past history. She thought back suddenly to those heady days when, at her grandma's house in Wolfe Street, she and Teddy had courted. And shared beds in the splendour of whole nights together. She had lived only to be with him then.

And the fruit of their union lay upstairs asleep now. In her own snug, brightly painted room, in this snug, brightly painted house. Wicked or not, mistake or not, she would never forget, or regret, the rapture of those times.

She reached out, fondly, briefly touched the lank dark head. 'He wouldn't be so smitten if he could see you now!' she grinned, and Dora gave a hoot of scandalized delight. 'Go on. Get your mucky self washed. Your supper'll be on the table, so be quick. And make sure you take your key when you go out. I'll be fast asleep long before you roll home. We haven't had the siren for over two months now!'

The young girl's vital happiness, her youth, had stirred memories both sweet and painful for Marian. My God! She chided herself. You'd think you were an old granny. You're only twenty-three, girl! But, as she glanced round at her neat kitchen, she knew she was not envious of Dora's exuberant freedom. She would be content never to leave this semi-detached haven. It was only the constant ache of her loneliness and love for her husband which assailed her, and which caused her eyes to moisten as she bent to light the twin rows of pale-centred blue flames, and prayed that, wherever he was right now, Teddy would know how deeply and permanently her thoughts were with him.

5

The packed bodies swayed, and arms clutched at others' shoulders as the wagon shuddered to a shrieking halt. Immediately those nearest the wide double doors began pounding with their fists and yelling to be let out. Teddy Wright, who was sitting with his back against the opposite side of the goods wagon, his knees drawn up against his chest, held up his arms to fend off the buffeting forest of limbs about him. He struggled to his feet. They heard the echoing clanks fading as the long train came to a stop, and the roar of escaping steam. German voices began to yell a series of orders, and the prisoners inside the wagon ceased their shouting.

Teddy felt the ache of his restricted limbs. The air inside the packed space was fetid, the heavy smell of urine and excrement predominant, even though the two sanitary buckets by the doors were, thankfully, not full yet. He glanced about him in the gloom, looking for Andy Macaulay, who had managed to trade for a pocket watch before they had left the camp near Rouen which had been their home for nine months. How many hours had they been travelling? Daylight no longer showed through the narrow slitted vents just below the flat roof. They had set off in the pre-dawn darkness and, apart from two fairly lengthy halts during neither of which were they allowed to descend, they had rolled steadily, if slowly, east. They must surely have crossed the border into Germany by now.

Teddy felt the bitterness he had fought to suppress well up once more. He had vowed that he would make his bid for freedom before they left France. 'You stand a much better chance of getting away from here,' he had argued forcibly just days ago. 'We're right near the coast here. And there's bound to be some folk who'd help out, get you on a boat.'

Not that they'd seen much evidence of sympathy from the local population during their months of captivity in northern France. From the few fleeting contacts they were able to make, there seemed to be, if anything, a resentment towards the British, as though the evacuation had been a matter of choice, leaving them in the lurch.

There hadn't been much resistance among the POWs either, in those early days of captivity. Most were still too stunned, and too thankful at still being alive. The chaotic days of the retreat seemed almost unreal now. Teddy's own unit had been working further north. Very close, in fact, to where, twenty-three years before, his father, and thousands like him, had fought and died in the Flanders muck. They had quartered at Ypres for a few nights. It had disturbed him to think of his father walking the same streets, visiting the same cafés. He could still remember the visit here as an uncomprehending seven-year-old, with his mother, and John, and Aunt I. Being hoisted aloft, to stare at a high, white building, with a big arch, covered in hundreds of neatly chiselled names, one of which they told him was his dad's.

They were busy with the logistics of preparing bridges for armoured vehicles to cross the rivers of the much fought over terrain, working with the company of Royal Engineers. Then, all at once, they were pulling out, loading gear hurriedly on to trucks, abandoning a great deal of it, heading south, on to roads choked with fleeing civilians. Then the strafing and bombing had begun.

It was unnerving, but Teddy had at least endured some of it before, in Spain. Some of the lads were demoralized at the sight of the first casualties. Pumping blood, severed limbs, scorched and shredded corpses. They had their own casualties, too. A truck caught on the highway, left blazing. Sergeant Rogers, with his face burnt, a stinking, bubbling black, his eyes gone. Others, unrecognizable bundles, smoking, the smell of burnt flesh stuck in your throat, clogged inside you no matter how many times you hawked and spat, or retched.

They ended up marching, trying to keep off the roads, linking up with the remnants of an armoured group which still had a couple of tanks — for a brief day or two. Then on again. Teddy, as a corporal waiting for his sergeant's stripe in the near future, found himself in charge of a makeshift squad of a dozen men. They were told to tag on to a bunch of Jocks — Cameron Highlanders, part of the 51st Highland Division. The nearer they got to the coast, the more Jocks there seemed to be, and at last there seemed to be some sort of order restored. Teddy and his group became quite hopeful. They heard about a mass evacuation being planned. A fortified beachhead was being established further east, men already assembling to be lifted off by the navy.

An infantry captain told Teddy cheerfully, 'You just doss down here, corporal. Stick with us. You'll be back home before you know it.'

They became more and more uneasy, though, as days passed and there was no sign of the fleet. They were there, at that place, St Valery-en-Caux, camped out on the harbour side. They had to keep under cover. Enemy planes attacked during daylight, but they could tell most of the action was happening further east. The buzz went round that they were picking up men by the hundreds from the beaches at Dunkirk. 'We'll be next, lads!' another officer told them confidently.

Then, on 2 June, in a cruel symbolism of the confusion of the military situation they were caught in, a thick fog descended, coming in like a wall from the sea, strangely lit by the last of a disappearing sun in the early summer afternoon. It rolled over them, adding to their feeling of isolation and entrapment. It didn't lift the next day, nor the day after. Meanwhile, the sounds of the battle rumbled ominously nearer, the Scottish infantry began to dig in around the small port.

'You men are assigned to me,' a second lieutenant said. He looked like a rugger-playing sixth-former. They were placed at the corner of an old, open-ended warehouse. The first they knew of the attack was when a shell smashed through its roof and fragmented, setting the building alight and killing two of Teddy's men and wounding another three.

Rifles were no match for tanks, and they

raced back over the cobbles towards the quayside, where they crouched in shallow dug-outs and endured several hours of deadly shell and mortar fire, only the oily water at their backs. Unbelievably, there came a cessation of fire. A cool breeze got up, and, for the first time in three days, the banks of fog parted, cruelly showing their avenue of escape but with no means of using it, other than swimming.

Everyone was too tense, nerves strung out by the bombardment they had endured, even to chat. They crouched and waited, and at last, as dusk began to fall, a lone figure came with white flag and megaphone, to announce the surrender. They were too bone weary and dazedly thankful to be alive to feel shame as they stood, filed out to lay down their weapons in the ever-growing pile, while their enemy stared with grinning interest.

Their first night was spent in one of the barnlike sheds near the harbour. Hundreds of them crowded together, lying on rolled up coats and kitbags on the stone floor. 'Do not worry.' A smart German officer addressed them in very creditable English, while they ate a meal of thick soup and coarse bread and sat docilely at his feet. 'You will soon be going home. You will be back with your families. When we have taken England.'

But it hadn't happened. Somehow, Germany had failed to capitalize on their rout of the British Army, and Teddy had spent the intervening months in 'temporary quarters', under canvas in a large, barbed wire enclosure a few miles from the city of Rouen. Discipline was harsh but quite fair. Food was adequate. They even received news from home, irregularly, it was true, but it came through eventually. Teddy was delighted at that first mail — letters from Marian, his mother, Aunt I. One from John, filling in for him the unsavoury details of Uncle Dan's death. For a day or two, Teddy carried them about, read and reread them, and felt wonderfully close to their world again. Then reaction set in, almost disastrously. The full helplessness of his situation drove in on him, and he found himself wishing savagely that he had heard nothing from home. It was days before he could bring himself to reply to any of them.

He was not the only one affected. A few days later, one of the Jocks — most of the inmates were from the 51st — walked steadily towards the wooden barrier by the guard-house at the gateway to the camp. He stepped over the line which marked the outer perimeter of the prisoners' area, ignoring the astonished cries of the sentry, and broke into a lumbering run. He didn't stop even when the dust was kicked up by the shots fired to deter him. His arms pumped high, he increased his speed, until more lethal fire broke out from the raised platform, and he was cut down, to lie twitching, then still, until a hastily convened stretcher party ran to him and bore him away.

Suddenly, there was the sound of the outer bars being drawn back, the wrench of the doors as they were dragged open, and a blessed wave of chill, fresh air wafted in to them. 'Raus!' came the shouts, and gratefully the prisoners began to jump down from the high truck, stumbling on their stiff limbs after the long hours of confinement. High lights had been rigged up on slender poles. They showed a large area of bare ground, earth and gravel, which had been penned off crudely by thick rolls of barbed wire. The men from the neighbouring wagons were spilling out, being herded into this enclosure by the shouts and gestures of the armed guards.

The first prisoners were ordered to take shovels from the large pile waiting for them. They were led to assigned spots, to begin digging latrine pits. The guards cursed at the great numbers of men who rushed to the edges of the level space and relieved themselves against the coils of wire. The steam rose in the pale light of the arc lamps, and the men sighed with the release, ignoring the barked reprimands of their captors.

'So much for the effin' riff-raff!' Tony Ellis jerked his curly red head at the rows of lamps to indicate the lack of any attempt at blackout, even though these makeshift pens were right alongside a railway track. His contempt for the Royal Air Force was not new. It had been prevalent among the POWs since the days before their capture during the retreat and the agonizing days of waiting at the beachheads, when they seemed to be at the mercy of the strafing Luftwaffe, with not a British fighter in sight to protect them. There had been rumours since before Christmas of raids being carried out by bomber command into the very heart of Germany.

Tony's face, the freckles showing even through the coating of dirt, looked absurdly young. Teddy recalled the first time he had seen it, twisted and lined with fear, in the first hours after their capture, when they had sat shoulder to shoulder, hundreds of them, in the damp summer darkness. Two Britons, one an officer, the other a sergeant, had tried to make a break for it and been brought back, slumped in the rear of a small army vehicle. They had been badly beaten. Their limp bodies were flung out on to the ground, in front of the appalled prisoners. There had been an underswell of muttering, but no one moved as the guards stood over them and menacingly raised their weapons.

The two half-conscious figures, faces swollen and blackened with their blood, had been tied to some kind of frame, against the long brick wall of one of the warehouses, and then, before the horrified gaze of the seated mass of prisoners, had been shot, folding over against their bonds suddenly, bowing low in obeisance, then hanging, inert bundles of clothing.

The clicks of bolts being pulled back sounded obscenely loud all around them, and their guards had stood tensely, their weapons trembling, ready in their hands. For a few minutes, there was a palpable feeling that a massacre was to take place. That was when Teddy had first noticed Tony, and been distracted by the pale features, the glistening trail of tears standing out on his pale, thin face. What's that boy doing here? Teddy had wondered. He couldn't be more than fourteen or fifteen. Then he realized the youngster was in khaki, just like the rest of them. He had reached out impulsively, grabbed the shivering lad's wrist, noting how thin and delicate it felt. Tony had reached for his hand, sought it out, clasped it tightly, reinforcing the impression of childhood, holding on as if his life depended on it, shaking and weeping very quietly. Afterwards, he'd wiped at the tears with the back of a sleeve, and smiled sheepishly, yet somehow not attempting to hide his weakness, and thus adding to his impression of extreme youth.

Teddy had become a kind of father, or at least avuncular, figure. The boy was indeed a soldier, a regular who had joined up as a boy, and was now almost eighteen, had been in the army since before the outbreak of hostilities and posted to France, like Teddy, with the BEF. He was with the Service Corps, attached to one of the Highland regiments, and working as a messman in the officer's mess at divisional HQ. He had become a kind of mascot looked after with rough affection, treated as a child. The Jocks referred to him as 'the wean', they all addressed him as 'Young-un'. Even Teddy.

Now, Tony sought the comfort of his presence, sticking close to him and Andy Macaulay as they joined the shuffling group of men spreading over the area of the enclosure, which was rapidly becoming crowded. They found a spot covered with sparse grass and squatted, making their own little encampment, placing their bundles possessively around them. Teddy and Andy had their haversacks, bulging with the items of clothing that had survived with them, and with their mess tins and mugs tied to the strapping. Tony had a wide canvas holdall, a gift from some officer in happier days, and a paper carrier bag which already looked in danger of disintegration.

'I don't think we're gonna get much effin' chance to do a runner from here,' Tony observed, staring round at the man-high rolls of barbed wire, the high lights, and the numerous German sentries.

His words stirred a feeling of resentment, and guilt, in Teddy. For all his talk, he had done nothing to put into operation any of his plans to escape, in spite of the many hours of conversation they had taken up with Andy and a number of others. Mind you, neither had anyone else, Teddy consoled himself.

'Will you stop your effing and blinding, Young-un?' he protested, with a real edge of irritation in his voice. 'I've told you. One of these days I'll wash your mouth out with soap and water for you!'

'Yes, Daddy!' Tony answered, with that fetching, cheeky grin, and his screwed-up little expression of fond mockery.

'Well, at least all these bastards are being kept occupied here,' Andy muttered. His soft, mild Scottish accent as usual seemed to give added weight to any of his remarks. 'That means they're not shooting the bollocks off some other poor pongo.'

Two lorries drove into the enclosure, scattering scrambling prisoners like the bow wave before a ship. Trestle tables were lifted out, and with swift efficiency a field kitchen was set up. In a short time, the POWs were lining up obediently to take their ration of soup and bread dispensed by the surly cooks.

'What's up, Fritz? Rather be tucked up with your fräulein, eh?'

'Fuck off, Tommy!' came the dull reply, without any animosity.

'Wonder where we'll be celebrating your birthday?' Tony said, scouring the greasy sides of his mess tin with the last of his bread. 'Think you'll get many cards?' Then his grin faltered, embarrassment was etched upon his face at his insensitive blunder. The product of a series of foster parents and children's homes himself, taken into care when he was only eight, Tony knew full well the importance of Teddy's family to him, had shared vicariously in it as Teddy had spent many of their idle hours talking of them. He had even read out bits of the letters he had got from his wife and mother and brother, whose features Tony knew well from the thumbed over snapshots in Teddy's paybook.

He was about to mutter his apology, but Teddy, with equal sensitivity, was already aware of his embarrassment and sought to alleviate it. 'Dunno!' he answered boisterously, finding refuge for both of them in the crude, prison-camp humour. 'But I know one present I definitely can count on, eh, Young-un?' He grinned lasciviously at Tony, and held up his right hand with his thumb peeping suggestively through the first and second fingers of his clenched fist.

The dark red curls tossed. 'Fuck off!' Tony answered roundly and happily, blushing this time with pleasure.

6

'Look what we made!' Marian proudly brought in the small, flat, round cake, and placed it in the middle of the table. A home-made frill of coloured paper, the edges cut into jagged fringes, had been secured round the rim of the plate, a single wax candle stuck in the centre of the well-baked, unappetizing mixture.

'For daddy's birthday!' little Teddie breathed, eyes shining, and May gathered her up, held her tightly against her, lifting her so that she could see. She placed her carefully on the chair which had been pulled out.

'Come on then. Let's light the candle,' Iris announced, and proceeded to do so using her solid lighter, with great ceremony.

'Blow out! Blow out!' Teddie shrieked, quivering with excitement, and Marian cried hastily,

'No! Wait, Sugar. First we have to sing. What do we sing, eh?'

'Happy birthday to you,' they all began vigorously, Teddie leading the way. Suddenly, Marian's high, clear tone faltered, died quickly as she choked, hiccuped, fighting not to let the tears come. May swallowed hard, putting up her own fight, but Teddie didn't notice. She leaned close, her cheeks ballooned, and blew noisily. 'Again! Again!' she demanded, hopping in ecstasy, and Iris obliged, sang with her again in her gruff contralto, giving May and Marian time to regain control.

'Make a wish. Did you make a wish?'

'Daddy come home!' Teddie cried decisively, and then it didn't seem to matter, and the three women were all talking at once, and laughing, and half sobbing, tears clinging to their lashes as they fussed over one another and the beaming little figure in her best party frock, and white ankle socks and shiny shoes.

'I don't know about actually eating it,' Marian said dubiously, but, on her daughter's insistence, she cut the unimposing object into sections, as small as she could make them. 'I *did* put some egg in, believe it or not!' Marian giggled apologetically. The cake tasted dry and flat, more like pastry, but they chewed gallantly through the few mouthfuls of their tiny portions. 'You don't have to,' Marian told them, still laughing, while Teddie chomped enthusiastically.

'Lovely, Mammy!' she asserted, and they nodded.

'Yes, pet.'

Marian had still heard nothing further, either from or about Teddy. Only the letter she had received over two months ago now, in February, which had been written a month before that. 'I hope he's got our letters and cards,' she said. 'They went off in good enough time.'

May nodded. 'They'll get to him eventually, even if he hasn't got them already. One thing's sure. He'll know we're all thinking of him today.' The air was heavy with emotion once more. May didn't want to change the subject. But she strove to lighten it. 'Twenty-five!' she exclaimed, with a little shake of her head. 'And John will be twenty seven this Christmas. It doesn't seem possible.' She glanced across at Iris, who was still chewing stoically. 'We're getting old, lass.'

'Don't I know it! And don't forget I'm two years older than you. It's the half-century for me next year!'

Teddy's still alive. He's safe. He'll come back. The thought came flooding into Marian's mind again, trailing with it guilt, as it often did, for she was sure her mother-in-law must be remembering, and remembering her loss. How on earth had she managed to carry on all these years, after losing her man? 'Doesn't John mind? Having his birthday on

Christmas Day, I mean? I don't think I'd fancy that at all.'

May smiled. 'Same birthday as Baby Jesus. That's what my mam and dad used to tell him. Made him feel a bit special.' Without knowing it, May's thoughts were running very close to her daughter-in-law's. Watching her little granddaughter's shining excitement, she was taken back to the boys' early birthdays. Teddie — May had given in, gracefully, despite her initial opposition to the diminutive for Edwina which Marian, with untypical obstinacy, had insisted on using — didn't know the father whose birthday she was vociferously celebrating. She would often accost any uniformed figure she saw with rapturous cries of 'Daddy!' But at least he was alive. May prayed earnestly every night that he would be kept safe, would come through unharmed to be reunited with them all, whatever the outcome of the war. And surely, then, she prayed every bit as fervently, he would at last realize and appreciate what was here for him: the unswerving, simple love of a wife, the gift of a lovely daughter?

It still pained her to contemplate the way Teddy had deserted the pregnant girl, only weeks after 'doing the honourable thing' and marrying her. Pained her all the more because she could never understand it. Nor, so far, had she really been able to forgive it, not in her own mind. She had wondered guiltily in the days after he had run away to Spain to fight in their civil war if it was her influence which had made him go through with the wedding. She knew how much of a close, self-contained unit she and her boys had been as they grew up. With Iris a part of them, she amended hastily. But then Iris had always gone along with anything she wanted or decided as far as the boys were concerned. It gave May both a secret thrill of pride and shame-faced pleasure to know just how devoted and unquestioning Iris had been. A helpmate in every sense of the word, through the long and happy years of the boys' childhood.

It was Dan, bless him, who, from time to time, had voiced his reasonable misgivings about her relationship with her sons as they moved into their teenage years. Over-possessive, he thought her, though he had never put it as bluntly as that to her. Secretly aware of the justice in his unstated accusation, she had at times burned with resentment, inflamed by guilt. They had even had serious fallings-out over it, which never lasted for long. May felt again that stirring of affection, and shame, when she remembered how, even after her marriage to him, Iris had roundly sided with her, attacked her husband scathingly at his mildly voiced cautions.

But she would like to think that it was not solely through her that Teddy had chosen to marry Marian. He had at least been taught what was right and wrong, and what decency meant. Even if he had broken its laws in his illicit sexual involvement with the girl. And, she could argue with herself wryly, Teddy had shown himself to be well and truly free of her apron strings long before that, when he had chosen to go and lodge with her mother and father soon after he started work at Swan's. And then compounding it by moving on to take up lodgings in Marian's grandmother's house, under the same roof as the besotted girl. And with such disastrous consequences.

No, no, not disastrous! The word smote her as she smiled at the happy child. It was true that May had been far from happy about his situation with Marian. Nelly Dunn's illegitimate daughter was not the girl she would have chosen as a suitable match for her son. But she was prepared to admit that the last four years had proved her wrong.

Marian was not the ideal partner, but then, who was? No marriage was perfect, many could not even be classified as happy. Look at her own sister, Julia, with her boozy, spinelessly easygoing Alf. And Cissy, Jack's sister, with her successful man, David Golding. The other end of the social scale, yet May could vividly recall the whiff of scandal attached to Cissy not long after they were married, her almost confessional confidences, and her bitter complaints at her husband's cold preoccupation with his business.

Even closer to home, it hurt to remember the deterioration of Iris and Dan's union, her heart going out to both of them. And in the shocking denouement that came with the awful circumstances of Dan's death, May had suffered from a deep sense of disloyalty to both of them, as she sided with Iris's bitter recriminations and suffered with silent, grieving sympathy at her brother-in-law's compulsion to be unfaithful.

Closest of all, in the very heart of her, was the pain of her memory of Jack, the sadness in his brown eyes when she had let all the bile of her bitterness and hurt and fear flow out at him when he told her of his decision to enlist. It was the only real, lasting animosity that had come between them, and she was helpless to stop herself, even though part of her knew he was right when he argued that soon he would have to go anyway, that it would only be a matter of weeks, at best months, before he was conscripted into the forces. Weeks that could be spent with her, and his bairns, she had flung at him, and for days would not let him touch her, not even with the loving gentleness that sought only to comfort her. Thank God that love had prevailed, and she had had a chance to manifest it, before he had been taken from her for good.

Marian had her faults, too, there was no doubt of that. One of them was her passivity, almost servility, which had so enraged May as she watched the girl let Teddy walk over her. That timid, beseeching look, begging love, like an animal that comes to its master no matter how many times it may be cursed and beaten. Not that her Teddy was cruel. At least, not consciously so. He surely could have no idea of how much he had hurt Marian by his seeming need to escape from her?

When he had returned safely from Spain, May had been so relieved, and grateful, that at last he had come to his senses. Marian's adoring glow was enough for him, she thought. But then, within months, she had seen the signs, ached with a helplessness as she wanted to shake the girl, warn her not to smother him so with her blind worship. May was furious, but not, deep down, surprised, when Teddy had announced so abruptly that he was giving up his job at the naval yard, going into the army, leaving Marian alone once more, though not quite, this time, deserting her. He could even argue the sense of his move — a career in a rapidly expanding service, into which he would, in all probability, be compelled to serve anyway within a year or two at most.

It didn't help now to reflect that his forecast had been all too accurate. That had happened, now, too, to her elder son, her John. It sickened her, literally, to think that soon he would be facing danger, just as Teddy had, no doubt was still, as a prisoner in the hands of the enemy. The old bitterness rose, as it so often did now, and had done in the past, chokingly, a purely sexist hate of the world of men and the huge folly of their violence, which humanity was helpless to stop. She thought with savage irony of the peace rally she and Iris had attended at the city hall five years ago, the cards with the peace pledge which they had signed so eagerly. How foolish, and useless, it all seemed now, looking back at the way the world had slid inch by remorseless inch into a conflict in every way as apocalyptic as the one before it.

Sometimes, May turned away from a black cloud of terror she sensed looming in some terrifying corner of her mind. She could not stand another loss. Her beloved Jack had been taken from her. How could she stand losing her son? Or sons? How could she go on believing, praying fervently to a God who could do that to her?

She had thought she would lose her faith, in fact thought she had, in the weeks that followed Jack's death. But his return to her, in her dream, or whatever it was, had placed in her that tiny seed of certainty that there was some force, something beyond our lives here, some eternal, loving goodness. Not all-powerful. She could never conceive of a divine plan to rob her of Jack. But she could not face the notion of going on believing if another sacrifice of blood should be asked of her.

Her prayers were desperate now. Her world was a very personal one. Her flesh and blood, like this lovely child, and loved ones like Iris — they had to hold together, it was all they had, all anybody had to hold on to. That was what Teddy must understand. The minor miracle of his living through the horrors of last year, the fall of France, meant that he had been given yet another chance. Whatever hardships he was enduring now, would be called upon to endure, he must know and understand the love that was waiting for him, that held him, in all the dangerous uncertainty which lay about them.

'Da-ra!' Tony Ellis sang out the musical clarion of triumph, holding the dirty, battered piece of tray aloft with the mound of baked dough upon it. The thick tallow candle ground into its centre flickered precariously in the draught. 'Happy birthday to you, happy birthday to you,' he sang raucously. 'Come on, you sods!' he cried admonishingly, and a few voices, gruff with embarrassment, joined in the chorus. Teddy was embarrassed, too, on his behalf, but laughed heartily, and to save him face leaned forward and noisily blew out the flame.

'Where'd you get this, Young-un?'

'Been doin' a turn for Fritz again, have you?' someone guffawed.

Tony raised his eyebrows, tossing his red curls coquettishly. 'Never you mind! And his name's not Fritz. It's Ludo, if you must know! And he put it in specially for me. It's fresh from the oven.'

'Did he now?'

'I bet he did!'

The comments flew thick and fast, and Tony's head tossed, his shoulders lifted, while his freckled skin glowed pinkly.

'Ludo!' someone spluttered derisively. 'That's a bloody game, that is!'

'If you must know, it's short for some-thing!' Tony retorted.

'Short for dirty Jerry poof!' another voice growled, and there was a burst of hard laughter.

'Come on then. Cut the bastard. Here's a knife.' Teddy hacked up the fresh bread, passed it round, and they all chewed appreciatively. He looked down the long trestle table at the wolfish faces as they devoured the unexpected treat. Already this hut, with its rows of three-tier bunks, the black iron stove, its chimney soaring through a crudely fashioned hole in the wooden roof, was depressingly familiar. They had been at the camp, just outside a place called Bergedorf, less than ten miles from the city of Hamburg to the north, for three weeks now.

There must have been getting on for 400 prisoners there, the vast majority army, though there were a couple of huts of navy lads as well. The long rows of wooden huts were like a miniature regimented township. There was another, smaller camp for officers down the road. Some lieutenant colonel and a couple of lesser cronies came along to take parades every now and then, under German supervision, of course. Kept reminding them they were still in the army, still subject to military discipline. It seemed to work, so far.

Teddy still carried his rank of corporal, was addressed by most as 'Corp', and was in charge of Hut 25D.

'The dizzy heights of power,' Andy Macaulay gently mocked, in his dry way. Teddy's main duty was reporting his hut as 'all present and correct', at the 'appels', or roll-calls held each morning and evening, when they assembled on the bare earth outside their primitive home.

The late April weather was improving, and after their impromptu celebration, Teddy set off on his usual circuits of the compound. Most of the prisoners spent as much time as they could out of the confines of the huts. They were penned inside anyway for fourteen hours or more, after their early supper and evening roll-call, until 8 a.m. Games of all kinds were being endlessly organized, the most popular being the inter-hut soccer competitions. There was a match in progress now, the touchlines crowded with noisy supporters.

As usual, Tony fell in beside him as Teddy began his laps of the enclosure, hugging the low inner wire beyond which the prisoners were forbidden to stray. There was a stretch of ten yards leading to the high outer fence, with its angled iron posts surmounted by the strands of barbed wire, and at the two corners at the front of the rectangle which formed the camp, the wooden watchtowers, always manned, containing the machine guns and the searchlights. There were lights on high posts at the two rear corners, but no watchtowers. Instead, the area was patrolled irregularly throughout the hours of darkness by guards accompanied by fierce looking Alsatian dogs.

'Cor! Slow down!' Tony puffed. 'You always set off as if you're after the last bus!'

'I wish! A kid like you shouldn't be puffing and blowing like that. You're smoking far too much. You need more exercise, you unfit young bugger! I think I'll put you in the team for the next match.'

'Bollocks! You know I'm useless at those blood sports.' Tony gave an exaggerated shudder. 'All those rough, hairy, sweating pongos! Gives me the creeps!'

Teddy stared at him in wry amusement. He was sure Tony's lisp was becoming more pronounced lately. He had hardly noticed he was just a little short tongued when they had first been captured, but now the impediment seemed all at once very noticeable. Not that it wasn't attractive in its own way. Made his naturally thin, soft voice sound a little breathy. Almost sexy, even. Teddy was struck by his thoughts.

'You know, you're getting more like a party

every day. You'd better watch it. You're even beginning to look good!'

It was meant as a bit of teasing banter, the kind that Tony was used to, had to put up with every day. But now the youngster actually pinked, his eyelids lowered in an expression of part bashfulness, part provocation. He gave a peculiar little skipping shimmy as he walked alongside Teddy.

'You dirty old man! Just cos it's your birthday! You chatting me up? After that treat you were on about, are you?'

He gave a simpering leer, and put his hand lightly on Teddy's left shoulder, swaying in close until their hips bumped together. Teddy was shocked at his body's reaction, the throb of arousal he felt. He felt his face grow hot. He thrust the slim figure away, shoving him so vigorously he almost fell, staggering to regain his balance.

'Piss off!' he snarled, with real anger. 'You want to stop pissing about, Young-un! One of these days somebody's going to take you seriously and you'll be in real trouble. Just shut up if you can't talk normal!'

He strode out even faster, and Tony gazed at him, his mouth open, blinking rapidly at the sudden prick of hidden tears at the back of his eyes, his throat tight with hurt, before he trotted to catch up with him.

7

John Wright emerged from Austin Reed's in Regent Street into a mild but dull May morning. Rather tardily, he returned the salutes of two men in air-force blue. He was still unused to receiving the mark of respect demanded by his rank from other service-men. In fact, he had to stop his hand snapping up to his brow at the sight of a fellow officer. He tried to shrug off his feeling of guilt at the amount of money he had just spent at the military tailor's on his brand new uniforms and other items of equipment. Or, rather, what he would spend when the bill came through at the end of the month. His pay as a newly appointed second lieutenant would certainly not stand such expense, but with Aunt I's more than generous cheque in his bank account, he could well afford to play the gentleman, at least for a while.

'This is just a token of my pride in your achievement,' she had written, in the note accompanying it. 'We're all very proud of you. Blow it all in on a few wild parties if you feel like it. Or perhaps it can go in the kitty for a rainy day, especially as I know you're contemplating entering the matrimonial stakes before very long.'

He felt his stomach tighten with apprehension momentarily. He pictured how much she and his mother would be dismayed when they learned just how soon that was to be. And without either their presence or their cognizance, which was what would really hurt them, he suspected. It was not that they would object to his marrying Jenny. Far from it. He had been thankfully delighted at their support and even enthusiasm for his reunion with Jenny. But the secretive haste of the ceremony, in distant London, with no one from either family or any of their friends attending, gave him undeniable qualms. He had not voiced them in full, in view of Jenny's urgent pleading. But they were there, still.

He glanced at his wristwatch. Still over two hours to go before he had to meet Jenny at the office in Seymour Place. He decided to go back to the Royal Empire Society, in Northumberland Avenue, where they had both spent the previous night, in their respectably separate and even distant rooms. He had booked her in there, chosen for the reason that they allowed women (and not only servicewomen) to lodge under their roof. She had looked tense and pale when she walked into the unpretentious lobby carrying her modest suitcase. He waited in the bar while she went up to her room to tidy up, then they went into the crowded dining room for a substantial, but unimaginative, dinner.

'Mummy and Daddy were in a real tiz-waz,' she told him. 'Daddy was just embarrassed, but Mum really went on and on about me coming away. I'm sure she knows we've done the dreaded deed. That I'm now a fallen woman.'

She tried to assume a light tone, but John could see the uncertainty and dismay so close to the surface. He could imagine the scene all too well, in the Alsops' middle-class bastion in the Lakes. Sandy's gruff discomfort, his wife, Moira, taking the voluble lead as she so often did. He tried to match Jenny's lightness. 'They should be relieved then, when you get back. To find we've done the decent thing.'

Jenny rolled her eyes eloquently at him, and he knew she was just as nervous as he was about presenting their folks with the *fait accompli* of the marriage.

She had gone up to her room early, their goodnight kiss almost timid. When she joined him for breakfast, her face looked pinched, pale with tiredness.

'You slept about as well as I did,' he smiled, and she blushed.

'Do I look that bad?' But she returned his

smile at his hasty apology. She was wearing dark brown slacks and a heavy sweater. The May morning filtered greyly through the long windows, each pane of which was marked by the white X of tape, stuck there to prevent flying glass in the event of bomb blast. When she had placed her order with the waitress, she nodded at the newspaper folded beside John's hand on the white table-cloth. 'All gloom and doom?' she enquired, pulling a rueful face.

The press had been full of the Greek campaign, yet another disaster for the Allied forces. The evacuation had been completed, and attention was now focused ominously on the island of Crete. John shook his head vigorously.

'No, as a matter of fact. Quite good. The Lion of Judah is settled safely back home at last.' He was referring to the Emperor Haile Selassie's return to Ethiopia from his exile in Britain. 'Anyway, there's only one item of news worth bothering about today!' He smiled tenderly and reached across to take hold of her hand, and she blushed again, this time with pure pleasure.

'Go on! Off you go and leave me to start on the task of making myself fit to be a bride. Just make sure you're there at the office on time. Don't leave me at the altar, will you? Or the desk or whatever it is they use at registry offices.'

He reached again for her hand, held on to it. 'You don't mind? No church and bridesmaids and champagne popping?' he asked seriously.

She held his gaze, returned the tightness of his grip. 'Hey! It was my idea in the first place to sneak off like this. I just want to be Mrs Wright. The fifth, is it? Or sixth? I lose count!'

'The one and only for me,' he answered gallantly. He stood, nodded at the thin piece of toast and watery scrambled egg the waitress had just brought her. 'Not much of a wedding breakfast.' He bent, kissed her cheek. 'I'll be there. Eleven-thirty. Don't change your mind.'

She didn't. She was wearing a dark tweed costume, and a defiantly insubstantial swirl of a hat, pinned to the crown of her head, pale cream with a smoky wisp of veil gathered about a single white rose. John was in his brand new uniform, Sam Browne shining, buckles agleam. 'Such a lovely handsome couple!' one of the witnesses said, kissing Jenny's proffered cheek, and simpering comically when John returned the compliment. She was some sort of cleaner or caretaker, and her floral pinny showed through the dark coat she had donned for the brief ceremony.

The other witness was the elderly clerk who assisted the registrar. He simpered just as coyly at the pinafored cleaning lady as he stepped forward, displaying a set of stained and decaying teeth. 'May I be permitted to kiss the bride?' Jenny turned the other cheek, while the registrar eyed his subordinate sourly.

John had booked a double room 'with private bath' at the Abbey Park in Victoria Street, and, after an unostentatious lunch at a small table nestled snugly against a flowered wall in the busy dining room, they rode up in the darkly panelled lift. Jenny strove hard not to appear embarrassed at the knowing leer of the brass-buttoned bellboy.

'He knows!' she hissed, as they followed him along the corridor. 'They all seem to!'

'Do you mind?'

'Not really,' she returned, but her expression did not match her brave words.

John blew out his cheeks in a huge sigh of relief when they faced each other alone in the decorous comfort of their room. 'Well, Mrs Wright the Fifth! We made it. Our first home!'

He could feel her tension and he was startled, and full of love for her, when she murmured, 'Let's go to bed. Please!' She began to undress, almost hastily, carelessly dropping her new clothes on a chair, and he followed suit. Naked, she grabbed at her sponge bag and ran to the bathroom. She did not close the door, but called out, 'Don't come in!'

When she emerged, she didn't look at him, made to climb into bed, but he caught her wrist. 'No!' he said. 'Let me see you. Let me look at you. Please don't be ashamed. We belong to each other.' Her glance was full of uncertainty, of a shyness which moved him deeply. She sat on the edge of the bed, gracefully awkward, and he knew she was fighting not to try to conceal herself.

'I'm not much of a bargain, am I?' she whispered unsteadily. He knelt in front of her.

'I love you so much,' he said.

After they made love, they lay with limbs entwined, bodies touching in the warm cocoon, and John drifted blissfully in and out of consciousness. A light spatter of raindrops on the windows enhanced his feeling of insulated happiness. He was appalled at the sudden realization that Jenny was crying quietly, and he untangled himself from her, propped himself on his elbow, saw with dismay the tears glistening on her eyelashes, the small wet patch on her pillow.

She gave a crackling little sniff, and her hair swung across her face as she gave a little shake of her head.

'Sorry. I'm sorry. I . . . ' She shook her head again, as if she were struggling helplessly to explain. She half turned away, and he felt the smoothness of her curving body fitting into him, and he thrilled with renewed excitement and love.

'What is it, love? What's wrong? Tell me. Please don't be sad. Is it something I've done? You mustn't — '

'Johnny!' She turned, with a wounded cry, burrowed into him, and all at once the half-pent emotion gushed out. She sobbed, shaking violently, her face pressed against his chest until he felt the wetness of her tears. 'It's me, it's me!' she sobbed. He held her, his face resting against her sweet, tangled hair, held her until the violence abated enough for her to speak. 'When I think — I wanted so badly for you — I wanted you to be the only one. I swear it. I let you down so badly — let myself down. All I dreamed of — believed in . . . '

He was ashamed of the instinctive little freeze of immobility, the frantic fear that made him want her to stop, want this shadow that would always lie between them to go away. He hugged her closer to him. 'Come on, sweetheart. That's all over now. It's not important. How we are. How we feel now. That's important. That's all that matters.'

She stirred against his clasp, raised her head a little from the comfort of his embrace, fought her hand up to wipe at her tearstained cheeks. 'Please — let me talk. Just this once. I want to explain, want you to know — I never felt anything — nothing like love. It wasn't like that. Like this.' She moved again, the movement taking in the tender intimacy of their bodies. 'Nothing like this,' she whispered, her voice even fainter.

He felt the tiny shrug of her shoulders, the quality of genuine disbelief in her tone. 'Trouble is, I can't explain it, really. Not even to myself. I can't ever forgive myself. I didn't think — with Horst. He was so wicked — he showed me — brought out the wickedness in me. I mean it — I'm not good, Johnny! I'm weak. Something flawed . . . ' Her voice trembled, the tears came catching at her again. 'I'll always feel I've let you down. I don't deserve you. But, oh! I love you so much, darling!'

He held her, stroked at the back of her head, while she cried once more, and quietly, as unemotionally as he could, he told her about the drunken night in Berlin, about his fear, and relief after his release from the

German police. About the tour of the seedy bars and clubs, the strip joints. Of waking up beside Inge, his vague memory of having sex. And Horst's evil delight in his corruption.

'And here we are,' he said, after a long interval of silence. He moved her gently under him, let her feel his bodily excitement. 'He couldn't break us up, after all. And neither will his whole bloody nation, no matter how hard they try!'

* * *

Several hours later, he was wondering secretly if his provocative words had been taken up as a challenge. They rose as the sun was setting, shared a bath, inhibitions deliriously shed at last, a considerable time after their discarded clothes. They were dizzy with their love, and with the sexual freedom they discovered was theirs. They were enraptured with the glorious new world they inhabited.

They ate at the Ritz, he proudly escorting her to the table he had booked. He pulled a mock mournful face at the uniforms in the throng around him.

'Can't move for bloody brass hats! I think the *maître d'* was in two minds whether to have me flung out. You could almost hear him thinking what's a lowly second looey doing in here?'

They danced, though the floor space was so crowded they could do little more than shuffle feet and jostle the shoulders that bumped against theirs. The compère's voice boomed sunnily over the microphone, 'Ladies and gentlemen! I'm sure you'll be fascinated to know that the air raid warning has just sounded. The cellars are of course open, but we have no intention of stopping the party just yet.' He paused, and winked. 'But if you see us leaving the stage, run like hell!'

There was a great cheer, and the band struck up again. Jenny giggled, her lips brushing his ear. 'Look. No one dare leave now!'

The lively warmth of the clubs and pubs and the theatres and restaurants was in great contrast to the stumbling darkness of the blackout, and the dim slits of the hooded lights of buses and taxis. Jenny was happy to leave the frenetic gaiety of the Ritz, though outside in the anonymous bustle of shapes, each with the pencil stab of torchlight flickering about the feet, the war was unavoidable. Just in case this flickering blackness was not enough of a reminder, the searchlights played back and forth above the looming buildings, and there were the flashes and crumps of the AA batteries muted by distance.

'This is only my second visit to London,' Jenny told him. She remembered her schoolgirl excitement at a day spent sightseeing with the family before they continued their journey to a holiday on the south coast. 'I've never seen the lights. We'll come back, won't we? You'll bring me when this is all over. Promise?'

'Of course I will.' He shook off the shivery presentiment that came with her request. 'Let's grab a taxi. No point in walking in the blackout. I haven't a clue. How about a revue? There's a place the chaps were telling me about. The Windmill. Might be a bit *risqué*. Fancy it?'

'Why not? I'm a married woman now.'

The scantily clad, leggy girls were fine. 'They're lovely,' Jenny conceded generously. Though the audience was predominantly male, there were some women among them. It was when the check-suited, pop-eyed comedian came on, his made up red face glowing like a beacon, that John became truly embarrassed for his bride. The jokes grew steadily and more pointedly obscene. John stole an apprehensive glance at the figure beside him. She was gazing up more in open-mouthed wonder than outrage.

'Do you want to go?' he whispered.

She shrugged, gave a conspiratorial grin. 'It's all right. But you'll have to explain some of it to me afterwards!'

Soon, he touched her knee and nodded towards the exit. Even before they left the foyer, they could hear the noise of gunfire, and the heavier thumps of what they realized were bombs.

It was no trouble to find a cab, but as they headed down Haymarket south, they saw the night ahead garishly lit.

'Bloody hell!' the driver muttered. 'Getting a bit far up-river tonight. Cheeky sods!'

They could not even see the lions as they negotiated Trafalgar Square. At the bottom of Whitehall, they came to a halt in a long line of traffic. An ARP warden came over in answer to the cabby's shout.

'You'll not get down there,' he warned. 'They've only had a go at Westminster!'

'Be easier for you to foot it,' the driver advised. 'No point in you sitting here and paying to go nowhere, eh?' John thanked him and they got out. The sky was rosily lit by burning buildings ahead. Growing increasingly uneasy, they walked down the oddly deserted road, except for the clanging fire engines which streaked past, jarring their nerves at their urgent passage. In Parliament

Street, the roadway gleamed, the puddles reflected the flames leaping palely from the House of Commons, whose long roof was ablaze. Hosepipes tangled and coiled like thick snakes, flattened here and there, spurting fountains of drifting spray in the suddenly warm air. They joined the knots of people standing on the pavement, until a sudden roar, and a blast of hot air, full of smoke and the stench of burning, sent them scattering.

'Get down there,' a dark uniformed figure told them, nodding towards the narrow canyon of King Charles Street which bisected the Foreign Office building and the Ministry of Health. 'And get off the streets!' he added, in an exasperated tone. 'The raid's still on. Go down St James's.' They followed several other hurrying shapes. Soon they came to the entrance to the underground station and streamed down the steps with the others. John wondered briefly if he looked as scared as Jenny. She was staring wide eyed at the crowds standing about the entrance to the platforms. Beyond the iron barriers, the platform itself was covered with humanity, not an inch of its surface showing, up to a distance of about four feet from the track. Even this narrow space was encroached upon in places, hiding the white line which had been painted there.

'Not supposed to cross the line till half ten. After the last train's gone,' a bystander told them. 'Then they'll be kipping on the tracks themselves, once the electric's been turned off.' He nodded towards the tall gateway at which a collector still stood. 'Get yourselves a three ha'penny ticket and you can kip down an' all till morning. That's if you can find enough room, eh? Packed like sardines. Some families get down here dinnertime. Start spreading themselves out. Look at 'em!'

Blankets, pillows, even mattresses, were laid out. The mass of bodies curled up in cheek-by-jowl intimacy. The children, and even some of the women, were in night clothes. Cooking paraphernalia, photographs, and other incongruously homely items, were set up on boxes and cases, making miniature familial enclaves.

'They come here every night?' Jenny asked incredulously, staring at the stretching ranks of bodies in the gloom.

'Too true!' their informant nodded. 'Come up the West End regular nowadays, just like the toffs.' He grinned at them challengingly, recognizing John's smart uniform, Jenny's expensive outfit. His smile faded, and he nodded to the roof, hidden in darkness almost. 'Can't get away from it, though, can you? And now they've gone and blown up Parliament itself. Even bleedin' Guy Fawkes couldn't manage that, eh?'

8

'I'm not pregnant!'

May was taken aback at the blunt statement from Jenny. Her face pinked, as did her son's, whose arm was placed defensively about his new wife's shoulders.

'Good Heavens, of course not!' May answered automatically, as though the idea had never occurred to her, and recalling her own words to Iris as soon as she had received the shocking news of the wedding from John over the telephone. 'Just like his brother. The young fool's gone and got her pregnant!'

'Well, doesn't much matter if you are now!' Iris chipped in, in her hearty manner.

May knew that, clumsy though she might be, Iris was attempting to lift the atmosphere of tension which had gripped all of them since the young couple's arrival minutes ago. But she was determined to let them see how hurtful their action had been. 'It's just the secretiveness of it. I can't see the need for it. It's not as if we would have disapproved.' The wounded reproach showed in her eyes as she looked at Jenny. 'You know we were happy for both of you, being together again.'

Jenny gazed back appealingly. 'I know. It was my fault,' she went on gallantly. 'After all the trouble between us. Losing each other. Then, after all this time . . . I just wanted to be married to John, to have it done with. Without any fuss, just between us.' She reached up for the hand she could feel resting on her shoulder, and John's grip tightened on her. 'It was more my folks really,' Jenny offered as an olive branch. 'They'd want to organize things. Have some sort of do. I remember Rosemary's wedding.'

'I'm sure they'll be upset too. They'd have liked to be there. Like us.'

Jenny swallowed hard, dismayed by the choking lump that rose, and the tears that stung behind her eyes. 'I'm sorry,' she muttered. 'We didn't mean to cause any upset.'

'Well, it's done now, anyway,' John said, a little more forcefully than he had intended. 'We have your blessing, don't we?' It came out almost as a challenge, and with it came the sensation of guilt he could not escape.

'Of course you do.' May's breath caught in a half sigh. 'You young beggars! Come here.' She reached for Jenny first, hugged her, they laid their cheeks together, then she turned and embraced her son, and now the catharsis of smiling tears was a relief, and all four were hugging and kissing, the tension dispelled.

Ruby was more forthright when she came back to work later in the afternoon. 'Ye young scallywags! Ye want your ears boxin', the pair of ye!'

Jenny was already anticipating the fraught scene she would face at her home when she and John travelled to Keswick the following day. When she had broken the news to Moira Alsop on the phone from London, there had been a shrilly dramatic cry in the ear-piece, followed by accusing tears. 'Oh, Jenny! How could you?' The receiver had been passed over to Jenny's father, for his wife had been too distraught to carry on.

'You *are* happy for us, Daddy?' Jenny pleaded.

'Of course we are!' Sandy had replied stiffly. Jenny could hear her mother still weeping in the background, and understood perfectly his gruffness.

'We'll be home on Wednesday. We're travelling up north on Tuesday, staying the night at Hexham, then we'll come on Wednesday morning. All right?'

'I'm dreading it,' Jenny confessed, sitting on the bed in the guest room of The Tea Cosy. She was wearing a blue silk nightgown. John tried not to let his eagerness for her body show too obviously.

'They'll be all right,' he assured her, far from convinced himself. But now other, more urgent and far more pleasant matters occupied him. Jenny clutched at his exploring hand with pretended decorum.

'Ssh!' She nodded at the door. 'They'll hear us. We'll have to behave ourselves tonight.' But under the covers, with only the dimness of the bedside lamp in its tasselled shade cosying the shadowed room, she shiveringly allowed his hands free access to her. 'Five nights of married bliss!' she whispered. 'Aren't you sick of me yet?'

His movement was sufficient answer. Soon, she clutched at his wrist, gasped at the excitement his touches were raising in her. 'Don't — you shouldn't!' she breathed, with helpless pleasure and a genuine fear at the storm of sensation he could arouse in her. She was close to weeping at her shocking passion. Her hips moved, her limbs opened, surrendering herself further. 'You shouldn't touch me like that! I can't — I — ' She turned her head into him, burying herself in his warm chest to muffle the cries she felt seeking to escape from her.

'I love you,' he said thickly, his mouth, and his hand, claiming her, and she sank down, let herself go to the tide of sensual pleasure engulfing her.

Next morning at breakfast, the outside world, in all its uncertainty, pressed hard upon them. 'I report back to the holding depot outside Basingstoke on Friday,' John told his mother and Aunt I. 'It won't necessarily be the Fusiliers I'll be posted to. Could be any infantry outfit. Wherever there's a vacancy. Could be a matter of days or weeks.' There was an awkward pause. He glanced apologetically at Jenny. 'If — it's an overseas posting, I'll get some sort of embarkation leave. Seventy-two hours or something.'

'And what about you, Jenny?' May asked. 'You'll still carry on teaching, will you?' Last month all twenty and twenty-one-year-old women had been called on to register for war service. Legislation was expected any day to increase the age range to be included. Jenny would be twenty five in September.

Jenny coloured slightly, looked briefly embarrassed. She shrugged. 'I'm not sure. I think — I might get into war work. Join one of the services. Or they might call me up.'

'But you're married!' May declared.

'Well, they've included married women without families in this last lot.' The blush deepened, but she plunged on into the silence. 'We're not planning on having a baby. Not yet. Not till things are — more settled.'

'The best laid plans!' Iris quoted laughingly, then shied away from her recall of her own distasteful efforts to make sure she did not conceive during her marriage to Dan.

There was another charged silence. 'I don't think it's right,' Jenny continued, almost desperately, aware of her burning face and clumsy speech. 'Not with everything so uncertain. Having to be apart, and everything.'

May gave a grim smile. 'It's a good job your father didn't feel like that,' she said quietly, addressing herself to John. She stood up. 'Well, we'd better clear away,' she said dismissively. 'You'll have to be off to the station soon.'

Jenny kept her head down, blinking rapidly at her plate. She sensed the sudden rift once more between her and May, and was both pained and resentful.

After an awkward cross-country journey of several hours before she and John reached her home in northern Lakeland, Jenny was surprised and gratified to find that her fears had been exaggerated. Though her mother fell on her neck and wept in brief abandon before regaining control with much lacy dabbing and delicate sniffing, the reunion was far less painful than her daughter had anticipated. The extra couple of days to absorb the news had helped, together with her father's subtle, calming influence, and Jenny conveyed as much of her gratitude as she could in the embrace they shared.

Moira Alsop was less skilful at hiding her surprise than May Wright had been when, at dinner that evening, Jenny made the announcement for the second time that she was not expecting a baby. Embarrassment made her flippant.

'I feel I ought to make plain that I am not in a delicate condition,' she told the assembled company, which included her older sister, Rosemary, married with two small children, and her husband, Gerald, so far secure in his occupation as bank clerk with the National Provincial. Also present was the youngest Alsop child, sister Joan, a month away from her nineteenth birthday, who blew out her rouged cheeks in a splutter of shocked delight. 'So there's no need for anyone to start counting off the months on their fingers,' Jenny finished, with a calm she was far from feeling.

'Well!' Moira's eyes widened, her mouth opened and closed, incapable of forming words for a second. 'What a thing — Jenny! Really! There's no need for such . . . '

She glanced helplessly towards her husband, who could do nothing but shake his

106

head in equal embarrassment.

'Just in case anyone had wondered,' Jenny smiled maliciously, beginning to enjoy herself, in spite of her unease.

'Just you wait, little sister!' Rosemary retorted, as though Jenny's remark had somehow cast a slur on young motherhood. Which had, John thought privately, studying her flushed features, rather coarsened his sister-in-law's appearance. She had been a pretty girl, in a large-boned way, when he had first met her. Now her face and figure had thickened, and it was as though she were parading her matronliness proudly. 'It won't be long, I bet, before we're knitting bootees!'

'I don't think so,' Jenny said pointedly. Joan giggled and Mrs Alsop cast warning glances at all her daughters, clearly intimating that decorum was being threatened by the direction the conversation was taking. In a spirit of wicked rebellion, Jenny ignored her. 'It's not really the best of times to be bringing forth babies, is it? John and I are going to be separated. Nobody knows what will happen. We have to face it.'

Rosemary's high colour deepened. 'You can't let the wickedness of the world dictate things!' she returned agitatedly. 'Even if — whatever happens.' Her brown head jerked in John's direction. 'That's what marriage is for, isn't it? The blessing of children. It's more important now than ever. There's danger for all of us. Not just the fighting men. We're all in it. Even if Gerald has to go — I know he'd be proud to do his bit, as we all are. But I'm more thankful than ever that we've got little Maureen and Alex.' Her head of pompous steam ran down, and she gazed around her challengingly.

Doing our bit! Jenny echoed savagely inside her head. Gerald and Daddy fire watching once a week at the pencil and the shoe factories, and us brave Alsop women gossiping and bitching at the WI, knitting socks and scarves and bottling fruit. She was ashamed of her cruelty, but she couldn't help it, when, inside, there was a rage of love, and fear of what might happen to her and Johnny and their precious, precarious happiness.

Within days of their being parted after their all too brief honeymoon, Jenny's anxieties were highlighted by the war news. Along with the proud declaration of victory at sea, with the sinking of the German battleship *Bismarck* came rumours of the loss of a British capital ship, HMS *Hood*, and almost her entire crew. Already proclaimed on *The Voice of Germany* by the traitorous Lord Haw-Haw, this proved tragically to be true, with only three lives saved from a ship's company of over 1,400. Less than a week later, the last remnants of the British forces in Crete were being evacuated, and, at home, clothing coupons came into being alongside the already established ration books for food.

On a purely personal level, Jenny's nerves were finely stretched as she waited daily to hear where John would be posted. She felt guilty as she prayed fervently each night that it might be somewhere safely within the United Kingdom. One of her favourite fantasies as she drifted towards sleep in the familiar surroundings she had known since childhood was of their fighting their war together somewhere, in a vague setting, military but pleasantly rural, she enlisted as a junior ATS officer, and with a cosily romantic room for their off-duty hours in which they could share the passionate love that held them.

'No regrets?' he had asked her tenderly, as they passed through the sandbagged barrier leading on to Keswick station, and their farewell.

She knew that he knew the answer. 'Only one,' she said, and watched his dark eyebrows lift. 'That I wasted five whole years before I got where I wanted to be.' She was determined not to shed any more tears after the unburdening of grief in the quiet night when she had wept in his arms. They were there, prickling behind her eyes, but she smiled with aching resolve, leaning back, her body pressed against his, staring into his eyes. 'Mind you, you'd have never got your degree if we'd wed at college.' She thrust her front with discreet boldness into him, clinging to his shoulders. 'I wouldn't have been able to leave you alone long enough for you to do any studying. You've no idea how wanton you've made me!'

'And you've no idea how much I'm wanting you!' he grinned bravely, returning her explicit movement.

She pulled a face of mock rueful painfulness. 'Oh, I think I have!' she murmured salaciously.

Afterwards, dabbing at her face with her handkerchief, walking back alone through the morning normality of the town, she blushed for her coarseness, and for the nagging shame her defiant words aroused. Making love with John was wonderful. But always, like a phantom hovering at the far reaches of her happiness, was that abiding remorse, and the memory she would always try to shun, of the sick excitement which the young German had initiated, and revealed, inside her.

★   ★   ★

June brought early summer in earnest to the Lakes. High, white fluffs of cloud, on a deep blue that seemed to sparkle, with a freshness that matched the fresh greenery of the woods around Derwent Water, and the billiard nap of the grass leading to the craggy slopes above them. And it was Jenny's own future which was thrust unavoidably at her, with the politely regretful tone of the letter she received from the Education Committee.

She tried to quell the petty spirit of confrontation she felt when she broke the news at home. 'Well, I'd better start thinking about which mob I'm going to join up in,' she declared, waving the letter at her mother, who was busy in the kitchen.

Moira turned, gaping, from the oven. 'What? They can't have — not call-up papers, surely?'

Jenny shook her head, dropped the sheet of paper on the table. 'Not yet. But it can't be long now. It's from the Education Committee. Giving me notice. Apparently the rule about not employing married women still applies. At least it does in Cumberland.'

'What? That's ridiculous! Wait till your father hears this! He'll have a word. With — '

Jenny felt a mean surge of triumph. 'Don't bother. I'm not surprised, really. I'd been expecting it. I'm glad, in a way.'

'What?' Moira exclaimed helplessly for the third time. 'You knew? And yet you still went ahead and got married?' She sat down at the long table, picked up the letter, stared at it without taking in its short message. She shook her head in incomprehension. 'Why on earth? Why didn't you wait? John's going away anyway. What's the point — '

'The point is I wanted to be married to him!' Jenny snapped. She was shaken at how angry she could feel towards her mother these days. She couldn't properly understand it herself. It was as if she was suddenly rebelling against all the conventions of middle-class respectability her mother represented. As if she were blaming them, and Moira, for the almost disastrously dreary course her life had taken over the past four years — her corruption by Horst Zettel and the loss of John and of her happiness. 'I lost him once. Through my own wicked, stupid fault! I didn't want to lose him again! Couldn't bear the very idea of it!'

Moira's cheeks were red. She held herself rigidly, as she did when anything untoward or distasteful reared; a literal stiffening of her spine, a locking of muscles, to repudiate it. Untypically, she had never pried into the reason for the sudden breaking off of her daughter's engagement, or the excruciatingly embarrassing atmosphere between Jenny and that nice, perceptive German boy who had stayed with them at that time. Something had gone on. Something involving her daughter and the two boys. Yet Moira's curiosity was stifled, warned as she was by her good sense that this was an intensely private area it would not be proper to probe. Several letters had come from Germany over the subsequent months. 'How is Horst? Is he well?' she had asked. Jenny's minimal answers made it clear it was a subject never to be discussed.

Now Moira said, with that polite half laugh of reasoned disagreement, 'Oh, I'm quite sure he would have waited. After all, it was him who came back, wasn't it? He came looking for you. With no encouragement from you at all.'

'Yes, thank God!' Jenny answered. Tears welled up, stung in her eyes. 'I couldn't believe it. Me being given a second chance like that.'

'Oh, come on,' Moira protested, her cheek bones prominent in that well-bred half sneer. 'He knows how lucky he is — '

'I don't deserve him! I never will!' Moira was shocked at the raw emotion unleashed in the cry. 'But I want to do my best. I might lose him yet. But at least I can do my bit, too, while he's away. I'm going in to see about joining up tomorrow. One of the women's services. I hope they'll take me on right away next month when I've finished teaching.'

She hurried out before the emotion should overflow into tears. Moira sat blinking, the tide of resentment at Jenny's outburst rising, to compete with her dismay and compassion, and her deep-set anxiety for her girl's suddenly uncertain prospects.

9

It was mid-June before John got his posting. His earlier speculations about North Africa proved to be correct in that it was the theatre of war to which he was heading, but inaccurate in his estimation that the campaign might have ended in victory long before he had an opportunity to take part. The Greek adventure had been costly in more ways than one. Though it was an honourable gesture, the dispatching of troops to the Greek mainland, and subsequently to the island of Crete, had disastrous consequences for the desert war. The impetus of the British advance against the Italians was dissipated by the diversion of men it entailed. And there was another new and vital factor thrown into the equation — General Erwin Rommel.

The tank commander who had distinguished himself in the French conquest had been sent out to North Africa in February, to head two divisions which were the basis of his soon to be famous Afrika Korps. His mission was to stop the rout of the demoralized Italians. He had already done so. Australian and British troops were besieged at Tobruk,

General O'Connor, the architect of the earlier Allied successes, had been captured.

At the briefing when their postings were announced, John and his fellow officers were told of the seriousness of the situation. 'At this moment, our forces are counter-attacking to try and relieve the garrison at Tobruk. But it doesn't look too good. We need you chaps out there urgently. We've got to try and rebuild our strength. If this blighter Rommel pushes any further east, the whole situation in the Middle East could be threatened. You're the chaps who have got to stop him.'

'You're being posted to fiftieth div.,' the captain in the regulating office told John. He smiled. 'That's the Northumbrian Division, so you'll be among your own kind. D Company, Second Battalion, Durham Light Infantry. Hundred and twenty paces to the minute, so you'd better get practising!'

The draft was to be a large one, almost 3,000 men. They were assembled in the holding barracks and organized into two provisional battalions. They were transported *en masse* to a wooden-hutted encampment on Salisbury Plain, where they began training together while they waited for their embarkation date. They had been forbidden to break the news of their destination to families or friends, and there was no leave. One of John's duties was the reading and censoring of the men's mail in his company. The officers were taken on trust, though they signed to say that they would divulge no secrets which might jeopardize the outcome of the war.

'It's probably what I thought,' John told Jenny in his weekly Friday evening telephone call from the inn a mile and a half from the camp. He hoped that any listening operator was not over curious or an enemy spy. 'A bucket and spade job,' he continued cheerfully.

His wife's voice sounded tinnily in his ear. 'You've had news?' she asked anxiously, and he cut in quickly, again with enforced heartiness.

'Yes. Like I said. Buckets and spades, just as I thought.'

Belatedly she understood the allusion. 'Oh — yes,' she murmured, her throat constricting. 'When?' she said, her heart fluttering.

'Oh, fairly soon, I expect. I'll get a seventy-two, I should think.'

She was already familiar enough with service jargon to know that he was referring to a three-day period of leave, which was all they would be granted instead of the usual seven days. Allied forces in North Africa had been reduced by over 30,000 because of the Greek excursion, and Wavell, the C.-in-C., was desperate for reinforcements. His efforts to relieve Tobruk were doomed to failure and, in fact, before the new replacements had embarked, General Wavell had been replaced. His successor was General Auchinleck.

The happiest piece of news for Britain at this time, though not everyone appreciated its significance, was Hitler's turning on his former, uneasy ally, in his invasion of Russia on 22 June. Two weeks later, as John stood on the parade ground with his men under a gently remorseless summer drizzle, loaded down with kit and feeling less than enthusiastic about the route march planned that morning for C and D Companies, they were surprised at the order to stand easy while the whole battalion, with much yelling and doubling back and forth of NCOs, was assembled on the square. Steel helmets gleaming, the rims beaded with tiny silver droplets, they waited with increasing anxiety and excitement.

The colonel himself addressed them, immaculate beneath the umbrella held over him by an acolyte. 'You'll be happy to know you're on the move at last. Your company commanders will give details, so stand fast. And good luck. I know you'll do us proud.' The men roared out with real fervour when the three cheers were called for, then the ranks buzzed with excited chatter until the apoplectic WOs and sergeants bellowed them into silence.

They were to sail on the *Stirling Castle*, within the next ten days. John's company was scheduled to proceed on seventy-two hours embarkation leave from 0800 hours the following day. While the men raced off like kids at the end of term, John and the other junior officers had to spend most of that day helping the harassed regulating staff to sort out the mounds of paperwork involved with organizing the pay and travel documents necessary for the mass departure.

It was after four o'clock before he could start on his own task of packing. Everything had to be taken, for they would not be returning here, but had to report directly to Liverpool at the end of their leave. Although this did not begin officially until the following morning, John found an enterprising colleague had managed to wangle a lift all the way to London that night, and generously offered him a place in the crowded military truck.

Frantically, he tried to place a call to Jenny to warn her, but there were queues for the phones, and he had to be content with leaving a worded telegram with the duty office who promised to get it off as soon as possible. By 2 a.m. he was one of a small crowd pestering a weary Transport Officer at King's Cross. Ten hours and three over-crowded trains later, he reached Keswick, light-headed with fatigue and sticky with perspiration, lugging his heavy suitcase and canvas holdall, his creased battledress blouse bisected by the broad webbing of his gas mask. The July sun beat down on him as he stood on the forecourt of the station, at the end of its covered walkway, and glanced round as though waiting somehow for Jenny miraculously to appear.

He sat on his case and waited, almost apathetically by now, for a further twenty minutes before a taxi could be found to take him to the Alsops' villa, where a delighted Moira insisted he stay for a sandwich and a cup of tea, followed by a quick bath before he set off for Jenny's school. The telegram warning them of his arrival came while he was still splashing in the warm water. 'You must wear your uniform,' Moira insisted. 'Mind you, she won't be free until four o'clock.'

In spite of his bravado, John was more than a little nervous as he approached the pleasant, grey stone building, through the pillars marking the gateway from which the green iron gates had been removed several months ago to help the war effort. The railings atop the stone wall surrounding the yard had also been removed, and there were rough daubs of cement marking their excavated roots like carelessly filled dental cavities running the length of its surface. The smell of stale milk, of dust and chalk, the mote dancing shafts of sunlight, the chanting voices, a distant piano and stern professorial tones, mingled nostalgically, and John found himself recalling Beaconsfield with a clarity and a fond regret he had scarcely felt over the past ten months.

He stood indecisively at the top of the central corridor, just inside the taped glass of the inner swing doors, searching for the head's room. Then Jenny came out of a doorway on the right, and saw his figure darkly silhouetted against the light behind him. She gave a sharp scream, dropping a pile of rolled papers, and hurtled towards him. They clung, he crushed her to him, and they kissed avidly, before they began speaking, gasping, both at once.

'Sorry I couldn't let — '

'Johnny! What is it? What's happened?'

'It's my seventy-two! We're off.'

'Oh, my God! Why didn't you tell me?'

She tugged him by the arm, led him into her class, where nearly fifty ten-year-olds stared delightedly in shocked silence as 'Miss' clutched at his hand, her face red, traces of tears in her eyes, and introduced him with breathless pride. 'This is my husband. Lieutenant John Wright.' And they began to giggle and whisper, while she held on to his arm and faced them, half laughing, half crying. 'Tell them about fighting the Germans!' she urged him. 'I'm going to find the head.'

He stared after her helplessly. As the door closed, the level of noise rose alarmingly. He cleared his throat. 'Right now, you lot!' he announced firmly. 'Settle down there, all right?'

He thought he was portraying his best parade-ground manner, but a whispered voice somewhere near the back, its sing-song Tyneside accent betraying the presence of one of the many evacuees, declared contemptuously, 'He's norra soljer! He's a teacher, man!'

★ ★ ★

May studied her daughter-in-law surreptitiously. She was a pretty girl, and her thick, dark blonde hair fell attractively down the right side of her face in a rich wave, the favoured imitation of trans-Atlantic film stars.

She thought of her niece, Julia's daughter, Dora, whom she and Iris had seen only two days ago, on their regular trip over to Marian's at Low Fell. Dora's hair was a much lighter, more brilliant blonde, its brilliance not entirely the work of nature, as the girl conceded cheerfully. But she was not cheerful about the newly enforced brevity of the hairstyle, for the ordnance factory at Birtley had insisted that, as well as being bound in a turban during working hours, the hair had to be trimmed short, to the disgust of the numerous would-be Veronica Lakes.

'Bloody cheek!' Dora had scowled, a cigarette bobbing at her lip (just like her mother, May had reflected) and perfectly aware of the effect her unladylike language would have on the two visitors. 'What I do with my hair's my business!'

'Not worth being scarred for life over, though, is it?' May had answered reasonably, to be rewarded by the tossing of the blonde locks and a sniff which, in its eloquent condemnation, was again reminiscent of her mother.

Dora's face, attractive as it was, was sharper, more worldlywise than this girl sitting across the table from May, even though Jenny was some seven years older. Jenny's unblemished skin, only lightly adorned by restrained touches of make-up, bore favourable comparison with the younger girl, whose complexion, doubtless marred by the daily coating of grime to which it was subjected at work, was heavily disguised by all the artifice powder and paint could provide. There was, too, the evidence about the eyes of the long hours of shift work and inadequate sleep, which was due not only to the exigencies of wartime but the imperious demands of pleasure to be squeezed from the few hours of leisure she could enjoy.

May conceded that, just at this moment, there were shades of darkening tiredness about Jenny's violet eyes, too, then almost blushed at the unbidden thought that they were caused by a very recent sleeplessness, occasioned by the previous night spent in the arms of her husband.

She strove to shy away from such indecorous conjectures, but was shocked at the strength of physical excitement stirred by her thoughts. And by the sharp pain of what she realized, with another shock, was simple envy. She had never so much as shared a passionate kiss with any man other than Jack. She had been a widow twenty-four years. Helplessly, her mind continued mercilessly to supply the statistics she had always banished from her conscious thought. Twenty-five years, near enough, since she had last made love.

For a long while after Jack's death, it had seemed that her body was numbed as well as her mind at the enormity of her loss. But then came nights of bitter tears at the shameful rekindling of bodily desire, so that it seemed at times almost a curse that she had known the fulfilment of sexual love, for it was a solitary, dead desire, fanned and then, finally, relieved by her own ministrations, in spite of her lonely torment. Sublimation came again, of another sort, with the precious comfort of having Iris close to her, literally. May cherished the blessing of the asexual bond which could still bring so much ease at the contact with that strong, reliant body, the tenderness of touch, of hugging embraces in the no longer lonely intimacy of the night. Moments of sexual deprivation were fewer and fewer through the years. Which was why, when they caught her unawares, as now, they were all the more disturbing, especially after a quarter of a century of celibacy.

Oddly enough, along with the jealousy, came a rush of warmth and closeness, deepening the link between her and the girl she acknowledged she still hardly knew, even though it was seven years now since they had first met. She found herself wondering as she had so many times what it was that had split the young couple and made them go their separate ways for more than two years.

She had guessed that it had something to do with that young German boy, something between him and Jenny, though the engagement had not been formally broken until after John's trip across to Germany as Horst Zettel's guest. The time of John's foolish, dangerous involvement with David Golding's plans to assist one of his Jewish relatives. Now, more than ever, May realized how lucky John had been to get away with no more than a few hours locked in a Berlin prison cell. At first, he had intimated that it was largely through Horst Zettel's intervention that he had escaped so lightly. But from that time the friendship had ended. It seemed that on that fateful trip John had learned the truth, in more ways than one.

That he loved Jenny, had never ceased to love her, was abundantly clear, even through the long months of their separation. Later, May was ashamed, would not even recognize her inner feelings of relief. She felt even worse at her son's clear unhappiness, though he refused to acknowledge or even refer to it. When his call-up papers had come last September, her tender conscience had won the day. She was glad that she had urged him to go and seek out Jenny, although she suspected he had already half made up his mind to do so. And she was glad, she assured herself fiercely, that his quest had proved successful, that he had at last won the girl he so clearly loved.

Conscience was certainly pricking tenderly tonight. She upbraided herself for her instinctive reaction when she had got his phone call yesterday, telling her that he was already at Jenny's, that they would spend the night there before coming across country to Hexham. How could she possibly be hurt, she scolded herself, that he had gone straight to his wife? What else could he, should he, do? And they were here now, both of them.

'What are you going to do?' she asked Jenny now. The slim figure looked more youthful than ever, snuggled in the loose folds of the dark siren suit. The narrow white feet were drawn up on the sofa, tucked under her thighs. May saw the vivid darkness of the painted toe-nails, felt again a sudden quiver of sexuality whisper through her.

'I finish at school in a fortnight,' she said. Her face was flushed, she sounded defensive as she answered. 'I've been told that if I put my name down for the Wrens I stand a good chance of getting in. But I'll have to wait a while. If I want to join the ATS I can go more or less straight away.'

'Are you really sure it's what you want? To get mixed up in it all?' May asked. Her expression reflected her troubled concern. 'It can't be easy. You don't know where they might send you. And — well, the girls you'll meet. They won't all be like you — with your background.'

Jenny nodded. 'I know. I'm a bit scared, I'll admit.' She looked directly at May, who felt a stab of compassion at the appealing, ingenuous look she saw on the young face. 'But the boys have to do it, don't they? And I will have to do something, sooner or later. I mean, I won't have any choice.'

May sighed, nodded sadly. Why don't you just let him get you pregnant, you silly girl? she thought strongly. But, of course, she did not say it. With her natural, conventional reserve, May would not utter such an indelicate observation. Just as she would never enquire even from her own son exactly what it was that had almost broken the two young people's lives together for good.

At that point, John came into the room from his bath. Out of uniform, in an old sweater and his dark grey flannels, he was far more familiar, and May felt a flooding tenderness that included the uncertain young figure curled along the sofa, towards whom he advanced straight away and plonked himself down beside. She squirmed as he reached out and playfully seized one cold foot. They were together and happy, that was all that mattered. May prayed fervently, against a cold shadow of panic she could feel swelling within her, that they would remain so, in the face of all the dangers she knew loomed ahead.

10

John leaned on the rail, screwing up his eyes against the sun glare which came off the sea. A darker smudge on the horizon, with just a hint of green, was Ireland. The movement of the ship was hardly discernible; the slightest suggestion of a rise and fall, and, of course, the quiver of the diesel engines beneath his feet and their ceaseless thrumming which had kept him awake most of last night. He was on the port side of the vessel, in the after section of what must have been in happier times the promenade deck. As passenger boats went, the *Stirling Castle* was no ocean giant. At 25,000 tons, she was less than a third the size of the 'Queens'. Even so, he could imagine how pleasant, at least for the passengers, a sea voyage must have been.

This trip would be different. As a troop-ship, most of her former luxury accommodation had been gutted to make room for the almost 4,000 personnel she was carrying. As well as the replacements for the embryo Eighth Army General Auchinleck was in the process of forming, there were almost 1,000 'odds and sods' aboard, including a large RAF detachment, and, even more eye-catching, a contingent of female warriors, made up of naval and army nurses, and a batch of ATS, which numbered over 150. Originally, he suspected, a boat of this size would carry no more than a few hundred passengers at the most.

He was sharing a tiny cabin with five others. Two rows of three-tier bunks, with about a foot and a half of space between them, and all their luggage stowed in the alleyway outside. The bathroom was similarly lilliputian, with three metal handbasins and two metal tubs in which you could only sit upright, and a coffin-sized shower stall, all to be shared by eighteen officers on D-41 'flat', which was naval parlance for the section of the deck occupied by the three cabins crammed with officers where he now lived. The three lavatories they had to share were now referred to as 'heads'.

Privately, John thought he was little better off than the men of D Company, quartered in a vast gallery on the starboard side of the ship, where hammocks were slung in their hundreds, fading into the hazy distance. His mind had been effectively diverted from his personal gloom by observing the antics of the majority of the men as they struggled to rig their sleeping devices, following a grinning crewman's instructions.

Now, after a virtually sleepless night, the depressing thoughts drifted like shadows waiting to claim him once more. The tiny edge of insidious excitement he had been feeling ever since they had got their orders for the off made him more guilt-ridden than ever as he recalled the agony of the farewell scene in the shabby impersonality of the Liverpool boarding house. Was it really only two nights ago?

It had been a mistake, he acknowledged that now. He should have left Jenny at the end of his leave, seen her on to the train to Cumberland and left it at that. But after reporting to the *Stirling Castle,* and with another four days to wait while the rest of the replacements returned from their embarkation leave, he had followed the example of his company commander, Captain Dolan, and brought Jenny down for the bonus of two more nights together. 'There hasn't been an air raid for nearly a month,' he told her. 'We could have Monday and Tuesday nights together. We sail on Wednesday.'

Jenny had been as eager as he was, in spite of the difficulties it would cause her at work. 'I think they've given up on me, anyway,' she said, more lightly than she felt. 'I'll leave under a bit of a cloud, but it can't be helped.'

'Well, if it's going to be too difficult . . . ' he offered, clearly intimating his expectations, and was warmed by the vehemence of her denial.

However, the grief they had shared on their final night together still hurt like a throbbing wound as he relived it. Her distress had appalled him. More, it unmanned him, and he joined her in tears, while they clung desolately together in the lumpy, creaking bed. They had made love the night before, striving to lessen the obscenity of the squealing springs, until Jenny had been seized by a fit of hysterical giggles. On the Tuesday night, after she had filled a tediously long day wandering about the bomb-ravaged city waiting for him to come from the frantic hours of last-minute preparations aboard ship, her brave attempts at bright talk petered out.

When she came back from the bathroom, clad in her long blue housecoat and clutching her towel and sponge bag, his body was racing with passion for her. But he felt a tremor of alarm at the misery on her white face as she stood gazing at him from the bottom of the bed. He was sitting naked on the counterpane. With sudden embarrassment, he reached for his striped pyjama pants, hid his loins beneath them.

'I'm sorry. Do you mind? I think I'm starting my monthlies early.' Her hands folded protectively over her belly. 'I'm sorry,' she repeated, and then her face crumpled, she began to cry, hopelessly, and he fumbled quickly into his pyjamas, went to hold her. 'Hey! Come on. It doesn't matter.' He tried a joke. 'It's just as well, isn't it? We'd be in a panic if you weren't. It's all right. Come here.'

And it was all right, at least as far as not having sex went. It meant they could be even more tender; they lay and held each other, stroked and kissed, gently, comfortingly. Except that after a while the comfort was gone as they both faced the awful prospect of the imminent parting and the vast nightmare of unspoken fears that lay between them.

'Look,' he whispered against her hair, his heart torn by the violence of her grief. 'You really don't have to worry about me, love. I swear. I'm not the stuff heroes are made of. You know me. I'll find myself some safe little billet. I promise. I'm learning all the dodges. I'll sit it out safe somewhere. And you've got to promise me you'll do the same. *I'll* be worried about you, you know. Even though I am proud as Punch of you.'

'Oh yes, my darling!' She clung even more fiercely to him. 'I just want to be with you.

Tell me we'll be together again soon.'

'Of course we will. I promise.'

John did not know how closely this scene echoed that which his parents had endured twenty-five years earlier. It was as well, for the pathos of their love, and their uncertainty, was hard enough for them to bear.

He was doubly glad now that he had not attempted to get a pass for her to watch the *Stirling Castle* pull away from the quayside on the poignantly sunny July morning. There was a select little group on the deck, gazing up with brave smiles and fluttering handkerchiefs, as well as a depleted band to play them off, and a sturdily cheering knot of dockyard mateys at the very end of the last wooden jetty they slid past on their way down river. He was not sure he could have borne watching the white blur of her face, her diminishing figure shrinking away from him across the oily surface of dark water. It was a little less painful to think of her dressing in that impersonal room, packing her small case, sitting self-contained in the carriage, gazing out of the window, holding back her tears. It might almost be a benefit that she would have the discomfort of her period to distract her from her mental anguish. But then he chided himself for his ignorant assumption. How on earth could he know how it made her feel? It might simply add to the enveloping misery of her situation. After all, even his limited experience had taught him such times could be emotionally unstable, too.

Reflecting on Jenny's biological make-up added further to his own depression, for he found himself wishing profoundly that he had left his seed planted and fertile within her. Was it a comfort to his father in his last moments to know that he had not left May alone, that part of him lived on in his two sons? For the first time, John felt a sudden chill of real and imminent fear that his life might soon end, that he might never see Jenny or his mother again. He pushed it away, shocked and disturbed by its novel, momentary power.

Two days later, they were at anchor to the north of Northern Ireland, in the company of several other vessels, waiting for the convoy of more than fifty ships to gather. The weather had changed. The *Stirling Castle* wallowed, rolling ponderously to the heavy swell, while grey rain sheeted down in continual squalls. Below decks the stale air carried the aroma of cooked food, oil, and, increasingly, vomit, as the majority of the 4,000 troops succumbed to seasickness. John wasn't sick, but after twenty-four hours wished that he could be, for his head throbbed, and his stomach heaved. He spent as much time as possible on the upper deck. So far, the confined nature of life on board ship meant that duties, compared with their normal routine in camp, were light. He had time to spare, a novel concept in service existence, and he began to keep a scribbled diary, as well as writing pages of a letter to Jenny which threatened rapidly to become the size of a fat novel.

Diversion was at hand. That night in a packed wardroom, the ship's chief executive officer, with the three gold rings of a commander in chain-link design on his sleeve, designating him as a member of the RNR, the Royal Naval Reserve, seconded from his peacetime occupation in the Merchant Service, broke the startling and generally unwished for news that they would be 'taking the short cut' due south, back through the Irish Sea, across the Bay of Biscay and down the coast of Portugal.

'We nip through the Straits of Gibraltar and give you the bonus of a Mediterranean cruise before we put you off at Alexandria or Port Said. Thus sparing you the horrors of a long haul round the Cape and up through the dreaded Red Sea.'

There was a low buzz of excitement from his audience, and he smiled. 'With a bit of luck, we'll have you there in ten days or so.

Luck being the operative word,' he ended with heavy emphasis, then added wryly, 'that and the vigilance of our escorts, of course.'

Though British successes at Taranto last November, and in the spring of this year, at the battle of Cape Matapan, had severely reduced the effectiveness of the Italian fleet, the Med was acquiring a reputation as a bit of a 'bomb alley' because of the proximity of the Italian and Sicilian airfields, as well as the threat from marauding U-boats.

'Better get used to sleeping in your clothes with your life-jacket round your neck,' one of John's fellow officers advised. Such advice was taken seriously by a great many once they reached more southerly waters.

The other ships, at least in their vicinity, all seemed large, and well capable of steaming faster than the ten knots which was convoy speed. There were plenty of escorts, but, apart from two sleek destroyers, the rest seemed extremely small — sloops and converted trawlers. They raced back and forth fussily, sending up fine bow waves, and the increasingly edgy troops envied their apparent busyness.

Their senior officers did their best to ensure that time should not hang heavily. Boat drills were frequent, and soon changed from the light-hearted episodes they had initially been. Once they reached Atlantic waters, the threat of enemy submarines was disturbingly real, and the more imaginative stared out at the relatively placid green sea and conjured visions of the gliding menace lurking beneath.

There were the daily physical jerks, the packed ranks so close that there was scarcely room to raise their arms without making contact with a neighbour. The men were not required to change into sports kit, except for the canvas shoes, which most of them wore permanently anyway. Braces dangled in pale loops from their trousers, and many actually wore the life-jackets throughout the period of exercise, much to the amusement of any mocking crew who happened to be close by. There were weaponry drills, and lectures to occupy both forenoon and afternoon on all kinds of subjects from first aid to map reading and war gases. These lessons were usually conducted in any free corner of the upper decks. Platoon commanders had to bear the brunt of the informal teaching periods, and John dutifully swotted up from his Forces' Handbook. He found he quite enjoyed them despite the difference from his earlier teaching experiences.

One afternoon, it was his turn to deal with aircraft recognition. He passed around the well-thumbed cards with the black silhouettes on them, then collected them in, and showed them at a distance, letting his squad work in pairs to try to identify them.

'Yeah, don't worry. You'll get plenty of chance to see this one,' Private Ron Maudsley quipped, in his flat Teesside accent, when John held up the card of the Italian BR-20, a twin-engined bomber. 'The real bloody thing!' He was an acknowledged mouthpiece of the platoon, and the novelty of the relaxed atmosphere which came with shipboard life made him even freer. 'We won't have any bother recognizing enemy planes. It's our own lot we'll never catch sight of!'

It was a common complaint. John had heard it often enough from veterans of the Dunkirk evacuation. The complete lack of apparent air cover for the convoy had been adversely commented on frequently, too. There was an uneasy tension developing between the RAF personnel on board and the soldiery, which, the officers knew, had to be stamped on.

'Thing to remember, Maudsley,' John said patiently, 'is that the air force lads *are* on our side. We're supposed to be fighting Jerry. Not each other!' They laughed tolerantly.

They slipped through the Straits of

Gibraltar under darkness. There was no sign of the Rock at daylight, only a sparkling Mediterranean under a hazy blue sky. At stand-easy, the troops brought their mugs of char up on deck and stripped off from the waist up, spreading themselves where they could on the hot deck plating. 'Go easy,' the NCOs warned them. 'Remember, sunburn is a punishable offence. Self-inflicted injury. Jankers if you report sick, lads!'

'I'd settle for a nice drop of roughers,' one of the deck officers muttered to John, glancing up at the blue spread overhead. His words proved prophetic. Just before lunch, they heard the distant, rapid thumps of gunfire, and saw, miniatured by distance, tiny black puffs of smoke, then a dappled carpet of white, stretching like an isolated cloud. The clanging bells for action stations set their nerves jumping.

'Clear the decks!' a petty officer bawled, and the half-naked troops, some of them already donning the ever-near life-jackets, grumbled as they moved quickly below.

'They will tell us if this bastard's sinking, won't they, sir?' Maudsley asked. He was not smiling.

John's platoon were lucky that they were not quartered on one of the lower decks. They had only one companionway to climb to get up top. Still, it was nerve-racking enough to squat inactively, listening to the increasing volume of the gunfire, then to feel the sudden, heavy thumping of the engines as speed was dramatically increased. The vessel heeled over; they cursed as loose objects went skittering across the sloping deck. They felt the sea smacking with solid force into the hull, which lurched again at a violent change of course.

The rapid bark of Bofors rose to a frenetic hammering for a few minutes, though it seemed a lot longer to the tense, crouching figures, then faded into the distance. The weaving changes of direction ceased, though the ship continued to steam at her new speed for some time, a fact that the men found very comforting. 'Get the fuck out of it!' Maudsley muttered graphically.

The second air attack took place soon after daylight the following morning, and there were three more before the end of the afternoon watch at four o'clock. A squad of men, under John's nominal charge though in reality, like him, under the supervision of a petty officer from the crew mysteriously referred to as 'cox', was designated to form part of a damage control party, so that they remained on the upper deck, waiting on the port side, in the section of the promenade deck normally reserved for the officers' recreation area. It afforded them a fine view of the arena of conflict.

They watched the hazy blue swiftly blanketed by a layer of pale puffs as the AA guns, including their own fixed on the superstructure below the wings of the bridge, put up a barrage which kept the enemy planes high above. Even so, they saw a V of tiny black dots, like a flight of birds, and briefly heard the engine throb over the noise their own side was making. The black shape of the vessel steering parallel to them, made small by the distance, was surrounded by slender white fountains of water, then disappeared completely until the eruptions subsided, and she steamed on, apparently unharmed.

The buzz that they were going to put in at Malta persisted as they ploughed on through the summer heat. 'Gonna drop some of them nurses,' one of the squad asserted knowingly. He winked. 'Get a chance to get ashore, eh?' he leered. 'Get up the Gut for a bit of how's-your-father.'

His hopes were dashed. They continued eastwards. The convoy was much more widely dispersed. They could see only distant smudges of smoke, only two other ships being near enough to show as distinct shapes. They were also maintaining a much faster speed. 'We should be in Alex some time on Sunday,' one of the naval officers informed John at dinner in the crowded first-class salon that served as the wardroom.

The two-ringer glanced over in the direction of a party of nurses, who sat at one long trestle table near the wide double doors. The girls were not of officer rank, but a concession had been made. They looked uncomfortably self-conscious for the most part, though one or two kept sneaking glances about them. 'More's the pity,' the navy man murmured, smiling.

The other ATS girls were billeted somewhere up forrard, or, rather, down forrard, John amended, for they were way down on E-deck. A night guard of two men was detailed to stand watch outside their mess. They were changed every two hours, and, for once, there was little grumbling at this extra duty. Some lurid and, John surmised, highly exaggerated tales were told of their experiences, though several men were already on charges associated with their female colleagues. There was even a rumour that a couple had been caught in highly compromising circumstances in one of the tarpaulin-covered lifeboats, where they had been spending most of their nights together. 'That's the kind of boat drill I wouldn't mind having a bash at meself!' Maudsley opined judiciously. 'Fourteen days in the glasshouse. Who gives a toss where we're going, eh?'

Part II

Promises To Keep

11

Teddy stared unblinkingly at the slender figure bathed in the brilliance of the stage lights. The brief white silk covering the torso, the long black stockings, the high-heeled shoes, created an all too real sexual allure which the crudely made, long red wig and the flamboyant make-up did nothing to dispel. Teddy felt his body's throbbing reaction, and was overcome with disgust and fury. The growls and laughter of the German officers in the front rows and the similar roars of appreciation from his own officers behind them caused a thick bile to rise in Teddy's throat.

'She looks the part all right tonight, eh?' Andy Macaulay's voice whispered in his ear in the dimness of the hut and, for a second, Teddy felt his rage turn against his friend. He grunted, never taking his eyes off the slim figure of Tony simpering his way through the provocative song and dance routine. His stance, his movements, were wickedly femi-nine, his heavily painted eyes flashing, the glistening cupid's-bow lips pouting so sugges-tively. Even his voice, reedily thin and with that breathless little catch and lisp, sounded far too authentically girlish.

The audience hooted and cheered at the end of the number, howling for Tony to reappear, until he was pushed back on from the tiny wings and he and his partner went through the whole routine once more. The applause at the end was even more rapturous. They were still whistling and stamping their feet when Teddy rose and pushed his way along the row, making for the exit. 'It's all right for Corp,' he heard a voice say behind him. 'He makes sure he gets his bit, don't you worry.'

Outside, the night was clear and freezing, the stark surroundings under the high arc lamps eerily pale with frost. Above, in the contrasting deep blackness the pinpoint stars flickered, infinitely distant and alien. He thought of Marian, and his mother. He wondered if it was a clear night at home, if they would be glancing up into the night sky. He felt the ache and the loneliness swamp over him, the residue of his sexual hunger tormenting him.

His second Christmas in captivity. How many more? One of the guards had taunted them earlier in the day with the news that Hong Kong was about to fall into Japanese hands any day. There had been a buzz of hope through the camp a couple of weeks before when a rumour had spread, and been quickly confirmed, that America had entered the war against Germany after the bombing of Pearl Harbour. But it was followed almost immediately by the announcement at morning *appel* that two British battleships, the *Prince of Wales* and the *Repulse*, had been sunk off Malaya. It seemed a perfect reflection of their life as prisoners, see-sawing between hope and despair.

At least this Christmas was far less unpleasant than the previous one had been in France. They had even got mail and some precious Red Cross parcels through and the atmosphere was much more relaxed. Hence this festive concert and the suspension of their nightly curfew. Though even that dug grittily at Teddy's conscience. The air of peace and good will to all men smacked shamefully of collaboration, he thought sourly.

Back in the hut the guards took the roll-call easily, letting the men chat through it all. They grinned at Tony's unoccupied bunk. One of the prisoners winked lewdly. 'She'll no be back for a while, Fritz. She's got to get a' that warpaint off, an' say goodnight to your boss, eh?'

Andy came over as Teddy was folding his

clothes under the thin mattress. Like most of them, he was wearing his khaki sweater over his underclothes. The POWs slept in most of their garments, for there was not enough wood to keep the stove burning all night and the hut soon became icy. Andy's normally soft tone was even lower than usual, scarcely more than a whisper. 'Ye know, you'll have to have a word with Young-un. Tell him to take it easy. There's one or two are getting really incensed over his messing about with the Jerries. He'll have to watch it.'

Teddy thrust his face close, his expression showing the emotion he felt. 'Christ, man! It's no good me talking to him. You think I haven't tried?' He jerked his head bitterly towards the rest of the room, struggling to keep his voice low. 'There's half of them think I'm shafting him myself anyway!'

Sleep eluded him, as he knew it would. The bunk creaked, the boards' hardness thrust up through the thin stuff of the mattress; divided rectangles of light played over the hut from the beams of the searchlights which swung irregularly from the towers. The crude comments and the guffaws died gradually, to be replaced by the grunts and snores, and moans and whimpers, of the dreaming occupants. No doubt there were some who, like him, could not find temporary relief in the oblivion of sleep.

The vision of Tony's assumed femininity would not be driven from his mind, reviving the sexual desire he tried hopelessly to keep at bay. His thoughts drifted to his wife, so that in desperation he strove to recapture the sight of her body, the smooth texture of her skin, the stirring warmth of her gladly given flesh. But it was overlaid cruelly with a much more recent memory, all too vivid, of Tony, the thin body twisting playfully beneath him in his grip, the head flung back, the red curls tumbling on his brow, the mouth flung wide open, warm and moist and red, the teeth white and even as he laughed.

It had been an Indian summer of a day, of real heat, so that the prisoners had discarded their outer clothing, lounging in shorts and vests, or stripped to the waist, to enjoy the unexpected late sunshine. Teddy had for once enjoyed the intimacy with Tony, the boy's innocent flirtatiousness. He had shown him the photos of his family again, talked about the café at Hexham, about John and Jenny, and Marian and little Teddie.

'You're dead lucky,' Tony said, with ingenuous pathos. 'Having your family and that.' He had told Teddy many stories of his own deprived childhood, his progress through various children's and foster homes, until his escape to the army school at fifteen.

'You'll have to meet them all when we get out of this lot,' Teddy told him, and Tony had blushed, his grey eyes misting with emotion. 'Course I mean it!' Teddy urged. 'You'll have a great time up north, I promise.' He had even read him the less intimate portions of Marian's letter, and the carefully neutral tones of John's missive, posted in Alexandria.

'You're a real toff, aren't you?' Tony said teasingly. 'Your brother a bleeding officer, your mum running a caff!'

Soon the horseplay grew boisterous, then mock-violent. They wrestled on the sandy earth, Tony puffing and laughing, and very soon relaxing his feeble efforts to resist Teddy's onslaught. Teddy pinned him down, lay on top of him, capturing the thin wrists. And the joke turned sour, ended abruptly, as Teddy felt the thin body, felt his own excitement, stared at the laughing mouth, the long, thin, upturned throat, smelt the faint fragrance of some kind of perfume on the youngster's smooth skin, and abruptly thrust himself clear, rolled away, appalled at his thoughts, and his physical arousal.

That had been almost three months ago. Since then, Teddy had seen and felt the danger many times, pushed it from him. His moods, and treatment of Tony had alternated wildly from that same unexpressed intimacy to sudden and brutal rejection. Often he had been pained himself at the pink-faced hurt he had seen on the young features, the undisguised pain as he turned away from him. Now, he lay in the Christmas darkness, listening for the rattle of the door, which was not locked, waiting for Tony to return. He did not come back. It was almost dawn before Teddy drifted into sleep.

A few days later, Tony moved out of the hut altogether. His freckles showed under the flushed skin, his eyes flickered from Teddy's gaze as he explained. 'They've got me working over in the guard office and the commandant's block. And they want me to do a night duty over in sick bay. Just for emergencies. They want me to kip over there.'

'The little queer's only doing a turn for the Commandant himself!' someone asserted vehemently when the news got round. 'I knew old Meyer was an arse bandit, but from what I hear Young-un didn't need no persuading. Bloody little nancy's loving every minute!'

In spite of all his efforts to curb his temper, Teddy could not contain his anger. He soon found himself embroiled in a bitter argument which led inevitably to blows. Later, he wondered what instinct had prompted him to try to defend Tony, for he was not sure whether the general condemnatory attitude towards the youngster wasn't correct. Maybe it was his own confused guilt at his secret, perverse, attraction to Tony that made him act so volatilely. A way of punishing himself. Whatever the reason, he fought a brief but furious battle with one of the Jocks, and gave a good account of himself. It resulted in a week's solitary, which he would have enjoyed were it not for the biting cold, for there was no heating in the bleak little cell, and outside there were four inches of snow on the January ground.

After his release back to the POW community, there was a scene which, for him, held a large degree of farce. He was summoned before a captain and a warrant officer from the Allied officers' camp across the road and informed that he was demoted to the rank of private and must remove his twin stripes forthwith. 'A note will be made for the record. You've put up a bad show, Wright. You're supposed to set an example to your men.'

The pale patch on his battledress where the stripes had been earned him a good deal of sympathy with his colleagues. Even his opponent in the fight came over and shook his hand, much to Teddy's private amusement. But tension flared suddenly again some two weeks later when the whole camp was called out on a special parade after lunch one Wednesday. The whispered word buzzed swiftly from mouth to mouth as the POWs lined up in a grey drizzle. 'Some blokes have given young nancy Ellis a good seeing to over by the hospital.'

Tony had indeed been seriously beaten and then sexually assaulted in the ablutions hut next to the sick bay. The culprits were never found, and the whole population suffered considerable hardship. The huts were turned over, the prisoners' few possessions flung and scattered carelessly in the mud. The already meagre diet was reduced for more than a week, and random selections were made from each hut, the victims being sentenced to two weeks in solitary.

Teddy went over to the sick bay in an attempt to see Tony, who had not even been attending roll-calls since he had left the hut soon after Christmas. He was refused entrance. There were no further sightings of the youngster, even at a distance, and eventually it was ascertained from one of the guards that Tony had been transferred to another camp. 'No doubt he'll be doing all right wherever he is, the brown-nosing bastard!'

'I bet you miss him, eh, Corp?' They still

gave Teddy the courtesy of the title even though he had lost his rank.

Teddy, wiser and less impetuous, merely smiled. In some ways, he had to admit to a feeling of relief that Tony had departed from his life for good. 'How could I,' he answered, 'when I'm surrounded by such gorgeous types as you?' They roared with laughter and left him to it.

★   ★   ★

'What's the matter? You'd not be doin' nowt wrong, ye know, just going to the pictures! Me mam's already said she'll come and watch the bairn for you. There's a good film at the Majestic. And we can pop in for a few drinks at the Canon or somewhere after.' Dora's pretty young face stared at her almost aggressively.

Marian felt herself pinking. 'Oh, I dunno,' she offered doubtfully. She was really torn between acceptance and rejection of Dora's invitation. She knew that Dora had arranged everything, and Marian felt both tempted and disturbed at the thought of going out with Jim Moody. And that's what she would be doing, going out on a date, with a partner. Dora would be with her Ray Lambert, and she would be with Jim.

She still shivered with both guilt and excitement when she thought back to New Year's Eve. It had all seemed so innocent, cleaning the house from top to bottom, the preparations for the party, the extra rations and 'goodies' which Dora had somehow managed to procure. 'It'll be a good laugh,' Dora had told her. 'They're a good crowd. You'll enjoy it. A chance for you to get dressed up in your glad rags. Put your blue dress on. You look smashing in that.'

She had let Dora arrange her newly washed hair, which she had allowed to grow long again. 'Hey, Kidder. You look like a film star!' She had felt the usual twinges of guilt and sadness when she thought, as she so often did, of her husband, but then Dora rallied her. 'Howay, man! He wouldn't want you to sit moping all on your own, would he? Not on New Year's Eve. He'll be hoping you're not feeling miserable and on your own. Enjoy yourself — for his sake!'

The guests came late, from some pub or other, so she had been sitting nervously on her own in the festively decorated living-room, more and more uncertain and uncomfortable. But then they came flooding in, most of them tight already, and with loads of booze to see them through a long night. Night and dawning — Jim Moody had been

159

the first foot, standing on the step in the freezing starlight, with Ray Lambert and several others to keep him noisy company, and with quieter but convivial groups in the neighbouring gardens and no wardens to complain about light spilling out into the night. There were no factory or ships' hooters from the Tyne, but no martial sirens either to disturb the celebrations — air raids had been infrequent for the past three months and more.

Those inside opened the door on the strokes of midnight, and Jim was thrust into the hallway, with his bread and salt and lump of coal. His lips stabbed in hasty embarrassment at Marian's proffered mouth, and she blushed and laughed, and was soon kissing all the menfolk, not minding the boldness of some of their embraces. The party went on, with games and impromptu concert turns and singing, and dancing. May and Iris had presented Marian with a gramophone player as a Christmas present for her and for Teddie, but the meagre stock of records were mostly unsuitable for the kind of dancing the party guests had in mind. 'Tune in the wireless,' someone urged. 'Geraldo's on, I think.'

They found the station, and soon entwined couples were shuffling round the limited space, with the furniture pushed back against the walls. By now, Marian had had far more to drink than she was used to. Her head spun as she moved around in one set of arms after another, her knees gently bumping, now and then her thighs rubbing against those pressed close to her. She noticed after a while that Jim Moody had commandeered her, refusing to let others have their chance, and she was shocked at how pleased she was at his attention. Then she discovered that Dora and Ray Lambert were missing, and stayed missing as the early hours passed. She found, again shockingly, that she didn't really care.

She went upstairs to check on Teddie, paused outside the small back bedroom which Dora used. She heard a soft snoring. She did not try the closed door, guessed that it would be locked. She slipped into the lavatory at the head of the staircase and as she came out, still shaking down her dress, Jim was waiting. He grabbed her and bundled her back inside the toilet cubicle, thrusting the door shut behind him without letting go of her.

The kiss this time was raw, and brutal in its hunger. She returned it, opening her mouth, taking his invasive ferocity, reciprocating it until they thrust savagely together, only breaking contact when they were both breathless. His hand clutched at the softness of her breast, the other dug into her buttock, held her loins to his. 'Don't!' she wept, and surrendered her mouth to his once more, the kiss gentler this time, exploring. She could feel his belly pressing into her, felt herself move, accommodating him, returning his thrilling pressure. She was panting, without strength, clinging to him. She began to cry. 'Please don't.'

He kissed her neck, his lips biting, burning, and her whole frame trembled against his. With a groan, he released her, turned away, leaning against the cold wall, his face resting on his uplifted arm. 'I'm sorry. I couldn't help it, lass.' His voice was thick, the words muffled. She sniffled, brushed at her wet cheeks, slid past him, dragging the door open and easing herself out. She went along the landing to the bathroom, went in and bolted the door.

He kept away from her for the rest of the long night. She chatted to the girls, and busied herself with food and coffee in the kitchen, and towards dawn went upstairs again. She tapped on Dora's door, shook the handle, knocked louder, until at last she heard groans, bedsprings stirring. The door opened a crack, and Dora's screwed-up pale face, make-up smeared wildly, appeared. Marian could see one bare, bony shoulder,

162

innocent of clothing, a woollen dressing-gown concealing the rest.

'It's your party!' Marian hissed. 'Get up and see to your guests. I'm off to bed. It's four o'clock.' She left her, went along and lifted the warm, sleeping bundle from the cot, carried Teddie back along the landing to the main bedroom. The little girl whimpered but did not wake, and seconds later Marian, still in her underclothes, crawled in beside her and hugged her in the dimness while she smothered her tears in the pillow.

Two days into 1942, a letter had come from Jim Moody apologizing for his behaviour. Though the wording was stilted, the sentiment seemed genuine enough, and when Dora asked if he could call for Sunday tea a week later, in company with Ray Lambert, she agreed, though not without some misgivings. 'I don't want him to get any wrong ideas, mind,' she warned Dora.

Dora grinned. 'Don't be daft. He knows you're an ould married woman, for God's sake!'

He had visited several times since then, always with Dora and Ray, who were now an acknowledged 'couple'. 'You be careful,' Marian frequently cautioned.

Dora gave her usual knowing chuckle. 'Don't worry, Kidder. I'll not get caught out.

Not like you were! Anyways, Ray would marry us like that if I gave him the chance.' She snapped finger and thumb together. 'But I'm in no rush. I'll wait a while yet. I don't want to end up like you,' she added cheekily.

But now, in the early March gloom of the cosy kitchen, Marian's face reflected her uncertainty. This was different. She liked Jim. It made her uncomfortable even to admit it. He had behaved with gentlemanly decorum since that one slip. But she knew he liked her all right. Maybe more than liked her. And she had to admit the idea gave her a girlish kind of thrill when she thought of it. She studied herself in the glass in the privacy of bed or bathroom. She had lost some weight in the last couple of years. Though not where it mattered, she told herself, with a guilty grin, eyeing her full breasts with ashamed pleasure.

She missed Teddy, more than anyone could realize. It was just coming up to two years since she had seen him. Since they had last made love . . . since anyone had looked at her in that way . . . desired her. 'I dunno,' she repeated, staring at Dora with that appealing, troubled expression.

Dora abandoned her teasing role. She reached across the table, briefly touched Marian's wrist. 'Jim's a nice lad,' she said warmly. 'He knows the score. He knows you love Teddy. He just likes being with you. There's no harm in it. Come on.'

Marian drew a deep breath. She sat up, gazed at her friend. 'Oh, all right then. As long as you're sure. He knows where we stand.' She was startled at how breathless and trembling she felt inside.

12

Jenny tugged at the knot of her black tie, tried to centre it neatly between the points of her white shirt collar. Even after six months of practice, she still had difficulty in fastening the tie satisfactorily. The knot was usually too small and chokingly tight, or too large and flopped loosely. For Sunday morning divisions and special parades the girls tied one another's neckties. It was much easier to do someone else's. She flicked her hair away from the collar. It was fine. Not even Chief Wren Lidell would be able to find fault with its length — yet.

She adjusted the round hat, squaring off the HMS lettering at her brow, then glanced round the 'cabin' with a deep sense of well being. The four iron beds were made, covered with the identical counterpanes with the large encircled anchor symbol dead centre. Pyjamas and dressing gowns were folded carefully over the raised hump of the pillows. The bedside lockers were tidy, with personal items safely stowed, except for the few framed photographs on their tops. She checked to make sure there was no sign of any dust, smiled at the grinning image of John leaning against the side of an army vehicle looking lean and tanned in his desert rig of shorts and short-sleeved khaki shirt.

She could still recall the enthusiasm with which she had written back in December to tell him of the end of her basic training, and of her delight at her new surroundings at the Signals Training School at HMS *Mercury*. There had been times during basic training at Chatham when she had pondered on the wisdom of holding out for entrance into the Wrens. She had felt guilty before joining up at the secret comfort she took from the generally held view that 'you get a better class of girl altogether in the Wrens'. In the rough and tumble of life at HMS *Pembroke* she had often wondered if the widely held belief had any truth.

The large, draughty Victorian barrack block destroyed all notion of privacy. The double-tiered bunks stretched to seeming infinity down the long wooden-floored ('deck' they had to learn to call it) room. You dressed, undressed, bathed, ate and slept in the company of forty-five others. It was a shock. She smiled wryly when she thought back to the days when she and her sister, Rosemary, had created a fuss every time they were required to share a room when visitors came to their Keswick home. She was no prude, far from it, but she cringed inwardly and sometimes blushed outwardly at the behaviour and attitudes of some of her fellow trainees.

Nora Graham, a statuesque, busty individual from somewhere near Blackpool, had been her particular *bête* — not *noire*, for she was a dazzling platinum blonde — at least as far as the fashionably waved locks adorning her head were concerned. 'You want to see me natural roots?' she would grin lewdly, when, naked, she would display the dark triangle between her fulsome thighs. She was a leader, and a bully, all too ready to launch into physical violence, a trait which, right at the end of their long period of training, had got her into deep water and, probably, a discharge from the service, though Jenny had not heard any further news of her. After one of the nights of celebration, Nora had broken the nose of some unfortunate who had crossed her path once too often.

Jenny was afraid of her, as were many of the other girls, though she did her best not to show it, with some success. Nora had taken a swift dislike to her because of her accent — 'snooty drawers' was the epithet Nora quickly applied to her, and to any others whose speech did not reveal any marked regional accent. Another was 'Miss', as soon as she found out that Jenny had been a teacher. 'Ello, Miss. How are we today, Miss?' However, she was, perhaps, just a little bit in awe of the bravura of Jenny's polished condescension, and of the fact that, at twenty-five, Jenny was almost four years her senior. And, above all, Jenny's status as a married woman. The twin rings on the third finger of her left hand carried an authority which, Jenny noted with considerable private amusement, all the recruits deferred to.

Not that the blonde girl made it obvious. She would often refer to Jenny's married state in a manner which secretly infuriated Jenny, despite her assumed enigmatic smile. 'Bet you're missing it, eh, Miss?' Nora would chortle, then turn to the others, who would snigger dutifully. 'This one knows it's not just for peeing out of, eh, luv?'

But the wariness was mutual, and Jenny had survived the sometimes seemingly endless twelve weeks without seriously clashing, even when she was appointed 'recruit in charge' of their barrack room, to Nora's chagrin and loudly expressed disgust.

The move to *Mercury* had been a blessing though, in more ways than one. She glanced one last time around the spick and span room, for, as 'duty wren' it would be her responsibility if anything was found amiss. And 'hawk-eyes' Lidell was nothing if not thorough. Another four weeks and *Mercury* too would become history. Their specialized training would be over and they would be posted.

She had no doubt that she would successfully complete the signals course and earn the right to sew the wings on her tunic. Although she was excited at the prospect of a posting, and truly beginning to play her part in this war, she would also regret the end of this phase of training. There were no Nora Grahams to cast a shadow over life here. The girls were great, and she had made some good friends. In fact, she hoped that some of them might continue to stick together, for it was almost certain that the numerous shore establishments both at home and abroad would require more than one additional signals rating on their complement.

Not all the girls were looking forward to a foreign posting. In fact, most of them seemed to favour the Admiralty itself, and the heady attractions of the capital, especially now that the days of the Blitz appeared to be fading. Jenny was torn with indecision. Although there were no longer any official drafting preferences to be taken into account, there was a strong rumour among the girls that a sympathetic ear might still be inclined towards any particularly urgent desires. That might be simply wishful thinking on the part of the prospective draftees, but she had let it be known in several quarters, including her divisional officer, Second Officer Gallagher, that she would be delighted with a posting to Flag Officer, Mediterranean — say in Alexandria, for instance.

Now she was not too sure. The vagaries of John's life and career in the past months had shown just how unstable the whole situation of the British land forces in North Africa was. In a letter written last Christmas, he had jubilantly let her know that they had just completed 'a long trek of 300 miles or so'. She had soon realized that he was referring to a spectacular advance, and she worked out that the letter had been written in the newly reliberated Benghazi. Less than a month later, the Allied forces had been pushed eastward again. At the moment he was, as far as she could tell, bogged down somewhere in the region of the infamous Tobruk once again, along with a detachment of New Zealanders, or 'Kiwis', as he called them.

He had managed to send her some photographs during their months of separation, but beyond an impression of dusty heat and vast, barren space, it gave her little idea of the reality of his existence. She knew only that it was fraught with danger, in spite of his earnest reassurances, and she was learning to live and cope with that leaden little core of sickness somewhere in the pit of her, the cold fear which she had constantly to thrust away from her consciousness.

She had begun to think lately that in many ways being out in Alexandria might be even worse, for there was no likelihood that they would ever be able to meet up, unless — Heaven forbid — he was wounded or sick. And even then, if it were serious, he might well be sent home.

There was a large naval presence in Liverpool these days, for the port was the chief centre for organizing the vital Atlantic convoys. They would need plenty of 'sparks' there, and from Liverpool it would be easy to reach her Lakeland home for off-duty weekends and leave. The thought stirred her feelings of disloyalty towards John, and she looked forward to the evening, when she would shut herself away in the reading room with pad and pen to pour out her love for him. Meanwhile, she was more than glad to have the busy distractions of her own new military career to occupy her mind, and she hurried off towards the 'schoolroom' with genuine eagerness to immerse herself in it.

The stench from the folded body hanging half out of the turret, and the cloud of flies which rose in an electric buzz as he reached for the corpse made John gag and swiftly turn his contorted face to one side. The bleached pale shirt flapped from the belted trousers, showing a small patch of the thin brown skin. The thin brown hair looked incongruously lifelike, stirring in the hot breeze and at John's hasty manipulations, in contrast with the feel of dead boniness beneath the clothing. One side of the face, the right arm and all the right side of the torso, which had been hidden when John had climbed on to the vehicle, had been burned, the flesh stripped and scoured by the flames, or perhaps by the shellburst which had disabled the tank. Averting his face, his lips pressed tightly together so as not to breathe in the noxious air, John fumbled at the pockets, quickly jumped down into the dust again, bent and hawked and spat, struggling to summon saliva to his parched mouth. 'No papers. Not even an ID tag.'

'It's one of them new Kpfw Threes, sir,' Sergeant Morrow offered. He pointed. 'See? They've still got their spare bogie wheels on the back. Crafty sods, aren't they?'

'Do we bury the Jerry, sir?' Ron Maudsley asked, nodding at the folded figure.

John straightened up, managed to look directly at him. 'There's another inside, I think. But not enough to recognize — just bits and pieces. Just leave it. But bury the poor sod on top there. Quick as you like. You'll need a handkerchief. He's been dead a day or two.'

'We must've got bloody close to stop the bastard,' Maudsley observed cheerfully, as he and a companion prepared to hack out a shallow depression in the brown earth. 'Our two pounders usually bounce off those things!'

John wondered wearily if he should reprimand Maudsley, but with no real intention of doing anything about it. After all, he was quite right. Rommel's Panzer divisions were better equipped, no one could argue. Their 88mm guns were devastatingly effective against the lighter Allied armament. Added to that, the German general seemed to be able to outsmart his opponents almost at every turn. Look how quickly he had reversed the Allied successes of November and December. They had lost all the territory they had gained at the end of the year, and were now expecting to be pushed back further day by day. The whole of North Africa was under threat once more, and there had been more disastrous losses at sea in the Mediterranean, including the aircraft carrier, *Ark Royal* and the battleship *Barham*.

There were all kinds of rumours flying about: British commando raids foiled up the coast; he had heard back at Field HQ their CO muttering darkly about a buzz that Jerry had somehow infiltrated Allied lines; that their plans were known to Rommel before they were ever put into operation.

Somebody found a sheet of charred tarpaulin to wrap the body in, but John could still see that flapping hair until they flung the sandy grit over it, and piled a few pale stones on the slight mound. They stood briefly, tugged off their caps while Sergeant Morrow, a Methodist lay preacher back home, said a short prayer. John looked from the anonymous heap of stones to the low gullies spreading out on either side. Only a few hundred yards away, he could see A Company going about the business of digging themselves in yet again, establishing yet another line in this fiercely inhospitable landscape they had fought and died over in the past two years and more. Though he had been out here for only ten months, already it seemed he had spent a lifetime in this heat and sweat and dirt, and bone-achingly chill

175

darkness sometimes, the smell of filth and violent death inescapably filling his nostrils.

The keen young officer who had chivvied his men on the *Stirling Castle* and at the desert training camp just south of Alexandria seemed a different, former self. Now, he was sick of it all, longed to be out of it, back with Jenny, to get on with the life together they had never really been allowed to start. He pulled his thoughts back to that pile of stones, to the rotten, burnt out corpse buried beneath them, and to Sergeant Morrow's sonorous words, meant to offer comfort and to hold out hope.

Did they mean anything at all? Methodist was inscribed on his identity disc, and in his paybook. He thought of all those unthinking hours through childhood, of chapel attendance, of Sunday school. He prayed now, at odd moments, before sleep. Half-formed prayers that he and Jenny would be spared to live their lives together, that Teddy and his mother would be safe, and all the rest of the family, and friends. Was there any presence out there, above this maddened earth, to hear him? Often, he was sure there wasn't. But then, in the frequent moments of danger he had faced, a fervently babbled litany ran in his brain. 'Oh God, keep me safe. Bring me through, God.'

One thing was sure. That poor, disfigured heap of young bones under the stones there wasn't his enemy. Even though they'd been trying to kill each other for months past. He recalled the action they had seen last September, their first real test in the line. General Auchinleck was still building up his Eighth Army for a push to relieve the beleaguered troops at Tobruk, when their division encountered a determined Axis offensive south of Sidi Barrani. A squadron of light German tanks was stopped in a shallow depression, for once the Allied gunpower superior and damaging. The infantry moved forward quickly, dug in on a low ridge and opened fire. A vehicle was burning below, dwarfed by the stretch of pale desert, and they watched the black, distant ant figures scramble out. Elliot and Burns on the machine gun began strafing, and the distant figures dropped immobile, still standing mercilessly out against the pale background.

'For fuck's sake!' Ron Maudsley had jumped up, careless of exposure, his weasel face twisted with passion. 'Let the poor buggers be, will ye? They've nowhere to go, for Christ's sake.'

Elliot had rounded on him angrily, his oppo, Burns, looked sheepishly guilty. 'Cease firing,' John ordered quietly. The dots were seen to be moving slowly, running up the long sandy waste. They would be lucky to make it back to their own lines, or be picked up by another crew. It was like being lost on an ocean once you abandoned your vehicle without support. Maudsley had nodded with aggressive vindication at John's command. 'We've got to conserve ammo,' John added, to save the machine gunners' face.

Since then, he had often heard an inner voice asking, What if we all just packed in and went home? Jerry and all? No more killing, we've had enough. He had had a surfeit of reasons for fighting — the forces of good against evil, democracy against fascism, civilization against utter savagery. But who was responsible for these acts which had plunged the whole world into war? He thought back to his days at college, when he had worked for the Socialist League, thought of the Jarrow marchers, the eloquent simplicity of the working class's demands. The right to work — and the right to live in peace. Tommy and Fritz didn't want to knock seven bells out of one another, to kill and maim. They wanted to be at home, a decent home, with their wives, their bairns. The homely word carried such simple truth.

The men moved from the graveside, their boots scuffing up the powdery dust. John roused himself. Such sentiments if expressed abroad would earn him a court martial, maybe a firing squad.

In the side of the gentle slope, already bathed in the sun's glare, the men were setting up the Aldershot oven, a crude but effective device, of brick sealed with mud. Lumps of dough were placed on a stone hearth which had been heated by a wood fire. When the oven was sealed, the dough was quickly baked into irregularly shaped but palatable loaves.

John carried on down the line. Slit trenches had been dug, a low, sandbagged redoubt marked the area acting as their company HQ. Lieutenant Coates was sitting at a folding table, with maps and documents fluttering in the hot wind. 'Mail's come up,' he muttered, his unlit pipe clenched between his teeth. An affectation assumed, John thought uncharitably, against the day when he obtained a more senior rank, for every general had to have his idiosyncratic trademark. Coates scarcely removed his pipe other than to eat, and yet John had hardly ever seen it lit. 'Sort your platoon's out. Several for you. At least one from your old lady. Jenny Wren.' He snickered at his witticism, as he always did.

John smiled dutifully. He shuffled through the piles of letters, and felt his heart thump at the familiar handwriting. But he was dismayed at the sudden painful thought that seeing it, and reading the heartfelt and often briefly passionate expressions of love for him, would make him feel the pain of their separation all the more, and the desolation of their enforced segregation ever more bleakly.

13

Tony came out from the bedroom and saw the hazel eyes of the girl fix on him with briefly searching curiosity. He flushed deeply, lowered his own gaze. For an instant, he felt a spark of hatred at the secret knowledge he read in that look, but then her face lit up with a smile, and she came across to him, her arm fully extended, eager to touch him. Her hand was soft, delicate and cool as the rest of her looked, but the grip was firm, her warm friendliness genuine. 'Hello, Tony. I'm Lucy Stratford. It's so nice to meet you.'

She had not waited to be introduced and he murmured a grateful reply. She was very pretty, even beautiful. Her hair, cropped short, lay in natural curls, and was a kind of burnished gold, quite dark and yet with the appearance of having been exposed for long periods to the sun. Her skin, too, had a shade; not a deep tan but a smooth, creamy tint, like very milky tea or coffee. It seemed to glow. He was ashamed at his speculation as to whether that faintly burnished complexion extended all over her body, then another unbidden, far more dismaying, thought kept the colour hotly at his cheeks.

He visualized the youthful figure who had followed him out of the bedroom moving and manipulating this girl in the same shamelessly clinical way to that which Tony had been subjected in the mechanics of gratification which had taken place so recently in the bed they had just left. Tony's anger swiftly dissipated. To be replaced by a sense of humiliation and hurt at the way Captain Meyer had handed him over, like an object, a piece of young, desirable flesh to be used. It stung him to acknowledge that that was exactly what he was.

But at least the prison commandant had been affectionate, even at first bumblingly inept and apologetic. And touchingly furious at the brutal treatment Tony had received at the hands of his fellow countrymen. 'They are animals!' Meyer had hissed, his voice unsteady with disgust. 'They will be punished.' But Tony didn't want them punished. He even knew who they were — they hadn't taken much trouble to disguise themselves in the darkness. Perhaps they guessed he would be too petrified to inform on them.

It wasn't that. Part of him felt that in a way he deserved what they had meted out to him. Not so much for being a homo — he had come to terms with that a long time ago, though he had hidden it well, at times tried to sublimate it even as he concealed it from his fellows. It was for consorting with the enemy, for his treachery, that he deserved punishment. First with Ludo, the guard, even though in many minor ways he had obtained concessions which had benefited many of his fellow prisoners. That was probably why they had tolerated it without wreaking vengeance on him.

But when the commandant had singled him out, that had been different. Tony knew it, and felt it. He had been astonished, and almost amused, at first. Captain Meyer must be pushing forty; plump, with flat feet that kept him out of the fighting line, and a fierce-looking wife and two smug children back home somewhere. He had taken to coming and lingering while they rehearsed the Christmas show, attracted by the spectacle of Tony acting, then dressing, like a girl. A tart, he corrected himself, with wry humour. He was good at it. Too good.

Meyer had sent for him, got him to work around his office, tidying up, then his private room; made up excuses to keep him there in the evening, courted him in his own embarrassed fashion. Tony had practically taken the lead, flirted with him, until their relationship quickly became a sexual one.

However much his conscience troubled him, Tony couldn't stop it — told himself he was helpless, a victim. It added to the secret pleasure he took.

But the beating, and the savage assault in the dimness of the bath house, were nightmares he still could not truly come to terms with. He might be queer, but he wanted love, or at least kindness and affection. Now, his role of traitor could in some way be rationalized. All right, he deserved to be punished. Well, he had been, and severely. And those brutes were men of his own side, fighting for the common cause. Freedom. Justice.

'I have a friend. A colleague. Working in Hamburg. Some of your countrymen work there. They are not really prisoners. They are volunteers. They support our policies. I can take you along. Introduce you to my friend. He might be able to help you. You should not be locked up, with those others.'

Tony was in awe when Captain Meyer took him in his staff car to the city. The commandant had spruced him up. Pressed his battledress blouse, found him a much better pair of khaki trousers than his own much-patched pair. And a pair of smart civilian shoes, brightly polished, which looked almost new. His heart was thumping with tension, and his first feeling when Meyer introduced him to his colleague was one of enormous relief, for the figure in the immaculate black uniform who stepped forward with a beaming smile appeared gracefully boyish, scarcely older or more robust than himself. Yet the older man seemed almost deferential towards him.

'This is the young man I told you about. Private Ellis. Tony.'

'How do you do.' The voice was light, the English studiedly faultless. 'I am Lieutenant Lipman. I hope we can work together. You do not mind if I call you Tony?'

That had been weeks ago. It had shocked Tony to discover that the 'work' involved being part of the propaganda service, the centre-piece of which were the daily broadcasts which went out from Radio Hamburg to many parts of the world, including the English language bulletins read by the strange Irishman — some said Englishman; he himself claimed to be half American — William Joyce, known in Britain as Lord Haw-Haw.

Tony struggled with his conscience, for a short while. This really was playing traitor. This was playing an active part in the fight against his own side. Not that his own side had done much for him. He still had the scars, both physical and mental, which showed what they thought of him. So be it. Besides, the real game was survival. And the life which had suddenly opened to him through the generosity of Captain Meyer was so temptingly desirable, compared with the bleakness of POW existence. In fact, his greatest fear became that he might lose it all.

He soon realized there was little he could contribute to the work being done. In the crowded rooms below the radio station, the mixture of nationalities employed in the propaganda machine were all far more educated than he was. They worked on the translation of articles, from German into other languages, and vice versa, or wrote reports themselves on various aspects of their nations' culture and characteristics. He stayed with several of them in a kind of hostel. It was hardly like a prison at all. He doubted if the doors were even locked at night.

He was quite happy to perform any menial tasks, like running errands in the large building, taking round tea or coffee, working as a cleaner or waiter. But then he was sure they could find plenty of German orderlies for those duties. So he was glad when he swiftly recognized the signs in Lieutenant Lipman's behaviour and words that indicated his interest in him. An interest that had nothing to do with his skill, or lack of it, as a fifth-columnist. After all, he came with a special recommendation from his former commandant.

Frank Lipman was not subtle. He clearly felt he did not need to be. And Tony responded, grateful only for the opportunity to remain part of this new, freer life. But he was surprised. He had thought from the young officer's remarks in the first days of their acquaintance that the slender figure was a womanizer. He talked about girls, referred to them in the crudest possible terms as sexual objects, with a deliberately shocking, smutty kind of glee which reminded Tony of his contemporaries in the army school and barracks. He constantly probed for Tony to reveal his own exploits. Soon, Tony decided he was sounding him out, and realized that Captain Meyer had given him a comprehensive account of Tony's sexual leaning.

'Do not worry,' Lipman assured him. 'We will find you something useful to do. When you — how you say? — learn the ropes. Captain Meyer tells me you are an accomplished actor. Perhaps Herr Joyce will find you something to do, some broadcasts, maybe.'

Tony's relief, and gratitude, were very real. And so his response to Lipman's advances was sincere, too. At first. But he was quickly disappointed, then repulsed, by the young German's total lack of sentiment, the coldness which was demonstrated even at the most intimate physical moments they shared. Always, the lieutenant was in control, always in command. Always, Tony felt, with increasing hidden dismay, emotionally detached, even at the very height of bodily satisfaction. He could be cruel, too. He liked to inflict pain. Not in any spectacularly violent way. There were no beatings, no whips or torture. But there were increasing instances of petty viciousness, of a joy in hurting, or insulting, that caused Tony growing moments of alarm. And he became more careful, more determined to please, and to act out his subservient role to the best of his considerable ability.

Tony was disturbed at what he saw as some intuitive knowledge of his relationship with the lieutenant in the eyes of Lucy Stratford, even though he quickly relaxed in the warm, ingenuous friendliness she portrayed. Lipman soon left them, directed Tony to escort her down to the canteen in the basement of the radio station. She took his arm as they went down the last flight of concrete steps and through the swing doors into the cafeteria, which was quiet at this time of the morning.

He felt proud as he noticed the swift, appraising glances. He was deeply attracted to her, delighting in the sweetness of her perfume, her beauty.

He had already heard her history, or at least the colourful version of it given to him by Lipman during the previous night and the early hours of this morning. 'She's English, though she has never visited England.' He smiled at Tony's baffled look. 'She is from your empire. From India. Her father is a wealthy planter. She was on her way home — the home she has never seen — on a passenger ship, which was sunk by one of our U-boats. Another submarine picked her up. She had been in a lifeboat for five days. The only lady, with five of the crew.'

He rolled his eyes, laughed lewdly. 'I am sure she enjoyed it. Apparently, she had already had a wonderful time on the ship with all the officers. And the little slut has only been married a matter of months, to some poor fool who went off to join the Indian army. She had decided to go off to England to fight her own war in the mother country. I think she has discovered she fights best on her back with legs in the air.' His hands were toying absently with Tony's compliant body as he continued.

'She seems to have accepted our cause with

remarkably little persuasion. Though possibly her latest inamorato — you can say that, for the man?' (Tony shrugged. He had no idea) — 'is responsible. He is a brawny Irishman, Shaun O'Brien. A dedicated enemy of your country. He has been fighting for his land's liberty for years. Now he is over here. He keeps Miss Lucy very happy, I believe. Which is nice, yes?'

Tony had expected to meet the immoral kind of tart Lipman had described to him. Instead, he was surprised and quickly captivated by her air of ingenuous honesty. They chatted happily across the wooden table, sipping the bitter wartime coffee substitute. 'The main thing is, it's all a matter of survival. Sufficient unto the day, I say.' She put her soft hand companionably on his wrist, her hazel eyes held his. 'We keep our lords and masters sweet. We are captives, after all.'

Her pretty face assumed a serious expression, and her honey complexion pinked slightly. 'It's the politicians that got us into this mess. Not us. I've never even seen England, you know. Except for films and photographs. I was on my way there when we were torpedoed.'

'Your folks must be relieved to know you're safe.'

The colour in her face intensified. She looked even more uncomfortable. She gave a helpless kind of shrug. 'I'm not sure if they know. The authorities here — I don't know if they've told them.' She paused, the light-coloured eyes gazed at him appealingly. 'When they took me from the open boat — I was very weak. The others, the sailors, were in a bad way. The submarine couldn't take them on board. The German commander told me later they probably wouldn't survive. The ship I was on was a fast passenger-cargo vessel. Travelling alone. She didn't sail in convoy. It was not on the normal routes through the Indian Ocean. That's why I chose it. It was supposed to be a quicker trip, to reach England.'

She hesitated again, appearing even more harassed and ashamed. 'I don't know what they plan to do with me here. I'm hoping — my friend, Shaun O'Brien, is training here. For some secret work, as an agent.'

'You mean a spy?'

She flinched, but nodded. 'He really believes — he's from Eire. He wants freedom for his country. I believe he's right.' That vulnerable expression was still on her face. She stared at him tremulously, with a childish defiance. 'I really — I'd like to go with him. Wherever they send him. So maybe it would be better if they didn't know — my family and everyone — that I've survived.'

She waited, expecting him to argue or protest, and when he said nothing she gave a shamed, grateful smile. 'I've done nothing with my life. Wasted it out there.' She continued her painful confession. 'Hughie — my husband — he's the same age as me. We were nineteen when we married. Far too young. It was all arranged, more or less. We just went along with it. I wasn't — I only grew up in the last few months. After we were separated.'

A messenger, wearing the same nondescript black garb without insignia which Tony was wearing, approached their table. 'Fräulein. Please come with me.'

She rose, smiled over at Tony. 'See? They call me miss. They don't count my marriage at all.' He stood, too, and once more she laid her hand on his arm, kept it there while she squeezed him. 'I'll see you again, I hope. I'm going to be kept here a while, I think. It's been so good to talk to you.' She leaned so close he thought she was going to kiss his cheek, prepared for it, dizzying at the scent of her, her closeness as her hair almost brushed against his. 'Be careful of Lieutenant Lipman,' she whispered. The tension caught both of them. Tony felt his skin prickle. 'He can be dangerous, I think. See you soon. Bye.'

He thought of her words often in the following days. He wondered how much of her warning was based on intuition and how much on experience. He met her several times in the crowded offices of the station, but not alone, so that the intimacy of their first conversation was not repeated. But she was always friendly, her face lit by that wide, warm smile whenever she saw him, and he remained captivated by her.

* * *

The bedroom which Frank Lipman used was part of the staff accommodation at the rear of the station building. Tony spent the entire night there when Frank wanted him. No one at the hostel made any comment about it, at least not to his face. In fact, to his private discomfort, several of his fellow workers adopted an almost obsequious friendliness towards him because of his relationship with the young Gestapo officer.

Then, one afternoon at five o'clock, at the end of another long day when Tony had been acting as an office boy and dog's body, Frank said casually, 'This evening we go to my flat. I have a free day tomorrow. We spend it together.'

The flat was again part of a complex reserved for military and government personnel, in Stellingen, quite close to the river, and the notorious St Pauli district, which Frank had promised to show him. 'I find a nice girl for you!' he had teased, and Tony had looked suitably abashed. The apartment was small, but newly and comfortably furnished, with bedroom, small living room and its own tiny bathroom and kitchenette. In the small hours, after their long lovemaking, and after a brief attempt to settle down to sleep together in the single bed, Frank thrust him away unceremoniously. 'Go and sleep on the couch. This is impossible, go.'

The couch was hardly bigger than an armchair. Weary as he was, he tossed and turned until dawn, his head resting on one upholstered arm, his feet sticking awkwardly over the other. He was up early. Wrapped in a towel, he padded about seeking out the breakfast things, laying the table. Then he began to tidy up the living room. He found a duster, moved to the modest bookcase, on top of which stood a number of mementoes and family photographs.

One caught his eye. It was in a simple leather frame. He moved it, cleaned the wooden surface beneath, put it back. He stared at the picture again, an ordinary black and white snapshot, of Frank and a girl, taken outside in summer. The girl was pretty, wore a short summer frock. Frank had his arm around her shoulder. He was dressed in shirt and shorts, ankle socks. When he rose some time later, Tony asked him about it. 'It was taken years ago,' he grunted. 'It was at a youth camp. Before the war. Long ago.'

He grinned, dropped sprawling into the upholstered chair, one leg hooked over the wooden arm, lewdly displaying his nakedness. Tony's eyelids flickered, his glance lowered in that characteristic manner, half shyness, half provocation. The colour deepened under his freckled skin. 'Her name was Gabi. She was first class.' Frank chuckled tauntingly. 'Ah! Those youth camps! Full of virgins simply dying to surrender their charms.'

He stroked himself, his gaze fixed mockingly on Tony all the while. 'But don't worry, *liebchen*. Not one of them could compare with you.'

He held out his arms and Tony moved obediently, and stood in front of the reclining figure. The lieutenant's hands shot out, pulled away the towel, and dragged him violently down on to his lap with his encircling embrace. Tony felt the shivering excitement of their intimate contact, Frank's hands, teasingly restrained, moving over his eager flesh.

195

'I suppose you prefer some massively muscled, hairy-chested brute, eh?' Frank's voice was deep, rich with his amusement. His lips brushed against Tony's ear.

Tony's own lips were against the warm smoothness of the pale, narrow chest. 'No way!' he whispered thickly. He shuddered with exaggerated conviction. 'Can't stand beefcakes!' His hands were moving, too. He could feel his partner's arousal, but Frank grabbed swiftly at his wrist, pushing the hand away, and Tony surrendered willingly enough to Frank's control.

The German clearly enjoyed prolonging things. 'What do you like, then, *mein schatz*? How about the girls?' He chuckled, nodded towards the photograph he had talked of. 'Are you as catholic in your tastes as I am? What about your pretty compatriot, Lucy Stratford? In spite of her professed passion for the Irishman, O'Brien, I'm sure she misses it while he's far away. There are some girls who really can't do without it, you know. She would be very willing, I'm sure. Why don't you try?'

A vivid memory flashed into Tony's mind. The twisting, weeping figure pinned down on the wet grass. The dirty white ankle socks, the torn frock pushed up in a band about her midriff. And most vivid of all, those thin, bruised thighs, the narrow band of startlingly black hair between them. Her cries had died to a soft, keening whimper by then.

The other lads from the home glared up at him wolfishly from where they crouched, holding her. There was no longer any need for force. 'Come on then, Tone! Get stuck in!' Panic-stricken, he had shrieked out a false alarm, pointing to the dark, looming shape of the bushes, and fled into the darkness, his companions following suit, crashing through the branches in all directions.

His breath was coming faster, his excitement quickening at Frank's stirring attentions. 'No thanks!' he breathed. 'Not interested. You know what I like!' He dipped his head, lapped reverently at the faintly damp, fragrant skin beneath his cheek.

14

August 1942 was petering out in a spell of wet and windy weather, at least in the north-east. 'Just when the farmers don't want it,' everyone moaned. Britain's crop growers and food suppliers were a lot more in the public eye these days. Once or twice, Dora had grumbled that she might well pack in at the ordnance factory and join the Women's Land Army instead. 'All that fresh air and good nosh. Bacon and eggs every morning, they reckon.' But Marian knew she would never leave the Birtley munitions works. The money was too good for a start. And with fellows like Ray Lambert around her day and night her life was far too interesting for her to change it willingly.

Dora's mother, Julia, placed her cup back in its saucer on the kitchen table and lit up another Woodbine. 'You off out Sat'd'y night then?' Her face was screwed up against the smoke, the thin tube bobbed at her lip.

Marian felt herself blushing, and turned, busying herself with the pots at the sink. 'Dunno. Dora was suggesting it, like. Just the pictures or somewhere.'

'Aye, go on. Why not? You're only young once, eh? Get out and enjoy yessels while ye can. That young bugger of mine never puts a night shift in these days, does she? Must think she's made of money. Doesn't need the extra brass any more, eh?'

'Oh, she's done a few,' Marian defended, still uncomfortable. 'And she works over three nights a week as it is. She doesn't get in till eight, you know.'

Julia gave a harsh bark of laughter, the cigarette still in her mouth. 'You're sure it's work she's up to? Or is she putting in a spot of overtime with that young lad, Ray what's-his-name, eh?'

Marian's discomfort increased by the second. She was convinced Julia knew far more about her relationship with Jim Moody than she let on, probably through Dora's carelessly loose tongue. The young girl thought it was a scream anyway. 'An ould married woman like you carryin' on!'

There were times when her teasing brought Marian close to tears, and she vowed she would not see him again. 'There's nothing like that going on between us at all!' she would deny vehemently. 'He's just a canny bloke, that's all.'

But her conscience was raw, for there *was* something like that going on, and she was deeply disturbed at the knowledge that Dora was well aware of it. Her face burned when she thought of how easily word could get around. She visualized Ray Lambert and the other men chivvying Jim about it at work, his mock sheepish confessions to them, Ray passing it back to Dora, their private sniggering.

She strove to check her own conjectures. She meant what she said. Jim *was* a canny lad, she would have had nothing to do with him if he wasn't. And for several weeks there really had been nothing more than friendship, just intimate chats over a drink, and round the fire after young madam Dora, bold as brass, pulled a grinning Ray by the hand up to her bedroom. Then an arm had been slipped round her shoulders in the dimness of the cinema, hands held during the walk home in the blackout, a kiss, hasty enough, on the lips at the front door as they said goodnight in the early hours. It didn't seem so outrageous, with Ray and Dora still asleep or even hard at it upstairs.

But then, one night, after they had been to a dance, and she had already thrilled to the feel of her body pliant against his in shuffling embrace on the crowded dance-floor, and after too many port and lemons which tasted sickly sweet and made her cheeks flush and her head spin, the kisses had started at the fireside, and they were not hasty, but breathlessly lingering, open mouthed and raw with passion, and suddenly she was sprawled on the rug, bathed in the fireglow, and his hands had been touching her, in those intimate places no man except her husband had touched her before, sliding over silk, ferreting through her finery, until she was almost past restraint, and only some instinctive reaction — decency or fear? — had made her suddenly convulse away from him, thrust him from between her limbs and huddle sobbing wildly in the red warmth.

She had thought that would be the end of their relationship. But he had written, then a few days later, turned up on the doorstep, at his own initiative and when he knew Dora would not be present. He brought flowers, and a present for Teddie, and was so contrite she hadn't the heart to turn him away. She didn't want to. Far from it, she was ashamed at her trembling remembrance of his touch on her, her fierce desire for him.

It would happen, soon. They both knew it. The kissing had started up again, and the clutching, and they could no longer pretend that it was anything other than this fierce physical need in both of them. She felt in her guilt that she had betrayed her husband already, had been unfaithful to him. Didn't the Bible say something about unclean thoughts being as bad as deeds? In that case, she was guilty all right. The only way she could stop it was to send him away, really for good this time. Have nothing more to do with him, never see him again.

But she couldn't. She wept helplessly, sickened at herself for her weakness. Jim knew, too. He was waiting, soon he would have her properly, she would be a true adulteress. She half suspected that Dora and her mother believed she already was. The older woman seemed to take a cynical delight in the idea.

Partly to escape her own thoughts, Marian said now, 'Eeh, isn't it awful about the poor Duke of Kent?' News had come through only that morning of his death in a plane crash. 'And that raid — where was it? Dieppe, in France. Mr Stokes was saying that reading between the lines it was a right flop. Umpteen of them Canadians dead, and nowt to show for it.'

Julia grunted. 'Just shows what would happen if they really *did* try to get an army across the water. Stands to reason, doesn't it? I mean, bloody Adolf couldn't do it two year ago, could he, and look at the state we were in then? That lot at the Home Guard were

202

training with bloody broom shanks, for God's sake!' As usual, she switched her mind to more local and immediate concerns. 'Dunno about our Dora not getting her overtime in. Since this bloody government took over the pits, Alf's working even more shifts and getting not a farthing more for it. I tell ye! Coalition my arse! They're all Tories when ye get down to it!'

There was the noise of a motor car, its engine roaring and dying right outside, and with a sinking heart Marian sprang up and ran across the hallway to glance through the front windows of the living room. She saw the black box shape, saw her mother-in-law's trim, fashionable figure climbing from the passenger side, Iris's bulk easing out from behind the wheel. Oh no! Not with Julia here! May and Iris were not expected until Thursday. 'It's Mam — May. And Iris,' she murmured, her stomach churning.

'Lord and Lady Muck!' Julia chuckled wickedly. Marian saw the joy of impending battle in her features and realized agitatedly that Julia was not about to depart at the arrival of her sister. 'It's a wonder they still manage to find petrol coupons for that thing!' Julia said cattily. 'Mind you, nobs like that Mayfield woman can always get what they want. Look at the size of her. Don't tell me that's just on the ration!'

Marian hurriedly opened the door, her cheek muscles aching with the bright smile she fixed on her face. 'Hello, Mam. Iris. What a lovely surprise!'

May came up the path, climbed the three steps and lightly embraced Marian, who caught the pleasant waft of her scent as she kissed her. 'Sorry, love. We didn't have time to let you know. Change of plan. We've got to attend a district meeting Thursday. WVS. Short notice. We just thought we'd pop in today instead. We can't stay long. Any news from Teddy?'

As Marian shook her head, Julia appeared in the doorway from the kitchen. She rested one hand high above her on the door frame, the Woodbine in her fingers curling its smoke in thin blue traces over her head. 'Well, fancy seeing you two here!' she smiled mockingly.

May's expression changed to one of instinctive caution, but she advanced swiftly and awkwardly embraced her sister, pecking hastily at her cheek. Julia didn't move. 'Hello, our Julia. How are you?'

'Keeping body and soul together. Like most of us.' She stared challengingly at the newcomers. Iris nodded a cool greeting, and entered the living room first.

'I'll put the kettle on,' Marian said, glad to

escape to the kitchen, but they all trooped through, crowding the limited space.

'We'll stay in here,' May offered brightly. 'No need to mess your room up. Teddie having her nap, is she?'

Marian nodded. She got them to sit down around the table, squeezed past to get to the pantry, setting out clean cups and saucers. 'Julia's brought some scones.' She set out plates, blushing a little.

'We've not long eaten,' May said. 'Keep them. Enjoy them later.'

'They'll not poison you. Us pit folk *do* know how to cook, you know.'

'And how to agitate and all,' May fired back, twin red spots appearing on her cheeks. 'There's talk of go-slows and strikes, I hear.'

'It'll be them Taffy buggers if anyone *does* come out!' Julia returned.

'Have you heard from John lately?' Marian cut in desperately. 'And Jenny. How's she settling in to her new job?'

Jenny was working somewhere outside London, at some secret location. All very hush-hush, they had been told. They knew little detail. 'Careful now!' Julia chortled mockingly. 'Careless talk costs lives, eh?'

May didn't rise to the sarcasm and they chatted a little stiffly. Marian grew increasingly uneasy. Her palms were wet, her body inside her clothing felt sticky with sweat. She prayed that Julia would go, but Dora's mother seemed grimly eager to carry on the traditional sniping antagonism with May and Iris. At last Marian could stand the tension no longer. She jumped up. 'I think I can hear Teddie,' she declared, and made her escape. She woke her daughter, who came down bleary and crotchety, to settle on her mother's knee, thumb in mouth and gaze resentfully fixed on the grown-ups round the table in the crowded kitchen.

'We'll have to be going,' May said presently. 'We really just came over to let you know we wouldn't be coming on Thursday. Listen. It's a long time since you were over at our place. The change will do you and Teddie good. Why don't you come over this weekend? Come Saturday. Or even Friday afternoon, if you like. We can come and get you, can't we, Iris?'

Marian reddened. 'Oh — well — that'd be nice. It's . . . '

'She can't. Not this weekend.' Julia's voice was blunt and flat. Clearly, she enjoyed making the announcement. Marian stared at her impotently. 'She's arranged to have a night out Saturday, haven't you, love? With Dora and her mates. Going for a bit of a dance. Or mebbe the pictures or summat.'

Marian could feel her face burning. Her legs moved, twisting with embarrassment against the weight of her daughter. 'Well, it doesn't really matter. I — '

'Howay, you can't let 'em down now.' Julia grinned malevolently. 'That lad — what's-his-name? — 'll be dead disappointed if you don't turn up. Our Dora told us he's taken a real shine to you.' She laughed, to show she was teasing.

Marian writhed again, her chest tight, the tears just below the surface. Her eyes, wide with apprehension, flickered to May's face, then lowered. 'Don't be daft,' she murmured in hardly more than a whisper.

'You take the chance, get out and enjoy yourself,' Julia said heartily. 'You don't want to spend all your time with old fogies like us. Does she, our May?' she flung out aggressively. 'We've had our day, eh?' she added, her glance directed now at Iris, who met her look coolly. 'We've just this minute fixed up for me to come along and look after little Teddie.'

'That's fine. Some other time then,' May answered.

They chatted for a few more minutes, then May and Iris rose.

'Give my love to Teddy when you write,' May said in the hall. 'I'm half way through a letter to him. But I know they limit them.

Maybe yours will get through first.' Marian was swept by a feeling of misery and guilt. She was strongly tempted to speak up, ask if she might after all accept May's offer to spend the weekend at Hexham. But she was afraid of precipitating an adverse reaction from Julia.

May was quiet in the car as they drove back. The rain had stopped but the sky held a leaden dullness, the roads still wet and liberally puddled. 'Sister Julia's as charming as ever,' Iris quipped lightly, to draw her out.

May nodded. 'It's not right, is it?' she blurted abruptly. 'I'm not just being a silly old woman. It's not right, Marian going out like that. When poor Teddy's shut away.'

Her voice was unsteady with emotion. Iris, attuned as always to her moods, took her left hand from the wheel, briefly patted May's leg. 'I'm sure there's nothing to worry about. It's probably Julia and Dora that's bullied her into it. The poor girl didn't look all that keen, if you ask me.'

May nodded again. 'You're right, I expect. It's just — she looked so — well, guilty. Scared, almost. You know what I mean?'

'She probably *was* guilty. Felt bad about it. About us finding out like that. She probably feels just like you do. That she shouldn't be going out at all. A married woman, her husband a POW. And as your damned sister pointed out, she *is* only young still. She hasn't had much fun lately, has she?'

'No one's having much fun just now, are they?' May countered, a hint of asperity in her voice. Then she gave a penitent little smile. 'Hark at me! I *am* a fussy old maid after all. There's plenty having fun, I guess. Especially now. Not least that painted little niece of mine.' She hesitated, shook her head, serious once more. 'That's what worries me. Poor Marian's not the strongest-willed of lasses. And young Dora's about as bold as they come, if you ask me. She can run rings round her. Look at the way she's moved in there. Got Marian skivvying after her like a maid of all work. She's a schemer, is our Dora,' May muttered darkly. 'Marian doesn't stand a chance.'

15

The excitement of being involved in something so 'hush-hush' was beginning to wear thin. The isolation of the old house in the extensive grounds of Bletchley Park, and worse, the spartan conditions of the low wooden huts which comprised their living accommodation, were getting Jenny down. She had never realized how much she valued her privacy until she joined the service. The girls were fine, on the whole, with a few notable exceptions. They had all been chosen for their skill and intelligence, though sometimes it was hard to keep that thought in mind when they sat through interminable watches, listening through headphones to the whines and crackles from the B-41 receivers, then sprang to life to scribble down frantically the spitting Morse jumble of incomprehensible five-letter groups, or streams of pointless numbers.

Pointless to them, though not to the cypher workers, both male and female, and the boffins who worked with their weirdly clicking and humming machines, surrounded by garlands of pinholed ticker-tape, or cards with their curious, pricked patterns. They were prepared to grub away round the clock, in a welter of coffee cups and a thick fug of tobacco smoke. Occasionally, they would go whooping, wild-eyed mad, crowds of them dancing about, hugging each other like kids at a party, even grabbing at Jenny and her colleagues, kissing them smackingly and taking untold liberties far from their normal, absent professorial behaviour.

'Put that Wren down!' First Officer Pearson, their divisional officer, would thunder. 'She's almost young enough to be your daughter!' And the boffin in her sights would generally retreat in blushful confusion.

But those break-through moments of celebratory elation were rare. Mostly, it was drudgery, sheer and unremitting, with duty watches that were often extended until life became an automatic round of babbling Morse, uninviting meals, snatched cigarettes, and cold but welcome bed. As they moved towards high summer, the beds became warmer, but just as lonely, despite there being half a dozen of them squeezed along each side of the mess.

That was another thing which added to the tedium of her cloistered life for Jenny. Talk centred with monotonous frequency on the other, far more zestful activities than slumber, for which beds might be used. Intelligent or not, her mess-mates' fancies turned far from lightly to matters corporal, and in graphic detail. Jenny herself took little part in such discussion, reminiscence, or speculation. She was far from prudish, she assured herself, but such topics still caused her to blush far too easily, in spite of her enviable status as a married woman.

'Go on, Jen! Tell us what it's really like!' someone would urge, and she would shy away with some laughing disclaimer. It hurt her sometimes even to think, let alone talk about it.

Partly to prove she was no prude, she joined the others in a titillating protest at their uncomfortable working conditions. At one end of their wireless office, in addition to the central bench with its double row of receivers which ran the length of the hut and took up practically all the space, one of the boffins had installed a metal contraption, full of whirring reels and flickering dials, about the size of a double wardrobe. The heat thrown out by this rumbling monster, along with eighteen wireless receivers and their operators, on baking July days and balmy nights, was nigh on intolerable. The fore and afternoon watches, under the eagle eyes of First Officer Pearson, could do little other than surreptitiously loosen knots on clinging ties, ease limp and sweaty collars, and perspire impotently.

But with the first and morning watches, it was a different kettle of exotic fish. 'I'm not putting up with this lot!' a pert brunette by the name of Anne Netherton declared, and before the astonished and admiring gaze of her fellow watchkeepers, she proceeded to remove tie, then shirt, then skirt, and, finally, the black shoes and stockings. She sat down at her set in brassière and panties. With an assortment of giggling cheers, her co-workers, including Jenny, followed suit. The unconvincing protests of the 'killick of the watch' were cut short by several of the bolder spirits volunteering to assist their nominal superior in her own disrobing — an offer she hastily declined, and so peace, if not decorum, was re-established.

None of the boffins, advanced in age or otherwise, objected, and knickers and bra became the regular rig of the day, or, rather, night, for those on duty from 2000 to 0800 hours. And thus it was that when Jenny first met Captain Martin Castleton, she was wearing a brief but fetching outfit of pale blue satin and lace which was definitely non-regulation issue.

She was merely one of twenty scantily clad

forms his gaze passed appreciatively over, and though the old, comforting adage about numbers applied, she was among several who blushfully reverted to a former, seemingly long-lost modesty, and shrank cross-legged and hunched into their seats and hid as much as they could behind the tall receivers, on the entrance of the distinctly attractive stranger.

He was in civilian garb, of dark suit and even dark tie with some insignia on it — school, college, or military outfit — grossly over-dressed by the relaxed standard of the staring, sniggering girls who surrounded him. Despite his clothing, he was undoubtedly a military type, and not at all embarrassed or put out at finding himself suddenly in the midst of a horde of underwear-clad young ladies. 'My God! Have I died and gone to heaven?' he queried, with an elegantly wolfish grin.

He had come to visit Leonard Garstein, the boffin directly responsible for the metal monster which had settled so invasively in their office. Garstein not only looked like but actually *was* a professor. Jenny liked him. Despite his lean, donnish frame and ascetic features, he was not at all stuffy, and treated the girls with an old-fashioned, avuncular courtesy which ignored any differences of rank. When he smiled, his face was twinklingly transformed to that of a mischievous schoolboy. Though slightly flustered when he first walked in on the informal undress of the first watch, he soon philosophically accepted their freedom — he even endured their draping of his beloved machine with various newly washed items of intimate attire which they would whisk away, dried by its throbbing heat, at the end of their spell of duty.

But the handsome Captain Castleton set daintily encased bosoms a-flutter with an altogether new intensity, particularly when it was discovered that he had apparently come from the mystic portals of some secret edifice in the distant capital. He became a regular visitor to Prof Garstein and his machine, especially after 8 p.m. and the 'sparks' on duty sported outfits under their soon-to-be-discarded uniforms worthy of the legendary Jane herself.

Jenny was startled, and pinkly discom-forted, one day, to be accosted by Martin Castleton when, dressed in the rather more conventional manner associated with daylight hours, she reported for duty on the afternoon watch at 2 p.m. The avidly curious stares of her colleagues at his singling her out added to her embarrassment. This was further intensi-fied when he suggested they should take a stroll through the extensive parkland, and, even more astonishingly, the idea was supported by a curtly permissive nod from the redoubtable First Officer Pearson. With a nervous foreboding she did her best to disguise, she fell in step beside the tall figure, and started as though touched by an electric shock at the light contact of his fingers on the smooth skin of her arm, a fraction above her elbow and below the neatly rolled sleeve of her dazzling white shirt.

He was in his thirties, she guessed, and something of a ladies' man, from his wide, confident smile and his light but assured touch on her arm. 'You're as tucked away here as we are,' he confided, without explaining the location he referred to. It all added to the air of glamorous mystery, enhanced by his next words. 'I like to get out in the open. My suspicious nature, I guess. But no one can snoop on you.' He nodded towards the distant lofty trees. 'At least not near enough to hear anything.'

His words, with their flavour of cloak-and-dagger and derring-do, should have sounded ridiculous, but somehow they didn't. And his grin was rather engaging, she conceded. He took a small notebook from a side pocket, and flipped it open, all without releasing his light hold on her. 'Now then, Jenny. You don't mind me calling you Jenny, do you? Mrs Wright sounds far too matronly, and you're far too pretty to be a matron.'

She felt the colour mounting in her and willed it not to show. 'No. That's fine, er . . . '

She already knew his name. 'I'm Castleton. Brown job, as it happens. Captain by rank, but I'd be delighted if you'd call me Martin.' His smile broadened, her blush deepened. All at once she thought disconcertingly of the number of times he had seen her in her underwear. 'You won't often see me in uniform. We MI boys like to play at Bulldog Drummond. Military Intelligence,' he explained unnecessarily.

'You come highly recommended, Jenny,' he continued, 'from quite a number of people. Including your divisional officer, of whom, incidentally, I am justifiably terrified.' He hesitated fractionally. His grip on her arm tightened. 'I'll get down to brass tacks right away. I want you for a special assignment. To work with me, and one or two others. All top secret stuff. You can of course say no right away and we'll leave it at that. Or you can wait to hear more and then say no. It's up to you. What's it to be?'

'I'd like to hear more, sir.'

'Uh-huh! You'll have to learn not to play by the book if you come in with me. Martin's the name, right?' She blushed again, nodded. 'You're a teacher. You're good with words. You're bright and imaginative. And most important of all, you're married. That's what I need. A girl who knows a bit about life.'

His words disturbed her, though she did not really know why. But they also intrigued her and she watched his face intently.

He glanced down at his notebook before continuing. 'So! You'll be twenty-six next week, eh? You must allow me to take you out to dinner somewhere.'

She almost stopped, and his hand moved her gently onward. A feeling of flustered outrage seized her, then she wondered why it should. Perhaps he was just being gallant. He had, after all, just mentioned her marriage. 'What's this all about, s — Martin?' she asked directly, in a belated effort to assert herself.

His light-hearted manner disappeared at once. 'Quite right. We've got ourselves involved in a piece of top flight intrigue. We stumbled on it through some of Prof Garstein's work. Your secret code malarky. It's linked with Special Operations, so all this is Official Secrets Act stuff. Breathe a word and you'll be Rudolph Hess's neighbour in no time.' Again, he flashed his brilliant smile, but she had a feeling that he was far from joking. 'We found out about a nasty piece of work operating in and around the American Embassy in Rome. An Eyetie named Donny who'd been passing information to anyone who might be interested. Before the Yanks got in on the war in December and had to pull out Donny hooked up with an American girl, one Maxine Trillo. Between them they made a very pleasant pair of immoral and amoral spies, but it seems they were very sweet on each other and Donny apparently trusted his little Maxi with some very useful rumours. When the Yanks shipped out Maxi was also forced to go back Stateside where we picked her up pretty smartly. But Donny doesn't know that Maxi is out of action, and that's an advantage that we intend to play.'

She was really intrigued now as she waited for him to go on. It seemed incongruous somehow to be walking in uniform beside this handsome man, in the middle of the shimmering English August countryside, and listening to such a tale of spy rings and subterfuge. It was like some game, a flight of fancy divorced from the sunny reality bathing them. But his deep voice had lost all trace of flippancy.

'What we need to do is to convince Donny and his new pals that his little Maxi is still sweet on him, and still working. From England. We know the code she would use to get in touch. And she would know the network to get her messages through. All we have to do is to make him think it's really Maxi he's talking to. That's where you come in. The woman's touch. We want you to be Maxi. Whisper those sweet nothings into his ear — through the air waves, of course. You'll be given all the gen we've got on the pair of them. Including some copies of their old correspondence, letters and so on. We can Yankify it a bit, if we need to. We've got somebody to do that for us, as well. But the female angle has got to be genuine. It'll mostly be just you and me working together. What do you say, Jenny? I hope you'll say yes. Apart from the fact that I'll cheerfully give my right arm to work with you.' He grinned down at her, and, once more, to her chagrin, she felt the warm colour mount to her face. 'I think it might really lead to something worthwhile. On the war front, I mean.'

He relaxed visibly, gave a deprecating little chuckle, and squeezed her arm companionably. 'On the other hand, it may all come to naught. But it'll be interesting, I can promise you.'

Her mind was spinning, she was still trying to take in the import of what he had told her. 'Does it — will I have to move — transfer to — '

'No, absolutely not. Certainly not in the foreseeable future. In fact, it'll be better to work from down here. Like I said, it's nicely tucked away. And we're keeping this well under wraps, even from many of our own bods. Our place up in town is a hotbed of gossip at the best of times. No. I'll come down and see you here. You'll still carry on as a sparks officially. We'll have to make up some kind of tale to cover for this little *tête-à-tête*, as far as your chums are concerned.'

She stiffened as he let his hand fall from her elbow and gently patted the small of her back, in a briefly intimate little gesture. His deep chuckle erupted again. 'We'll put it about that I'm an old chum of your hubby's, all right? He's a second looey in some infantry mob in the desert, yes?'

'They'll wonder why on earth I haven't mentioned it before,' she offered practically. 'Or why you haven't approached me before now.'

'We'll say I didn't know you,' he answered promptly. 'That I met him out in North Africa. Asked me to look you up. Keep an eye on you.' His quizzical look caused her further evident embarrassment. 'That'll help to explain my turning up here now and then, and taking you out for dinner. I don't get many perks in my job, but I must say you look like being one of them!'

She stared at him, once again feeling slightly affronted, as though he had done something improper, then reprimanded herself for being over-sensitive. He was the kind of egotistical individual who couldn't help acting towards any personable female in that manner. And she was honest enough to admit that she *did* look good in uniform — or out of it, she added, as the blush-inducing thought occurred that he was already aware of that fact from the several forays he had already made to the wireless office during her spells of duty.

*   *   *

As a subterfuge, the story worked all too well. When he called one evening at the Wrens' quarters, dressed in blazer and grey flannels with knife-edge creases, the girls were goggle-eyed, and some were cattily envious. The sporty little open-topped roadster merely confirmed the Lothario image, and Jenny's cheeks were hot as she climbed into the low passenger seat and gathered the skirts of her light summer dress about her bare limbs to restrict his appreciative view.

She had spent the intervening time, or most of the precious spare moments of it she had, studying the batch of papers in a cheap cardboard file Martin Castleton had left with her. In spite of her uncertainty about getting involved in this project, she was fascinated by the scraps of documentary evidence of the affair between the Italian and the American cypher worker. It was full of deviousness from the start.

Donny was supplying the Germans with useful items, both about his own Fascist government's dealings and Allied secrets too. The entry into the war of the Americans put a new spin on his espionage, but his movements became more obscure and Jenny could hardly make out what he was really up to. But then, she assumed, she was not being given the full picture. Not that it mattered.

She was primarily concerned with the more private and personal angle — the love affair, if that was what it was, which had now become part of the deception. 'He's hot stuff, as our Yankee colleagues would say,' Martin Castleton chortled as he handed over the file. 'It'll make interesting bedtime reading for you.' It did, though some of it made her face burn in the lamplit privacy of the reading room.

Castleton drove the way she would have expected, with a speed and dash that faintly alarmed and excited her. He took her to a country pub a few miles away from Bletchley.

'We're not exactly hiding ourselves away,' she murmured, aware of curious eyes turned towards them as they made their way through to the comfortable lounge.

Again came that disturbing grin. 'I don't want us to, Jenny. We're an item, remember. A bit of gossip'll be good for us. Besides, it might get you in the mood.' Her eyes widened, she stared at him, more amazed than affronted, until he chuckled, and went on, 'For composing a pash letter to your Latin lover. That's your job, and a tricky one it is. You've got to hit the right note. Put yourself into Maxi's . . . ' he paused deliberately, enjoying her confusion, before he added, 'shoes. You've got some idea what she was like. I want you to have a go at composing a billet-doux. We'll put our heads together. After we've had a couple of drinks, to loosen up.' He laughed. 'After all, this is only our first date.'

She glanced down, angry at the way he could make her feel so unsure of herself. 'I don't know what on earth John's going to make of all this. My husband,' she added, with a note of defiance.

'Nothing, my sweet! We're not going to tell him.'

Jenny was staggered at the bluntness of his reply, and his infuriating grin. 'But — I couldn't — not tell him. Not something like this. We don't — '

He reached across the low table and seized her wrist, held on to it and shook her hand as though she were a fretful child. 'You'll do as you're told, Jenny. That's an order. And I don't need to remind you you're a member of His Majesty's Forces. Even though you look devilishly cute in those civvy clothes. No channel of communication is entirely safe, certainly not those going overseas. So mum's the word, otherwise I'll have you clapped in irons for the duration.' He narrowed his eyes, his expression one of exaggerated lustfulness. 'Now there's a beautiful thought!'

16

John stared out of the train window. An Arab woman, covered from head to foot in flowing black, with only her mahogany-coloured, seamed features showing, thrust forward a tin plate full of thin, curiously striped reddish fish. In the centre of her forehead hung a metal coil. It looked suspiciously like a tuning coil from some radio part, and probably was. She smiled, displaying a few brown teeth and what she hoped was an alluring expression, held the pile of fish a little higher. He shook his head, her patently false grin was wiped off immediately. Muttering what was doubtless a curse, she moved further down the line of the carriages, towards the third-class coaches which were packed with bodies. Groups of sellers clustered round them, and John could see some Allied uniforms in the throng of passengers who were bartering.

Rather ashamedly, John was once again glad of his officer status, and the cushioned banquettes of the reasonably clean first-class compartment he was sharing with two other pongoes and a naval officer. There was also a floridly stout lady opposite who was dressed in European style clothes but who looked and sounded, when she spoke in complaint over something or other, middle eastern in origin.

John offered his bag of oranges round. The navy type shook his head. 'I'd be a bit careful of the local produce,' he warned, pursing his lips like a maiden aunt. 'Don't want to get a gyppy tummy. No joke at all.'

John stared at the pale knees over the white socks. He looked as though he hadn't been out here five minutes, silly sod. Too weary to argue, he leaned back, stared across the ramshackle huts to the bank of the canal on his left. On the other side, the desert stretched away in a sandy haze. Just here the sand was soft, and orange, sculpted into long billows of dunes, in true romantic tradition. Unlike most of the territory he and his comrades had been scrapping over for the past year now.

It was hard to believe that just two days ago he had been in the line at Alam el Halfa, and celebrating the fact that they had repulsed yet another Afrika Korps advance, holding Rommel at the Qattara Depression, where the Allies had the advantage of the clifflike ridges with the Panzer divisions bogged down in the salt marshes below. It was uncomfortably close to Cairo, but they had stopped him and even thrown him back. The new man,

Monty, might be about to make the vital difference after all.

They had lost a lot of men, though. His own company had been depleted. A number of familiar faces had gone for good, either dead or too seriously wounded to return to the unit. They had even taken part in a fixed bayonet charge, stumbling and screaming down the stony incline, John shrieking with the best of them and firing his revolver — with totally harmless result, he calculated later. But he had been involved closely enough. He doubted if he would ever forget the cluster of terrified faces in a shallow little hole, the murderous stabbing and hacking from his own men as the Germans abandoned the gun and scrambled madly to escape from the sandbagged enclosure.

The German push, and their own successful counter-offensive, had lasted three days and more. Three days of virtual sleeplessness, of grimly holding on, constantly rushing up more ammunition, calling up more armoured support, then the mad, short spurts of advance in the choking wake of the tanks battling it out ahead of them. John slept in his filth in a dugout with his men, when at last there was a lull. It was Ron Maudsley who had woken him, brought him the news in the early morn. 'You're off out of it, you lucky bugger, sir. Transfer out. Friends in high places, is it, sir?' The sharp features, half disguised under a thick stubble, grinned.

'Piss off!' John muttered, his heart beat quickening. 'Read my orders, have you? Where am I off to?'

'Way up the line. Back to Div HQ. No shit, sir. It's right enough.'

And it had been. He still couldn't work it out. He had to take all his gear with him. Report at 0900 hours on Thursday to Room 150 at Staff HQ, Cairo. He couldn't understand it. At Battalion HQ, his CO wished him luck, with a firm handshake. 'Sorry to lose you, Wright. You've proved your worth here. There's talk of you getting a commendation after this last scrap. But it seems you're too bright to be wasted on us. Transfer to Intelligence, I hear. Join the boffins, eh? Pity. I think we're in for the big push now. General Alexander's taken over, and with General Montgomery taking over the Eighth Army we're going to stop Rommel once and for all.' He gave a harsh laugh. 'Let's face it. If we don't you'll have Jerry breathing down your necks in Cairo. Have a large G & T for me, Lieutenant.'

He felt bad about leaving at such a critical juncture, felt as though he were deserting men like Maudsley and Sergeant Morrow, and the others who had come through unscathed thus far. But he didn't feel sad. He was not going to make any theatrical gestures of protest, or beg to be sent back to his regiment. He had had enough. They all had, even if some of them didn't realize it. He had not yet had time to absorb the full horror of this latest action at Alam el Halfa. But it hooked in the forefront of his mind, set his heart racing and his hands trembling when he thought of it. His last action? he wondered now. He found himself fervently hoping it would be. And he did not feel ashamed or cowardly, only honest with himself.

Cairo was a bedlam of carts and donkeys and honking motor vehicles, almost as unnerving in its way as Alam el Halfa. But at last the RTO at the station fixed up some transport for him and the two officers he had shared the compartment with. The navy type went off to his own particular section of the chaos, much to John's relief. He decided that the rough and tumble of desert life had eroded his social skills. He was glad when, at last, he could stand in sweaty solitude in a high-ceilinged room which was to be his temporary accommodation, and stare through the long window's slatted wooden shutters at a hedged garden with parched brown grass and some tall, slender palm trees through whose fronds he could see the shimmer of the mystical and slightly odorous Nile.

He stripped down to his underpants and lay gratefully on the narrow, creaking bed. He would tackle the problem of finding the ablutions and the luxury of a bathtub later. He stared up at the dingy, flaking ceiling, tried to work out when he had last slept in a room with a proper ceiling. His thoughts drifted guiltily to the desert he had just left, and the men he had shared it with for so long. He hoped they were bedded down somewhere not too rigorous, and that their night would be without danger. He realized his thoughts had formed into the pattern of a prayer. They so often did these days, and yet if anyone were to ask him outright if he believed, he would probably deny it, or, at the best put himself down as a 'don't-know', with a dismissive shrug.

His thoughts turned to home. He hoped that his mail would not be lost in his move and trail forlornly in his wake for weeks ahead. It was ages, or so it seemed, since he had heard from Jenny. Her letters had been less regular since she had been moved to that hush-hush place somewhere in the country. But that was not surprising; she was part of a watch-keeping set-up now — 'very nautical' she had quipped — and often worked on nights. He could imagine what a strain it must be, listening to the hissing and crackling radio waves, having to scribble down incomprehensible numbers and letters.

It was odd to think of her deciphering all those rapid Morse blips, and even odder to think that what crackled and bleeped in her ears came from the enemy. You couldn't get much closer to the foe! Thinking of her delightful ears made him think of the rest of her, the beauty which was all too vivid in his memory. He groaned softly, forced himself up from the bed, and dug into his canvas holdall, searching for the leather writing case which contained the last ten of her letters. He would have to make do with those expressions of love he had hungrily perused numerous times already until new ones were sent to him. He needed to feel that closeness, to sense that unique blending of flesh and spirit so exclusively theirs.

★   ★   ★

'How is she doing? Is she proving any help to you?' Leonard Garstein looked across at his junior colleague with real curiosity in his mild blue eyes. 'She seems a rather delicate little creature to me,' he mused fondly. 'Too delicate for your devious scheme!'

'Most of these blushing violets are a damned sight tougher than you'd think,' Martin Castleton replied forcefully. 'And I'm sure a barrack room full of Wrens has knocked a few prickly edges off. She'll be all right, don't worry.'

'Apparently she's a bit upset about not informing her husband,' Garstein continued in the same mild tone. 'I don't know if you'll be able to bully her into going on with it.' He smiled again. He could not help admiring Castleton's no-nonsense approach, even his professionalism, which was a refreshing contrast to the attitude of some of his own colleagues at Bletchley with their genteel fastidiousness — which he himself suffered from, he acknowledged. It showed in his sympathy towards the unfortunate girl who had got herself mixed up with their nefarious dealings, and was clearly having second thoughts about the business.

'We need a spot of the old stick and carrot touch,' Castleton smiled. 'I've already bribed her with the offer of helping to get hubby out of the firing line. He should be up in Cairo now. He's a schooly, and we need a few of them, as it happens. We'll have him transferred to Intelligence. They're moving him up to Palestine, I believe.'

'Is that out of the firing line?'

Martin Castleton grinned. 'Oh yes. You're more likely to get shot in the back up there.' He resumed airily, 'Anyway, it fits in with my plans to keep our Jenny sweet, and co-operative.'

'You're developing a nasty, conniving mind, Martin, my boy,' Garstein cut in, with a tolerant shake of his grey head.

'Goes with the job. So, Hubby's shipped off to Haifa. He'll run a few courses up at the university there. For military personnel — they're forming new units, from the locals. Jews and Arabs, mixed. You know — why God is on our side. What will happen in the brave new world when victory is ours. That sort of thing. In the meantime let him think he's a regular Bulldog Drummond. Ask him to keep an ear to the ground, real Intelligence work, that sort of stuff. There's a few of those types around. The Iraq pipeline ends there, you remember.'

Garstein shook his head. 'I'm glad, for the girl's sake. Things are going to get very lively in the desert. Showdown time, as our Yankee brethren would say. He's well out of it.' He shifted in his chair. 'So. You got the letter out of her. Clever stuff. Convinced me, anyway. Did she come up with it herself?'

Martin smiled with patently false modesty.

'A good deal of it. We worked on it together. I think we caught the right tone. It should be well on its way now, if not already in Donny's sticky little fingers. Let's hope they're trembling with passion. He clearly has a weakness for the ladies. After all, he talked his way into li'l old Maxi's panties, didn't he?'

'Martin!' The lean features had darkened, there was even a trace of genuine asperity in the mild-mannered voice. 'There's no need for such crudity. I hope you're a bit more subtle when you're dealing with Jenny Wright.'

The younger man laughed unrepentantly. 'She really is far tougher than you give her credit for. She's had her moments, I'd say.' He was almost enjoying Garstein's discomfort, and he continued teasingly. 'She's getting right into the spirit of things. As a surrogate floozy. I knew when I first saw her. Don't let that butter-wouldn't-melt charm fool you, Leonard. She's quite a girl is our Jen! That letter spelt it out pretty plainly, I'd say.'

'She's a perfectly decent girl, and certainly no — floozy,' Garstein answered huffily.

'Absolutely.' Martin grinned mockingly, and held up both hands in a gesture of innocence. 'If you say so. Pure as the driven snow!'

* ★ ★

Jenny was a little more wary this time, when Martin Castleton appeared in his motor outside the Wrens' accommodation block in the grounds. She had changed once more into civvies, to match his elegantly casual garb, but this time she had chosen a pair of dark brown slacks, and pulled her thick woollen three-quarter coat over her jumper, the dark honey waves of her hair falling below the tam she perched on the side of her head.

'Not exactly dressed for pash!' one of her colleagues commented. Several pairs of eyes studied her with critical envy.

'Must be quite a VIP, this boyfriend of yours, if he can get a pass into this bloody nunnery. What's your old man going to say if he finds out?'

'I've told you,' Jenny replied coolly. 'Martin's actually some relative of John's. A cousin of some sort. He happens to be working near here, that's all. Took the chance to look me up.'

'Twice!' her interlocutor emphasized teasingly. 'But who's counting, eh?'

'You, obviously,' Jenny smiled sweetly. 'But don't wait up for me. He's taking me for dinner somewhere so we'll be quite late, I imagine. I've not got the forenoon, so don't wake me. 'Night.'

She was meanly glad when she climbed into the passenger seat of the Austin that she had put on her trousers after all, instead of the dress she had considered. Martin Castleton was too ready to cast a less than neutral eye over her legs, as she had noticed the last time they had met. She had spent half the time tugging the hem of her uniform skirt down over her knees.

It had been an eye-opener in more ways than one. At the end of their long session — in a bedroom over the pub for goodness' sake! — she felt as though she had taken part in a gruelling assault course. His manner had stunned her, at times. She had known from their very first encounter, in the grounds of Bletchley, that he could be a forceful and downright blunt character if necessary, but, given the embarrassment of having to discuss and then come up with some very intimate details for the missive to Donny, she had expected a little more tact, and sympathy.

He had reduced her to wordless gasps of outrage several times during their *tête-à-tête*. Then there had been those unguarded moments, later on in the meeting, when, sprawling shoeless and tieless on the bed, which was spread with scribbled sheets of paper and was, perforce, the only item of furniture they could sensibly use for their efforts, she had caught his glance straying to her dark stockinged limbs, which did nothing to lessen her discomfort as she swiftly struggled up and tugged at her recalcitrant skirt.

She found now as she surreptitiously studied his handsome profile that she was uncertain of her feelings towards him. He had made no bones about the fact that, although they hardly knew each other, he found her attractive, and she could not deny that this gave her a secret thrill of pride. It was good to know that men could still find her desirable, even though she belonged to John now.

But then, this relationship with Martin Castleton was somehow unique, had been from its outset. It was based on their mutual knowledge of an extremely intimate secret, and their collaboration in exploiting it — she still grew hot and cold sometimes at the very notion of what they were doing. What she wasn't sure of was whether he realized just how significant her embarrassment was. He struck her as a man who would not dwell too much on the importance of moral niceties. There was a lusty kind of animalness about him, she felt, that would sweep aside such moot points. It was a quality she found both dangerous and guiltily appealing. It shook her to recognize she was rather frightened of him.

She wondered on later reflection if she had perhaps been spoiled by John's adoration of her, and by the general over-politeness of the young men of her generation and background. Perhaps that was why Martin's manner was such a shock to her. And this led on to even more painful and personal introspection.

It was a long time since she had allowed her mind to dwell on the most shameful episode of her young life, which had so nearly caused her to lose John for ever. She felt sullied, with a sense of haunted despair at this resurrection of the deep shadow which even now lay across their love. For him, as well as her, she was sure, although he had nobly denied it, swore that it made no difference to his feelings for her. As always, with the despair came a feeling of real bewilderment, or incomprehension almost, that she could have let such a terrible thing happen.

She had never felt love for Horst Zettel, not even as it occurred, when she allowed herself to be seduced. She would never forget, her flesh would never cease to crawl at the memory of that smug expression on that too handsome face, his wicked words, 'There! Now you are ready for love. Now you are a woman.' Like some bloodied trophy he had captured, a triumph to his animal maleness.

She had been helplessly, wickedly excited, driven by hunger, need, desperate loneliness, and a feeling of separation from John — all kinds of cloudy emotions, but never love. Intense sexual excitement — and gratification. That was the cruellest scourge of all. It consumed her with shame, so much that she always tried to push it away from her consciousness, to deny the baseness of such an animal instinct which was part and parcel of her nature. It was part of some feral, musty crudeness in her, emanating from that damply beating sexuality she felt between her legs which, without John, could not be graced with love. And, shocked as she was, she felt it now, fearsomely strong, in Martin Castleton's presence.

She was prickly from the beginning of the evening, for she felt uncomfortably dressed down for such a place. The other female diners were in smart cocktail dresses or evening gowns, the males suited. The head waiter raised his right eyebrow an eloquent fraction at her slacks and Martin's blazer and cravat, but Martin beamed at him. 'We're travelling to town, old sport. Just popped in to eat. On the spur of the moment.'

'Look, I'm not happy about keeping all this

from John,' she said determinedly, her cheeks red, after they had ordered the meal. 'I'm going to write and let him know. I can't keep something so important from him. We don't have secrets,' she ended pointedly.

'What? None at all? A sexy old thing like you? I find that extremely hard to believe, Jenny, my sweet. Your demure manner might well fool old codgers like Leonard Garstein but it won't wash with me. I'd say you're a girl who knows what's what, all right. Or am I wrong?'

She gaped, her mouth hanging open, blinking rapidly at his brutal directness. She fought to recover, to find her speech again. 'I — I — you've no right to talk to me like that! No right at all! How dare you? I think I'd like to leave, right now, please!' And then, excruciatingly, she burst into tears, fled the dining room and hid in the ladies', shaken by a sobbing fit that astonished her almost as much as it distressed her.

When she emerged in to the panelled lobby, Martin was waiting for her. 'Come on,' he said quietly, and took her arm. His tight grip was oddly comforting. He led her out to the car. She thought he was taking her back to Bletchley, and she was silently bemused by her ambivalent emotions at the thought that the evening was over.

She blinked round with genuine surprise when he swung to a halt outside the pub they had already used twice before. Again, his hand was firm on her arm and she was led inside. Next minute they were back behind the closed door of the bedroom, whose high double bed took up most of the limited space. He plumped up the pillows, arranged them in a pile, and pushed her firmly on to the patterned eiderdown. 'Get your feet up. Make yourself comfy.' He was even slipping off her shoes as he spoke, and still she made no objection. 'We need to have a heart-to-heart. We've got to get on with each other, Jenny. I need you. So. Where do we begin? Tell me about your John. And about you. All about you. Forget our other double-dealing lovers. Start at the beginning.'

She cried again, sniffled, blew her nose into his handkerchief — and talked. It was as though he had given her some kind of truth-inducing pill. Certainly he had released something, breached some dam within, for it all came gushing out — her love, her loneliness, the idyll of their time at Durham, the frustrations afterwards — and, finally, helplessly, the whole episode of her infidelity with Horst Zettel. Later, she wondered dizzily if he had known all along, that he had somehow hypnotically forced her confession from her, for it was to colour their whole relationship indelibly, from that moment on.

'He can't have been all that bothered. He still married you. Forgive and forget et cetera.'

'I don't think — *I'll* never forget it!' she murmured, her voice charged. 'Yes. He's forgiven me. That's the kind of man he is. But I know it did *bother* him!' Yet again she felt the surge of contrasting emotion, from a weary, confessional penitence to anger at his apparently casual rejoinder.

'Your precious hubby is sitting safely on his arse in some officers' mess in Cairo right now. And soon he'll be sunning himself on Mount Carmel like an Old Testament prophet, and delivering lectures to recruits at the university there. That was my part of the bargain and I've kept it.' His hand still imprisoned hers. She felt just as pinned down by those brilliant dark eyes boring into her. She could not look away.

17

May raised her glass. 'Let's hope we won't have many more wartime Christmases to face, eh?' Iris and Jenny copied her gesture before they all sipped at the golden liquid. May pursed her lips and laughed as she gave a little shudder. 'It's a bit dry for me. Be careful. I ought to warn you. Ruby's husband makes a potent brew. We both got tiddly on New Year's, didn't we? I don't know who put who to bed.'

Iris grunted. 'Come off it! I practically carried you upstairs!' She slapped at her broad, trousered thigh. 'That's something *you* couldn't do for *me*. You're nothing but a spelk.'

May smiled warmly across at Jenny. 'It's good to see you! It's been so long. Far *too* long! Not since John went overseas. That's what? A good eighteen months or more.'

Jenny nodded, pinked slightly. 'I know. I've felt so bad about it. But once I joined up I never seemed to have enough time for anything. Even this Christmas I only managed three days at home. I had to be back for New Year. We work watch and watch about, you know. But I was determined to get up to see you. I wangled this long weekend especially.'

'And lovely it is to see you.' Iris echoed May's sentiment. 'I must say you look very fetching in that outfit. You did very wisely to join the Wrens. Far and away the best uniform. Doesn't she look lovely, May? I hope you've sent John a picture of you.'

Jenny nodded. She smiled. 'This is my Number Ones. Best uniform,' she explained. 'You should see us when we go on duty. In this cold weather we all look like barrage balloons, we've got that many clothes on! Specially on nights.' Quite a dramatic change from the summer! she thought, but kept it to herself.

'It's hard, is it?' May asked sympathetically. 'I'm not prying,' she continued quickly. 'I know you can't tell us all your secrets. But it must be demanding work, I gather.'

'You don't have to worry,' Iris laughed. 'Any secrets are safe with us. We don't know any Jerry spies, honest!'

'Oh, it's mostly boring as hell,' Jenny answered quickly. 'Just sitting twiddling knobs and listening to static. Sometimes we tune in to dance music to relieve the boredom, but you're in for a right rocket from the killick of the watch if you're caught out. The one in charge,' she added, translating the naval slang for leading hand.

'I'm sure you're doing a very vital job,' May said quietly. 'And I know John's as proud as Punch of you. When did you last hear from him? We got a letter a couple of weeks ago, not long after New Year. I'm so glad he was posted to Palestine. I know I shouldn't be so selfish, but I was so relieved that he was out of it before Alamein and all that. Wasn't it wonderful? Hearing the church bells again, eh? Remember when we all thought we'd be hearing them to announce a Jerry landing?'

Her words made Jenny feel even more uncomfortable, but she was continuing animatedly. 'And the news is still good out there, isn't it? They've entered Tripoli. Let's hope that Winny and Mr Roosevelt can get things sorted. Bring this whole mess to an end.' She was referring to the Casablanca Conference taking place at that moment between the two leaders, and the optimistic speculations going on in the press for this new year of 1943. 'Get all the boys home again. John. And our Teddy.' Her voice quavered just a little.

Jenny felt wretched. Each mention caused her tender conscience to smart. Her involvement with the shadowy form of military intelligence represented by Martin Castleton had taken over her life to an unwarranted extent. Even this long weekend leave had been attributed by some to his machinations. Joyce Radcliffe, whom Jenny found hard to get along with at the best of times, had remarked bitchily, 'Off up the line again, Wright? This *cousin*' — she gave the word sceptical emphasis — 'has certainly got some pull round here, eh?' Jenny was becoming so guilt-ridden she even wondered if the girl might not be right. Now she groped in the pocket of her discarded jacket and took out the packet of Park Drive and her lighter.

'I didn't know you smoked!' May exclaimed, and the brittle Jenny thought she detected a note of criticism.

'Oh yes. I have for ages.' She offered the packet to May, who looked even more startled.

'No thanks. I've never been able to get away with them.'

'Glad somebody else has a few vices,' Iris chaffed, reaching over for one. 'I keep telling her they work wonders for your nerves.'

Jenny nodded. 'Helps to pass the time, specially at work.' The smoke caught her and she gave a throaty cough, angry with herself, and feeling a little foolish. She felt like a schoolgirl trying to appear grown up. But then her mother-in-law had that effect on her, even though she hadn't seen her for a year and a half. She acknowledged ashamedly that it was only her disturbed state of mind seeking scapegoats. Damn Martin Castleton, she thought, and not for the first time. He loomed constantly in her mind these days. Far more than he ought to.

Again, that sense of helplessness, which seemed to be associated uniquely with him, swept over her. She had seen him only three days ago, and it had been as stormily emotional as ever. 'He's hooked, well and truly!' Martin crowed as soon as they were alone. He held his fist in the air.

He had just told her that they'd received the third letter from Donny. He showed her a transcribed and clearly edited version. Over the months they had been working on the project, she had swiftly realized that Martin was making her privy to only as much information as he felt it was necessary for her to know. The last communication from her *alter ego* of Maxi had been much longer than previous messages, and therefore much more of a struggle to invent. Martin had found a way of getting actual paper correspondence through to the agent in Rome. She had wondered aloud how Donny could possibly be fooled if it was not in Maxi's hand. 'Oh, don't you worry your pretty little bonce!' he replied airily. 'We've got experts for all kinds of things, including other folks' handwriting.'

She felt even worse about it, inwardly writhing with shame at the explicitly sensual references she both helped to create and receive. 'It makes me want to puke!' Jenny said vehemently, at the end of their tortuous session in the pub bedroom, back in November, when they had penned her reply to a previous missive. 'I sound like a right little cock teaser!' she declared tearfully, flinging the crude phrase at Martin as a kind of defiance for her own feeling of self-loathing at what they were doing.

'You are, Sugar!' he grinned, capable yet again of making her gasp at his bluntness. 'But you can't help the way you look, eh?'

If his remark was meant to make her feel better, it failed. She was savagely glad she had put her navy slacks on and that her hair was a lank mess. The tears started when they came to the response to Donny's latest declarations. He had to bully and cajole a weeping Jenny for a long time before she would agree to continue. 'I can't do this,' she pleaded. 'I sound like such a scheming little bitch. It won't fool him. He must know this isn't Maxi.'

'Look,' he soothed, getting up from the crumpled bed and pacing the tiny length of the room. The blue cigarette smoke hung in rolling clouds under the shaded light. The confined space was acrid with it, underlaid with the scent of her perfume and the smell of alcohol drifting up from the bar. The windows were sealed against the cold night, the heavy blackout in place to add to the claustrophobic effect. 'Believe me. His male ego will convince him it's true. It's his weakest point, I know.' He chuckled encouragingly. 'We're all the same, us blokes.'

'No you're not!' she snapped back.

He laughed, unfazed by her attack. 'Well, you really *have* got the guy in a million then. And aren't you glad that he's tucked away safe up in Haifa, eh?'

The country was still buzzing with the rapturous news of Monty's desert victory at El Alamein. Jenny glared at him, full of disgust and a sudden hatred. As though reading her mind, he echoed the word which was ringing in her thoughts. 'Cos the rest of us are just cocky bastards!' he grinned.

He got his way in the end. She was too weary to argue. Her head throbbed, the gin she had been sipping tasted sharp and burnt sourly at her stomach.

At their last meeting three days ago, in the now familiar setting of the pub bedroom,

Martin had got his way once more, and, after an agonizing two hours and more, her latest promiscuous reply had been penned. Unnervingly, he changed his tactics on this occasion. He hardly bullied her at all and when, predictably, she felt the onset of tears yet again at the drained feeling of shame and taint these sessions gave her, to her bewilderment he folded her in his arms, held her shoulders while she laid her spinning head on his chest and let the storm of sobbing blow itself out. Even more bewildering, she realized how much she appreciated his gentle touch, and even the affectionate kiss on her temple as the sheltering embrace ended.

Belatedly, she focused her attention on May's words, to discover that her mother-in-law was suggesting a trip over to Low Fell to visit Marian and her little girl. 'I told her you were coming up this weekend. She'd love to see you.'

'Great,' Jenny answered. 'I haven't seen her for — Oh, goodness knows. Teddie was just a baby.'

'She's five now. Ready for school this year. Doesn't seem possible, does it?' A brief flicker of private pain passed over May's face, and Jenny felt a stab of real sympathy for her. 'When you think of all that's happened, eh? I wonder when the poor mite'll see her daddy again?'

★ ★ ★

Marian was clearly on edge, and Jenny thought at first that it might be because of her visit. She recalled a rather shy personality, a pretty girl, in a rounded, homely way, perfectly suited to the neat-as-a-pin semi and the new infant. And she knew from John's description that she was a diffident character, a little too ready to let others decide things for her. And utterly dedicated to playing her role of the little wife. Not that it had done her a lot of good, as far as John's brother was concerned. Jenny had expressed her indignation at Teddy's treatment of her, though she had only heard it at second hand from John, who agreed with her. 'She's always tried too hard,' he told her.

'Thanks. I'll remember that!' Jenny had answered.

The young woman she saw now certainly looked more mature. She had lost considerable weight. She was still attractive, but her face wore a constantly strained look. Her eyes flickered warily back and forth, from one visitor to another. Jenny recognized the aura of stress, for she was uncomfortably familiar with it. The smoking was just one sign; Marian scarcely ever let a moment pass without a cigarette in her lips or in her hand. Jenny felt almost abstemious in comparison.

'No Dora, then?' May remarked quizzically.

'No, she's going home this weekend,' Marian replied, the colour mounting. 'Time she spent some time with her folks.'

'Have you seen your mam recently?' May asked. There was a stiff awkwardness in her enquiry, and a mutual embarrassment as Marian, her face still red, shook her head.

'Not since just after Boxing Day.'

Nelly Dunn, Marian's mother, was a girlhood friend of May's — and an old adversary, from the time it was discovered that Teddy had got her daughter pregnant.

The reference to the recent holiday was itself a floating mine full of dangerous barbs. May had expected that Marian and little Teddie would spend most of the Christmas holidays at Hexham with her and Iris. But Marian showed unusual stubbornness in insisting she must return to Low Fell the day after Boxing Day. She had used the excuse of Nelly's visit as a reason for going back home, but when May had offered to run her across for it and then come and collect her again, Marian had agitatedly refused. Her daughter-in-law was nearly in tears when she guiltily told her that 'a bit of a do' had been planned for later that week, with Dora and her mother, May's sister, Julia.

Tense seconds of silence followed, which should have been filled in by Marian's invitation to May and Iris to attend. May was deeply hurt, and Marian guiltily wretched. She couldn't invite her mother-in-law, because Dora would be the only family member there. The others would all be Dora's work mates, including Jim Moody. Marian's lover. Her 'fancy man'.

She had held out for almost six long months. Weeks of intensely passionate kisses, and groping, and half sin. And bitter tears of shame and penitence. 'We can't go on seeing each other!' Marian sobbed, partly for the pleasure of having Jim's eloquent pleading to make her change her mind. Her penitence was real enough, especially during the long, lonely days and nights when she did not see him. She half hoped and dreaded that he would get sick of her, of her failure to commit herself fully, and stop seeing her himself.

He came as arranged the evening she came back from her Christmas stay at Hexham. Dora was away, still at her home — at least, that was where she was supposed to be sleeping during the four-day break she had from work. 'Uncle Jim!' Teddie called delightedly, holding out her arms to be picked up and paraded aloft.

Marian was still tensely emotional after her two days at the cottage, with all its reminders of Teddy from his earliest infancy, and his mother's seemingly constant references to her absent sons.

'All alone,' Jim said, from his seat by the fire, when Marian came back down after settling a still excited Teddie to sleep. He held out his arms. There was a pause before she moved to embrace him, and to sit as she usually did, on the rug, leaning against his legs, her head and arms on his knee.

'The neighbours'll think we're a right pair of floozies, Dora and me. What with you and Ray always back and forth.' She gave a strangled laugh that was almost a sob. 'I suppose we are. Well — *I* am, any road.'

He pulled her vigorously up on to him and they sprawled in the armchair, his arms clamped round her waist, his lips pressed to hers. 'I love you, Marian. Don't send me away tonight, love. I want to stay with you.'

She cried, abandonedly, while he held her, hardly daring to breathe, but her tears were of weary relief, for she could fight no longer against their mutual desire, their need for love. Though she knew that she would suffer torments of conscience in the future, maybe for the rest of her life, she was glad at last to give herself, to take with him, and there was a desperation in the haste in which they undressed and came together in the heat and light of the flames that dappled their writhing bodies on the carpet of the room sparkling with the festive tinsel.

18

John stared at the girl coming forward to meet him with outstretched hand. The no-nonsense manner of her handshake took away from the brief awkwardness of their greeting. He recognized the traces of the shy smile, the vulnerability of the expressive brown eyes behind the ugly round frames of the glasses. 'Hello, Sara. Long time no see.'

There was little else to remind him of the plump, sallow schoolgirl he had last met in England, more than five years ago. He had been intrigued when the letter came, especially when he saw the name of the sender, Sara Arad, and that it bore a local postmark. She was at the Kfar Netter, a *moshav*, which was a collective farming commune, on the coastal plain north of Tel Aviv. She had been there since before the outbreak of war, when the *moshav* had first been established. She explained that she had heard of his posting to Palestine from his uncle, David Golding, with whom she had kept in regular correspondence since her arrival in England.

It took two months for David to fix up a

257

convenient meeting. She had lost considerable weight, seemed taller, with an attractive
figure. The bleached khaki of her neatly
pressed shirt, and the dark olive skirt of the
same serviceable material, together with the
black beret angled on her short, dark hair, cut
straight across her brow and levelled at her
ears, gave her a military look. This was offset
somewhat by the fact that she wore no
stockings, only a pair of simple, strappy
leather sandals. Her feet were as tanned as
the rest of her limbs, the short, unpainted
nails standing out palely.

'My word! You look very fit. Wonderful!' he
smiled, just stopping himself from using the
word 'nice'. Which she was, he acknowledged.
Though her features were still plain, with the
simple, square hairstyle and the small, ugly,
dark spectacle frames, her trim, healthily
scrubbed outdoor appearance appealed to
him.

'Thank you. You look — very distinguished,' she finished, after a smiling pause.
He was wearing his tropical rig of short
sleeved shirt and knife-creased shorts, with
the three-quarter stockings, and his cap, of
course, which had the buckled shape and
sun-bleached texture of a desert veteran. He
was proud, too, of his flashes and the
regimental badge and shoulder tags. He had

not been required to change his infantry insignia. He was proud of their proclamation of a front line soldier, like his weather-beaten complexion, and the eye surrounds marked by the fine, wrinkled network of tiny lines acquired from peering, screwed-up, against the glare of rocky waste and the constant blow and drift of the particles of sand. It was different from the smooth tan achieved by hours of sporting on the Little Beach beside the transit camp close by, or the golden stretches of Netanya seaside further to the south.

He lightly took her arm, just above the elbow, as they emerged into the full blaze of the morning sunlight from the shade of the railway station. The heat shimmered and beat from the vehicles parked in the wide expanse of Plumer Square, and he felt a thrill of sensuous pleasure from the cool smoothness of her skin on his fingers. He steered her across to busy Kingsway, and they turned right, the haze of the sea on their right as they strolled. 'I thought we'd have a cup of tea. The YWCA's just along here. They have an excellent canteen.'

In contrast to the noisy chaos outside, the large room was quiet, and they found a secluded table next to the wide open windows, looking over to the crowded harbour. The traffic noise hummed mutedly as a background. He cleared his throat, decided to take the bull by the horns. Get the unpleasantness out of the way as quickly as possible. 'Have you heard anything? Any news of your parents?'

He saw the pain at once, though she did her best to conceal it. She shook her head. 'Nothing directly. Someone had news of them, over a year ago now. They were still — at home. But we've heard since . . . ' she paused, as though searching for words, and he waited tensely. 'They may have been forced to move. A lot of people are, now. Being sent to camps.' Again a hesitation, then her tanned face darkened, and the large eyes moistened. She went on hurriedly. 'There are some awful stories.' She gazed away from him, out over the dazzling scene outside, lifting her head a little. She had clearly fought to contain her emotion. Her voice was flat, almost harsh in its bleakness. 'I sometimes wonder if I'll ever see them again.'

He cleared his throat, made inadequate noises of comfort, and she continued quickly, as though to spare him. 'We can only wait, yes? It can't go on for ever. The RAF are bombing, every night — and day. And now the Russians are forcing them back in the east. When they open the second front in the west . . . ' Her voice trailed off, and, with a visible effort, she assumed a bright casualness. 'Your Uncle David was very kind to me. As you know. It was through his help that I got out here. I was so lucky to be chosen. We are still in touch. Of course, you know.'

The awkwardness returned, at least in John's mind. He had not discovered until much later that Sara Arad had emigrated to Palestine, an official immigrant into her new home, thanks to some of her distant relatives' and David Golding's influence. Not long after her departure had come the White Paper, or 'Black Paper' as Jews called it, severely limiting Jewish immigration into the Mandate for the next five years, in order to make sure that their population would never be a numerical threat to that of the Arabs. It didn't stop the illegal immigration, as John well knew. There was a crowded internment camp just down the road at Athlit. In spite of the known harsh treatment of Jews by the Nazis which had been going on for years, and now the growing reports of the horrors of forced labour camps where they were being literally worked to death, official British policy towards immigration had not changed at all.

In the last seven months there had been times when John had wished he could be facing the simple dangers of the front line again, especially now that the North African campaign had ended in such spectacular success, with the complete cave-in of the Axis forces in Tunisia. Though he might well have been involved in the invasion of Sicily, and the six weeks of fierce fighting it had taken to subdue the island. News of the end of enemy resistance had just come through in the last few days.

Up here, the issues were far from clear cut. Thousands of Jews were fighting for the Allied forces, many had gone as volunteers from Palestine itself. Yet clandestine immigrants were still rounded up when caught and put into camps like Athlit. The Arab and Jewish underground movements still carried out acts of murder and reprisal on one another. The notorious Stern Gang was still perpetrating acts of terror, and both Jews and Arabs felt betrayed by the British.

Meanwhile, John gave lectures at the Technical Institute about a rosily vague post war world and the wisdom of partition and power sharing. The debates he instituted at the end of his talks to the locals all too frequently ended in flashing-eyed, spittle-flying invective which was prevented from degenerating into a physical fight by the intervention of a cynical NCO, or the equally sceptical member of the police force on duty for that very purpose. 'I reckon we should just bugger off and let 'em tear each other to pieces, sir,' the sergeant observed, with prophetic wisdom.

And when John wasn't dispensing the party line to the uneasy cohabitants of this troubled land, he was imparting similarly vague and optimistic views of the brave new world to which his audience of British conscripts would be heirs in that magical era 'after the war'. He was fascinated by the mixed reactions of these young men. Clearly, there was an overwhelming desire for something better, something 'fairer' — he could recognize the issues which had mattered to those workers, or unemployed workers, of the north-east he had met in Welfare Institutes when he was at college. They pinned their hopes on men like Ernie Bevin, Churchill's Minister for Labour and National Service. 'A better deal' for the working man. And the other one, Bevan with an 'a', and his vision of a free health service for all.

John wondered privately what really would happen in this new world of victory, when all these disgruntled men, who had been plucked from their homes and families, made to face terrible dangers and hardships, got back to where they belonged. Surely the old order would, *must* change? And not only at home. Just down the road from where he and Sara were taking tea, was an Indian club, and near it a club for the African forces. There were hundreds of brown and black men in uniform in the busy port. Would they be content to return to their homes, to be faithful subservient members of the Empire, after all they had seen — and all they had been asked to do? 'The Empire true, we can depend on you.' Can we? he wondered. Will there 'always be an England'?

'Do you miss Europe at all?' he asked.

She shook her head. 'Not now.' Suddenly, he saw again that shyness come over her, fill those gentle eyes, the colour again mounting in her face. She leaned towards him earnestly. 'I'll always be grateful — I can't tell you how much — to you, for what you did. And for your uncle. Getting me away.'

He shrugged uncomfortably, stirred and pained by the memory. 'No. It was — I made a mess of things. It wasn't — '

'No, no. Not at all.' She reached out, touched his hand, and withdrew quickly. 'It was through you, I'm sure. The fuss you made. That's why they let my papers go through. I was so lucky.'

John thought of Horst Zettel. The wide, charming smile, his light laughing reference to the 'little Jewess'. He thought of his hands on Jenny, of his body . . . he shivered mentally, contracted with rage and hurt.

'There's so much to do here. There's never time — to be sorry for yourself.' She smiled. 'I can't describe what it's like — to feel proud. I've only been here five years — but it's my home. It always will be.' Again her tone lightened, sounding youthful and full of hope. 'I'm going to move. We're setting up a new kibbutz — you know kibbutz?' He nodded. 'In the Huleh Valley. Kvar Blum. There'll be some people from England coming.' She assumed a mischievous expression. 'Legally, of course!' He smiled sheepishly.

'It won't be easy,' he cautioned. 'After the war. It's hard to see what's going to happen. How the — you and the Arabs — how you'll work it out.'

The baldness of her reply shocked him. 'With our own war, I expect.' She gazed at him sombrely. 'We may be enemies, you and I.' Then she smiled. 'But *you* will go home, surely? When Germany is defeated. You'll go back to — Jenny, isn't it?'

He raised his eyebrows. 'My! You *are* well informed.'

He blushed as she went on, 'Oh yes. I always ask about you. Whenever I write to

David. What does she do while you are away? Do you have children?'

'No, no. We'd only just been married when I was posted overseas. We haven't seen each other for over two years now.' She tutted sympathetically. 'She's in the Wrens,' he told her proudly. He dug in his breast pocket for his wallet, and took out the photos. 'There she is. In uniform. She's working in signals — in England still.'

'Ah. She's beautiful.' She passed the snapshots back to him and he flushed with pleasure at her compliment.

'What about you?' He smiled teasingly. 'You're not married? Boyfriend?'

She pulled a face of mock exasperation. 'Ach, no. I am too busy. Life is very full, we work hard. But there are some nice boys.' She giggled. 'Maybe I'll find one from the new arrivals — an Englishman! You are so polite!'

They left the cool quiet of the YWCA and crossed back over the main railway line, approaching the harbour and strolling towards the long, low breakwater. 'What do you want to do?' he asked her. 'We can go for a swim at Bat Galim, if you like. There's a pool there.' He nodded ahead, towards the south. 'You can probably hire a swimming costume. We can get a bite to eat there. Or we could have lunch at the Officers' Club.' He was quick to notice her instinctive reluctance. 'I'm not much of a guide. I've been here since December and I hardly know anything of Haifa, apart from the servicemen's clubs and the cinemas.'

'I've visited once or twice,' she said. 'I'd like to go up the mountain. The Carmelite monastery. Have you seen the cave of Elijah?' In fact, he had, but he pretended ignorance, and they took a taxi up the long, curving road until they stood on top of Carmel, by the solid stone structure of the monastery, and the domed church in which was the grotto said to be the cave of the Old Testament prophet. Candles twinkled in the dim recess. A monk stood by. 'Aren't you going to light a candle?' she asked.

He shook his head. 'I'm not Catholic. I'm a Protestant.'

His Methodist background made him note with disapproval the gaudiness of the interior, the gold and the statues, with their somehow uncomfortable flesh-coloured paint and bright robes. He grimaced at his own inconsistency when he recalled suddenly saying to Jenny when they were at college together that the rituals of Roman Catholicism, the glitter and pomp of its ceremony, appealed to him.

He was glad to get out of the dim cool into

the glare of the sunlight. They crossed Stella Maris Road, and Sara glanced curiously at the two uniformed guards at the gate of a building almost at the edge of the summit. 'That's the military court,' he said, in answer to her query. 'Let's see if we can find a quiet spot to sit.' They moved through the low bushed scrub at the lip of the escarpment, found a spot shaded by some gnarled old olive trees where they could sit and gaze out over the bay.

The sight of the court building had jarred his memory. At first, he had treated as a private joke his other, unadvertised duty in Haifa of intelligence officer. Major Lilly, who was from the Corps and worked closely with the Palestine Police Force, had interviewed him soon after his arrival. 'Hot bed of intrigue here, Wright. Like everywhere else in this place. Got to keep your ear to the ground. Arabs, Jews, other nationals, too. Some of our so-called allies!' he grunted dismissively. 'Be aware of what's going on. You're not just assigned to Torch House, you know.' Torch House was the Education Centre. 'You're working for us, too.'

The only time he had been called upon to exercise this aspect of his duties had been in the building he and Sara had just passed. A frightened bunch of youths were sitting in one of the cells at the back of the building. They had been beaten by the British policemen, but a grinning army lieutenant with the Royal Engineers' insignia on his tunic told him, 'They've been brought up here to put the wind up them. Told they've been handed over to the military because we are empowered to execute them. The skinny one with the cut on his head is an Irgun suspect. Possibly his chums as well. Talk to them. Put the fear of God into the little shits and find out what you can.'

John did not enjoy his role as interrogator. He was not very good at it, he thought. The fear which he could smell on the suspects nauseated him. They were in their teens, some of them still at school. He doubted that any of them were members of the resistance movement, or that they had committed any crimes worse than daubing a few slogans on government property. Their voluble terror made him question the morality of the machine he was a part of.

He wondered what Major Lilly would say if he knew he was entertaining a young Jewish girl. Probably be pleased as Punch and tell him how splendidly he was 'keeping his ear to the ground'. He pushed such speculations aside, and basked in the pleasure of female company. Not that he had been starved of it, exactly. There were plenty of servicewomen around, from all three branches of the service. He had even danced with several at the Garrison Club and the YWCA. But not often. Unlike many of his colleagues, he did not go out of his way to seek dates with girls. He guessed that a number of his fellow officers thought of him as rather strait-laced. The idea of married status as a reason for shunning such leisure activities struck them as at best amusing and at worst downright bizarre.

When, after tea and sandwiches, he put Sara on the train southward, he realized just how much he had enjoyed spending the last six hours with her. Self-consciously, she leaned out of the carriage window and proffered her cheek. Just as awkwardly, he touched his lips lightly to her. There was no trace of perfume, even a slight hint of fresh perspiration, but he was shaken at how his body responded to the chaste embrace.

'Don't forget to write and let me know your new address when you move.'

Her face, still flushed, took on a concerned expression. 'It's all right? To write to you?'

'Of course! Good heavens! We're old friends, aren't we? Listen, we'll fix up another meeting, eh? Perhaps you could stay over-night — I mean — you know — the YWCA.

Or there's the St Andrew's Club,' he added hastily, embarrassed again until he saw her grin.

She nodded. 'I'd like that. Very much.' She reached out, he held her hand. 'Thank you, John. It's been lovely.'

It had. But as he made his way back towards the mess not far from the Institute where he worked, he found his thoughts drifting back to the circumstances in which he had first heard of her, of his trip to Germany and the trouble he had got into. The spectre of his former German friend and betrayer cast a looming shadow. What pained him most when he looked back on it was not his own fear when he had been held for hours in that Berlin prison, but his cravenly tearful relief at Horst's rescue of him, and the puppet-master control of the young German as he supervised John's moral degeneration, putting him in bed with the girl, Inge. And, worst of all, the sickening meaning behind that superior smile as Horst revelled in the secret knowledge that he had already corrupted Jenny, months before, with a kind of *droit de siegneur* wickedness. The thought of it, even after all this time, left John with a helpless, cold outrage, filled him with revulsion.

As he had so many times in the past, John

admonished himself for its power over him. It was all done with. He and Jenny had survived, scarred perhaps, but with their love intact, maybe even strengthened because of it. He wondered what had become of Horst, if he was fighting somewhere for the Fatherland. Somehow, the concept of noble self-sacrifice did not sit well with John's memory of that effete, good-looking personality. The chances were that he was alive still, somewhere, pursuing his coldly amoral ends to some nefarious purpose.

John felt an upsurge of loneliness and longing for his wife, translated into a physical ache. He recalled the gentleness of the past few hours, Sara's unassuming femininity which he had appreciated so much. He quickened his pace, eager to get back to his room and settle down with his writing pad, to share the events of the day with Jenny. To hell with Horst Zettel. He would surely meet his just deserts in God's good time. And whatever he had done, he could not sully the Jenny John alone knew, the priceless love they shared. He prayed that the thought of Zettel never entered her mind these days, to haunt her as it did him.

As he crossed Carmel Avenue, he glanced up to his right, where the huge slope of the mountain swept up, dotted with the pale rocks and dark scrub, lit by the mellowing rays of the late evening sun. He was surprised at the comfort he found in its massive bulk. It was no longer a symbol of this alien land, but a familiar, towering shape, a solid representation of cherished eternal truths.

19

Teddy glanced up at the louring sky, fumbled for the top button of his battledress blouse. The cold struck through his thin clothes. Already the autumnal nip was turning into the aching cold of another winter, though it was only early November. The top button fastened easily, his ragged clothing flapped loosely. He had had to tie up his trousers with string. The POWs all looked like scarecrows, their motley collection of garments, remnants of uniform supplemented with second hand articles from the Red Cross, hanging on their skeletal frames. He had to admit that, despite the grumbles of some of his fellow inmates, their officers down the road scarcely fared any better.

Their numbers were still increasing with depressing regularity. All the latest arrivals were Brylcreem Boys, RAF flying crew, NCOs who would soon outnumber the 'brown jobs' in the camp if this kept up. Four boys had come in only three days ago, from a Lancaster forced to ditch on a raid over neighbouring Hamburg. They had all been badly beaten, their features swollen, their bodies a multi-hued welter of bruises from boots and rifle butts. The nightly raids, and the daylight sorties of the Yanks, were evidently getting under their captors' skins.

A fine drizzle fell clingingly to his uplifted face as he stared at the low clouds. The freedom of the sky brought the weight of imprisonment down on him even more. He suppressed a groan at his longing to be away from here. The faces of his family appeared in his mind. Little Teddie. Marian. He thought of her accommodating, voluptuous body, her female softness entwined around him, absorbing his heat. With it came the now all too familiar scalding shame, as other images superimposed themselves on his physical want. The sharp-featured, boyish gracefulness of Tony Ellis, the lithe, warm sweetness, which, shockingly, he had lusted after. He thrust the picture from him, to suffer in turn an earlier but still vivid memory, of an equally slim, elfin body, and a hunger he did not suppress under the heavy Spanish night; the icy coldness of the impromptu bath they had shared at the water hole they had discovered; the feel of her wet, smooth frame clinging to him, her dark cleft opening, joyously, fiercely. Rosie. Like Tony, she was also lost to him now. Where were they? Conscience smote him.

Oh God, Marian! I never deserved you, never did right by you. And you've stuck by me, always been there for me. I love you! Just let me come safely home to you, and I'll show you, my love, I swear I will!

⋆ ⋆ ⋆

'You've had a letter, haven't you?'

Jim Moody's voice was accusing, as though she had done something wrong. Marian made to laugh bitterly, gave a snort like a sneeze as she fought back the tears. 'It's *that* obvious, is it?' she muttered. 'I'm sorry. Still,' she couldn't keep herself from adding, 'it isn't very often, is it? Once every couple of months if I'm lucky.'

He moved over to her, crouched awkwardly on his heels by the armchair, put out a tentative arm to her sloping shoulders. She stared at the glowing grate, avoiding looking at him. Her left shoulder twitched, and he withdrew his hand. 'Don't,' she said dully. Her voice quavered. 'I'm sorry. I can't just . . . ' She stopped, choked again by her grief. She had been about to say 'hop into bed with you,' except they didn't go to bed. Not at first, anyway, even if they were alone, which they usually were these days, except for weekends, when the four of them went out to the pictures, or dancing at the Oxford, or for a drink.

Dora and Ray, Marian and Jim. Two couples, acknowledged as such. Even by Julia nowadays. The thought of Dora's mother having that hold over her made Marian secretly furious — and afraid. She was an accomplice now, in her adultery. A willing one. Largely, Marian often thought with anger and terror, because of the sense of knowing superiority it gave her over her own sister, May — Marian's mother-in-law. 'Off out at the weekend?' Julia would ask, cigarette bobbing at her lip, and with that knowing leer which never failed to cause Marian to blush hotly. 'Don't worry. I'll mind the bairn for ye, ye don't have to ask.'

Ever since that first time, when they had made love in front of the fire, last Christmas — a year ago — it had become a ritual for them to come together on the hearthrug, scattering their clothes around them as they tumbled together. It was wicked, sinful — and drove Marian wild with a helpless excitement she could not remember reaching even in the first heavenly days of courtship with Teddy at her Gran's — and certainly never since they had married. Not that she had wanted it then. All she wanted as a wife was to please her husband, and show him how completely she loved and belonged to him. Would do anything he asked of her. She had never really thought of herself and her pleasure in sex.

It was shatteringly different with Jim. He made it so, made her think of herself, showed her how physically aroused her body could become, so that, in achieving release she forgot everything, even him, in the consummation of her need. It shocked her, made her weep when she was alone, to realize that it was the very sinfulness itself — the way he aroused her, the coupling on the carpet — that was a powerful element in her excitement. It was like a drug, an addiction. She hated herself for it, hated what she had become, spent hours away from him weeping in shame, loathing herself, but it was impossible for her to end it, no matter how many times she vowed she would. On the days when she knew he was coming, getting ready for him, bathing, putting on her best silk things, she could feel her body deep inside spasm with sexual desire.

When the rare letters came, when she saw the distinctive envelope lying on the doormat, it was like a searing torment. The tears came even before she picked it up sometimes. She was disgusted with herself at the reluctance which came over her even to hold it, her fingers shook while she forced herself to tear it open.

Teddie knew. 'Daddy!' she would exclaim, watching Marian weep, thinking that she cried for love, and loneliness. Which she did, Marian told herself wretchedly. Of course she loved Teddy, always would. But then, it wasn't just the sex that kept her with Jim. She wasn't that mindlessly basic. True, he drew depths, or heights, of physical sensation from her that left her totally exhausted and sated, but, afterwards especially, there was the tenderness, the kisses and the holding, the whispered words which meant as much as the caresses themselves. And to him, too, she kept on reminding herself. It wasn't just that she was 'a good poke', the crude phrase revolting her every time she thought of it.

In just over two weeks it would be exactly a year since she and Jim had first committed adultery. And two years since he had stepped in across the threshold at midnight on New Year's Eve, and snatched that hasty first kiss. She could still remember vividly the feel of his cold lips, her laughing, blushing, flustered embarrassment. And the first insidious beat of excitement which had led to all this.

Then the letter from Teddy had come this morning. Written over a month ago, in early November, yet it was as if he were in the room with her, his voice whispering in her ear. He had never written like this before. Every word tore at her, dug deep into her heart, and her conscience, and her love. His loneliness was a cry that rent her, his outpouring of love. And, most devastating of all, his admission of guilt, of his failure towards her, his acknowledgement of it.

I swear to God, Marian, I'll make it up to you and to our little girl when I get out of here and back to you. I never appreciated just what a treasure I had in you and the love you never failed to give me, even though I let you down so badly, deserting you even before our lovely little Teddie was born. I can't understand how you could ever have taken me back, forgiven me, after that. And then to leave you again — I know it is my own stupid fault that has landed me in this pickle, and that if I hadn't run off to the army I might still have been with you now. I just thank God that it's not too late, that you're still there, and that I will have the chance to make amends for all the hurt I've caused you. I love you, my darling. I'll never leave you again, I swear.

It was a terrible effort, but she moved, reached out for the letter tucked behind the clock on the mantelpiece. Her voice unsteady, often breaking altogether, sniffing, and with the tears streaming unheeded down her face, she read out every word while Jim listened in appalled silence.

She sat hunched in misery. 'It's — he's never told me — anything like that. I can't go on, Jim. I'm sorry. It's all such a mess.'

He pleaded, and argued, told her he loved her, too, that he wanted to stay with her, would stick by her if she would come to him. She was shaken, not so much by his sudden eloquence, but by his desperate sincerity. She had been utterly determined to send him away. She still was, but in the end she let him stay and make love one last time. Gently, she stopped him using his lover's skill to bring her to a climax. Instead, she gave herself to him, for *his* pleasure, unreservedly, knowing it was the last time.

It took him several days to understand the truth, that she had meant what she said, and that they were indeed finished. Desolate though he might have been, he stopped trying to see her, vanished from her life. She was sad, too, deeply, but she had the solace of knowing she had done right, enduring all Dora's incredulous scorn with shades of her old dumb passivity. She spent the Christmas week over at Hexham, to May and Iris's delight, stayed for their restrained New Year's Eve celebrations.

The dawn of 1944. Still no sign that the war would end in the near future, though there was a certainty now that the Allies would eventually be victorious. Next day, Marian realized she was several days late with her period. A grain of fear seized her, but the idea of such an appropriate nemesis seemed too melodramatic for reality. She had not worn her diaphragm for that last act of love. She had not been expecting it to take place, so resolved was she that she and Jim should part company. When it happened, it was a spontaneous gesture of nobility, and genuine feeling for him — a farewell as tender as she could make it.

She tried to dismiss her fear. It was just that her rhythm had been so disturbed — yes, painful as it was to face it, her sexual activity had come to such an abrupt halt with Jim's recent departure from her life. That's why she was 'all to pot', as she put it to herself. She tried hard to believe it.

But as the war moved into its fifth year, and the Allies' arduous campaign in Italy ground bloodily on, and the Yanks came over in droves to flood our southern counties, Marian could no longer be in doubt that she was pregnant.

20

Jenny felt the familiar stab of irritation at Martin's use of the word *Kraut*, the latest term of opprobrium for the Germans. She had heard it used frequently lately, picked up from the Yanks, she was sure. Trust Martin Castleton to seize on it. She was startled at the conflicting emotions he was capable of sparking off in her, not least these sudden bursts of illogical fury or disgust. Other times she felt a fascination; an attraction which she tried not to dwell on, it was far too dangerous. As *he* was. Her feelings for him were run through with fear, she realized. For him, or for herself?

She was closer to him than anyone else in her life now. She shared secrets with him, deep, shameful intimacies she could not share with anyone else, not even John. Her flesh shivered, goose-bumped with disgust sometimes, at their intimacy; the sick closeness of the relationship she had become enmeshed in, a perverted kind of triangle, or rather quadrangle, she thought, with gallows humour — her and Maxi, her libidinous *doppelgänger*, as she had become, and

284

Martin and Donny. It appalled her — and worse, at times thrilled her. More perverse because there was no physical gratification, only this fine net of sensual verbiage that bound them tightly together like lovers.

With a kind of dread, she found herself thinking more and more as the months of subterfuge dragged by that it would be more honest, less inverted, if she and Martin *did* go to bed together. He had made it plain that that was what he wanted, even expected, of her, though never without that underlay of jokiness, as an insurance. She insisted, with the same vigorous touch of lightness, that the very idea abhorred her. 'You're not my type!' she laughed. And he wasn't. Except that there was still that hidden, dreadful aspect of her nature which she tried to hide even from herself that challenged her belief; the wickedness deep inside her that the young German had drawn from her, revealed so shockingly to her, more than six years ago.

The irony was, most of her colleagues thought that that was exactly what was going on. A passionately lustful affair with the handsome figure of mystery who kept on calling and whisking her away for nights of sin. Somehow, word had spread about the assignations in the Fox and Hounds, and the bedroom over the bar which they rented for their rendezvous. Martin had chuckled when, pink with indignation, she had told him about the sniggering hint of scandal spreading about her. Predictably, he was highly amused. 'Great! Couldn't have a better alibi, could we, sweety? Just what we wanted!'

Her anger gave way to mind-spinning speculation. She began to wonder if he had encouraged such a misconception. He was quite capable of it, she knew that. 'I don't like being thought of as some good-time tart cheating on her husband while he's overseas!' she declared coldly.

Joyce Radcliffe had said as much, and more, in humiliatingly public surroundings, the other evening, when Jenny was making arrangements for duty swapping. 'Some people might think it's glam, but *I* think it's pretty low, if you ask me! Carrying on while your husband's risking his life overseas!'

Jenny froze, then was scalded with red hot rage. 'That's just your sick, pathetic mind running away with you again, Radcliffe! There's no carrying on, as you put it. I've told you — '

'Oh yes! That's why you book a room at the Fox and spend half the night in it, eh? And sometimes the whole night, if I'm not mistaken!'

It was true. The last time she had met

Martin, he had persuaded her to stay in the room. At first, she had been afraid, sure that he would be tapping on her door after a few minutes. But she was bone weary with the hours they had put in on her latest letter, and the idea of having the luxury of a room to herself won out over her misgivings. Besides, she had locked the door, and there had been no tapping. None that she had heard, anyway. Though she had blushed like a honeymoon bride on going downstairs in the cold darkness of early morning to find Martin already sitting in the tiny recess that served as breakfast room, signalling for her to join him, and welcoming her with enfolding arms and a hearty kiss which had the young waitress almost as beet-faced as she was.

While the others in the rec room stared in enthralled excitement, Jenny let out a helpless explosion of her frustration. Her fingers curled with urgent desire to fix themselves in Radcliffe's permed brown hair, or rake across that mean visage. Instead, she fled, sobbing with humiliation, leaving the moral high ground to her triumphant attacker.

As she threw off her coat and cardigan and tossed them carelessly on the chair, then sat on the wide bed and slipped off her shoes, she was overcome by a weary familiarity with the small room, its homely furniture, the scents of stale beer and fag smoke with which it was imbued. Martin smiled, and she recognized the hardness behind it, that glimpse of wolfishness that made her shiver. 'I think we've really got to turn up the heat, sweety. Come on strong with the old pash. Not too blatant, of course. But a lot of repressed carnality. Steaming breath and heaving bosoms — metaphorically speaking. Come on a bit more forcefully with the old verbal cock-teasing, eh?'

He flung the phrase she had used to shock him — so long ago, it seemed to her now. She grabbed the two pillows, placed them one on top of the other in the centre of the headboard and stretched out on the bed, propped up on them, her hands interlaced behind her head. She crossed her ankles, stared at her stockinged feet. She was wearing an old pair of cord trousers she used for walking when she was off duty, or just swanning about the grounds of the Park. An oldish, thick shirt, too, loose enough to be comfortable. Her relaxed dress was a kind of statement. A protest against what this relationship was seen as by others, against what the egotistical figure opposite hoped it might become. Yet, wickedly, part of her wondered if he found this pointedly casual and almost androgynous attire attractive.

'You're better at that than I am,' she answered. 'I'm too knackered to think straight right now. I had the first watch last night. Didn't get to bed till after 2 a.m.'

'Your language, young lady! Enough to make a commando blush. I know. War's hell, isn't it? I was out dancing at the Dorchester till after midnight.'

'I hope she was worth it. More of a pushover than me.'

'Oh, you know me. I like a challenge.' He came and sat down on the edge of the bed, facing her. He put his hand on her black-stockinged ankle, kept it there.

She forced herself not to jerk the limb away, and prayed that he would not discern her blush. She was quiveringly aware of his touch, moulding the rounded, slender shape of her, the thrust of bone. It burned her through the material of her stocking. She kept unnaturally still, afraid that she was beginning to tremble. He rubbed gently, his fingers pressing against the fragile swell of ankle bone, moving just a few inches upward, over the cool smoothness, displacing the cuff of her slacks.

She felt she couldn't breathe, even though her heart was pounding, the blood thundering through her. He moved in to her, the pulse of her excitement beat strongly, left her helpless to do anything but respond, as he grabbed at the back of her neck with his left hand and pulled her into him. Her mouth opened, thrusting blindly against his, savaging, searching, the harsh cry trapped in her long throat.

When they broke, they were panting, her breath rasping noisily. He reached forward, across her legs, his arms gathering her in again, mouth moving to her neck, and she twisted away, fought him, they wrestled until she was tumbled off the displaced pillows, lying on her back under him. Her breasts strained against her shirt, his hands burned her wrists which he had seized in their struggle. She arched her shoulders upward, like a wrestler refusing to submit, squirmed her body beneath him. She wept impotently at his brute superiority, and her base excitement at it. She was both revolted and thrilled that he did not do the gentlemanly thing and release her.

'You'll have to rape me if you want more!' she sobbed, her wild eyes glaring up at him, her head tossing on the cover.

'Will that make it OK?' he asked cruelly. He let go of her left wrist with his right hand, and thrust it between her legs, cupping it to fit round the curve of her crutch, pressing with lewd clarity into the soft pad of her sex under the thick stuff of her trousers. She felt the fierce beat of response. She lay still, except for her trembling and the violence of her weeping.

Now, he was totally calm again, relaxed and in control. He took his hand away from her, then his fingers began to work methodically, slowly searching out her buttons, and the fold of the zip fastener at her waist, drawing it down so that the waist band of her trousers slackened, and he could slip his fingers inside. His voice was calm, too, hypnotically so, soothing and reasonable, and her resistance ebbed, the tension of her locked muscles loosened. She cried quietly now, snifflingly, like a child.

'Let's put an end to this foolishness, eh? What the hell are you fighting me for, Jenny? We want it, both of us. You as much as me, sweety. For God's sake let's be honest with each other, even if we can't with anyone else. I want you. I want to make love to you. Have done for months. And you want me to. That's all there is to it.'

He tugged and drew her slacks down as he spoke, and she let him move her, ease them off over her lifted feet. She was embarrassed at the black stockings, the garters which were so workaday, the tops of the stockings rolled around the thick, ugly elastic bands, which had made red indentations in the winter white thighs swelling over them. They were not the stuff of seductive fantasy. Nor were the navy woollen knickers, naval issue, revealed under the rucked up tails of her shirt.

Part of her spinning mind was masochistically glad that it was so, and glad of her damp pungency as he stripped her, while she moved like some doll to his bidding. She wanted it over with, wanted to be taken by him, soiled, yet part of the shameful, shameless thrill was the wicked deliberation of his movement, the sureness of it. He pulled her gently up by the arms, and she stood naked while he swept back the bedclothes, climbed in at his bidding. Again, she felt weirdly childlike when he drew the blankets over her, shielding her. He was still fully dressed, and she lay on her back, her hair dark against the pillow, no longer aware of the tears trickling down her temples, wetting the curls above her ears.

She watched him undress, with the same measure of control, unabashed at her gaze, and now she began shivering violently, her vaginal muscles spasming in anticipation, desperate for him. She watched the rampant evidence of his excitement, watched with a kind of dread as he half turned, reaching over for his clothes, intent on the fumbling business of preparing and drawing on the sheath before he turned back to join her.

She lifted herself to him, opening her legs, trying to entwine herself about him, but he refused her passionate proffering of herself, eased himself off her a little, put his hands to her again, on her most intimate flesh. She cried out sharply, racked by shame. 'No! Don't wait! Please!' But mercilessly he ignored her, and she felt him moving with expertise, opening, caressing, until the stirrings of her release began and she cried out again, her head tossing back in the pillow, her limbs splayed, body jerking, aflame with mindless hunger, so that when he *did* finally move on to her and in her, she was frantic with need, lost to the sensations aroused and clashingly sated by their coupling.

She cried herself to exhaustion afterwards, and he lay curled with her, his nakedness fitted into her back, holding her. He said nothing, listened to her groans, and moaning, disjointed phrases, just held her firmly, letting her feel his warm body against hers, the gently firm joining of their flesh. She even slept, and woke, sore and heavy and pungent with their activity, her violent grief replaced by dull desolation.

'You were ready for me,' she croaked, through swollen throat, turning to face him.

'That thing. You knew. Known all along, I expect. Did it take longer than you thought?'

He grinned. 'You know me. An ex boy scout. Be prepared.' He chuckled, and she couldn't hold his gaze. She felt the prick of tears yet again, and thought wearily, oh no! No more. What good are they? And then he undermined her, by his gentleness, though it was somehow in keeping with his character. She suddenly vividly recalled that he had said nothing, uttered not a single phrase, while they made love, only the animal grunts of bodily delight. He held her for the first time like a lover, caressing her, so that the weeping *did* start again, and she lay against his chest for comfort.

'Come on, sweety. Yes, it was bound to happen. Some time. And yes. It was a bloody sight longer than I thought. And hoped. You're not meant for celibacy, any more than I am. You know that, Jenny. You've known it a long time.' She knew it was not a question. 'Right from the beginning. So don't whip yourself over it. It had to happen — '

'Two years!' She struggled up, stared tragically into his eyes. 'Two years, I've been — alone. Without sex. I love my husband. For God's sake . . . ' She shook her head furiously, lost in the maelstrom of her emotion, and fell back on the pillow.

'Two years of wanting it, of being alone. Torturing yourself,' he answered.

When she cried now, it was an outpouring of relief, almost as powerful as the orgasm she had reached. It was as if he had peeled the last layer of secrecy and shame away from her. She sobbed, clung to him, welcomed his love-making, sank into it with luxurious escapism as he stirred her once more, drew her to the storms of passion released only when they came together again.

It was after midnight when she crept along the corridor to the bathroom, then they sat naked in bed, the scribbled sheets scattered over their knees, and wrote the reply to Donny's letter. She had no more tear storms, and no arguments. She wrote almost at his dictation, contributing little herself, and when they had finished, around two-thirty, she wrapped herself in his arms, wearily submitting to her weakness and her failure, rejoicing in the comfort and thrill of his masculine body enfolding her.

Next day, back at work, she suffered all the pangs of shame she felt she deserved as she endured the girls' penetrating eyes on her, observing her worn out expression, her strained nerves. Joyce Radcliffe's gaze in particular shone with a mean triumph. She already brimmed with victory after their previous confrontation. She was not one to let slip advantage over weakness. 'Bloody hell, Wright! You look rough. Made quite a night of it, eh? Or were you and your *friend* discussing poetry till the early hours?'

If their audience had been expecting or hoping for a blazing row, they were disappointed. 'I know what you think of me,' Jenny answered, so quietly they had to strain to hear. 'And you're entitled to your opinion. In any case I don't want to fight with you. All right?'

Her opponent was taken aback at first by Jenny's apparent lack of spirit. From then on, she treated her with growing and cutting disdain. Her attitude had an effect on their colleagues, and Jenny, who had thus far been popular, found herself, though not ostracized, treated with similar contempt, to varying degrees, by the majority of her contemporaries. But it was only part of the despair she found herself in.

Martin called her a day later, inviting her to wangle the weekend and come and spend it in London with him. 'We'll dance, drink, and be decadent, my love!' he chuckled, his voice deep and purring in her ear. It sank to a whisper. 'Look. I can fix it for you, if you're really stuck. Just say the word. I can open sesame.'

She shivered, felt the beat of sexual desire, relived the power of his body and hers united. Her reply was scarcely more than a whisper, too. 'No. I can't. I — I need to think. To be on my own. Away from you. I can't — accept — what we did. It — '

'Oh, my poor Jenny.' His deep, knowing chuckle was a scourge to her. 'Not again, my love.' That was twice he had called her his love, she noted. And never before, that she could recall. Was she his love now? 'Why put yourself through all this again? Time for you to sort yourself out, sweety.'

Again! It was with a shock that she realized he was referring to her confession of her long-ago entrapment with Horst. The blood rushed to her face, its heat swept her body. How could he? Shaking, she crashed the receiver down on its hook, fought to check the tears. She moved resolutely to her cabin, delved in the locker for her writing case and hurried towards the rec room.

21

May studied Marian worriedly. She had lost more weight, and the healthy bloom of her fair complexion had faded. Her face looked gaunt now, etched with lines, her eye hollows deeply shaded. Even her body seemed bent, she moved slowly, gingerly, as though afraid of returning pain. 'What's the doctor say? What are they doing? Are you sure you wouldn't like a second opinion? I could book you in — the Brierton's very good. They look after you — '

'No, Mam. Honest. I'll be right enough, soon,' Marian cut in quickly, her voice taut. 'Doctor Leeson's fine. He knows what he's doing. This stuff he's given us is helping a lot now. I just need building up a bit.'

Marian's face flushed as she remembered the doctor's overtired features, his weariness as the stern expression softened at the anguish of her sobbing. 'I had to know, Mrs Wright. You've been lucky. You could have killed yourself. Apart from the fact that it's a criminal act.' He held up his hand. 'Oh, I know there's plenty of women resort to it. I don't want to know where you went or who you consulted. And I'll respect your confidentiality. I think you've suffered enough.' He paused, as though weighing up whether to go on. 'You'll get over it. But — whether you've done any long-term damage . . . ' He let his voice die with uncertainty.

Marian, her nose buried in her handkerchief, nodded. At the time, it seemed a fitting retribution. She had killed the life growing within her, now she would never bear any more children to the only man she had ever loved. She had dismissed any tenderness of feeling towards Jim Moody, condemned it to herself as sin. The 'original sin' — she had heard that phrase used, had a vague notion of its religious meaning which seemed all too appropriate — that had led with sickening inevitability to all the rest.

When she missed her second period, she was sure, though she told herself she had known long before. She cried, her mind crumbling before her horror at what had happened. She felt helpless, couldn't think of what to do. It didn't take Dora long to twig there was something seriously wrong. At first, she had thought Marian's strange mood was simply the result of her break-up with Jim, and her tardy and inordinate guilt at the affair. But then a sudden hysterical bout of sobbing when she tried to discuss it with her gave the normally heedless younger girl pause for thought. It was, typically, a very brief pause.

'What the flamin' hell's wrong with you? What is it?' She had raced upstairs after Marian, and now stood hands on hips staring down at the weeping figure lying prone across the bed. Tormented beyond control, unable to contain her despair and loneliness, Marian sobbed out the truth. Dora was shocked, as much at Marian's carelessness in 'getting caught' as anything else. 'Me mam!' Dora declared emphatically, at once.

'No!' Marian glanced up with streaming eyes, though, on reflection, she realized that having let out her secret there was no way it would remain solely with the first recipient. In any case, there was a huge relief at having confessed, at the feeling of someone taking it out of her hands, of deciding on some sort of action.

'Me mam'll know what to do. She'll know somebody.'

And Julia had. Marian's helplessness increased. 'Please, please, swear you'll never tell a soul!' she blubbered, more terrified at the idea of the news reaching May. The spectre of Julia using such a disaster as a weapon in her eternal battle with her well-to-do sister was a new nightmare to haunt Marian. 'Promise me!' she begged both mother and daughter, over and over, until both became angry at her refusal to be comforted. She wasn't so much worried about Dora, but she carried a terrifying vision of Julia blurting it out to May in her desire to strike at her sister and her 'toffee-nosed' friend.

The price of the solution was high. 'I can help out a bit,' Julia offered.

'No, it's all right. I can manage,' Marian told her. And she could. She had a good nest egg. There was the allotment from the army, and May and Iris were so generous, not only with foodstuffs but with buying clothes and other things for the house that Marian had been able to save regularly from her household budget. It grieved her that she had to take such a large chunk out of the savings, but that would just have to be piled up with all the rest of the guilt she was burdened with from now on.

Marian had expected that it would be a woman who would be the expert Julia arranged for her to see. She was shocked when it turned out to be a floridly distinguished-looking man, with silvery wings in his swept back hair, and a distant, comfortingly professional approach, as well as a practised confidence that made Marian guess that he was a doctor. The house, too, was far from the imagined Dickensian tenement. It was an unassuming but respectable old terraced house across the river in Heaton.

His questions, and even the examination which followed, were detached enough to lessen Marian's sense of embarrassment if not of shame. 'Right. Come on the twenty-fifth,' he said. 'That'll be the twelfth week. I'm glad you haven't left it any later. Shouldn't be too difficult. Make sure you order a taxi to take you back. Tell them to pick you up in Tankerman Street. Not from here,' he emphasized. 'It's only a couple of streets away. But you'll need it.' He turned to Julia. 'She'll be quite sore.'

Sitting on the tram as they rode back to Gateshead, Julia chuckled. 'I should ask our May and Iris to pick us up, eh? Only joking!' she added swiftly, punching Marian's arm, at the look of wide-eyed horror on the ravaged face.

The procedure was painful, and worse was to follow. He had explained that the expulsion of the foetus would take place hours after she had returned home. But he had inserted an instrument into her, probed agonizingly at the uterus, then left some kind of pessary inside her vagina. Marian clutched at Julia's arm, doubled over, and hobbling like a crone to reach the pick up point in Tankerman Street.

Back in her own bedroom, the pains swept over her, fierce birth pangs, against which the pain relievers he had given seemed to have little effect. They added to the nightmarish quality of the ordeal, for they made Marian's head whirl, her mind spin out of focus, so that she lost sense of time, of reality, sobbing out for Teddy, drifting in and out of sweat-drenched, burning awareness. She screamed, crouched in the final apocalyptic minutes over a bucket, supported at her elbows by a grim-faced Julia and a terrified Dora. 'Do you good, ye bugger!' Julia hissed at her daughter when this last part of the nightmare was over.

Packed with wads of cotton, Marian was put back to bed, the tearing pain a steady torment now. At last she felt some of the intensity easing as she drifted towards unconsciousness. She wept quietly, ashamed to discover she hoped she would die, aching with regret at the thought of losing her daughter and her husband, yet convinced she was unworthy of both of them.

Two days later, Julia sat on the side of the bed and patted Marian's limbs under the covers. 'There y'are, pet. All over now. Put it all behind you.'

But the nightmare wasn't over. Sometimes, she thought it would never be. The scars, if not physical, would be there inside her head. Dora's cruelly unthinking words were an early part of it. 'Eeh, it was amazing. Tiny, like — no bigger'n me finger hardly. But you could see a little head, curled up legs — ' she stopped, but too late, while her mother cursed her viciously.

'Shurrup, ye stupid little bitch! If ye've got nowt better to say, bugger off out of it!'

It was retribution, Marian thought, the sickness that dogged her, kept every muscle aching, made every action an effort. Bleeding didn't stop properly, there were spots on her underclothes, sometimes heavier floods. And constant, nagging pain. Now, she became worried that she *would* die, wanted to live for little Teddie's sake. She could not face going back to the abortionist, or feeling so helplessly under Julia's control, even though she guiltily acknowledged the older woman's essential guidance and help throughout her ordeal. Instead, she took a huge risk and went to her own doctor, Dr Leeson, a young man, married himself, with two young children.

He knew at once. After the internal examination, he left Marian lying there, covered by the sheet, and sent the nurse out of the room. 'What have you done?' he asked accusingly, and Marian burst into tears, stammering inarticulately. He waited, calmed her, and she told him, through her weeping.

'My husband's a POW. I let — I was unfaithful. I couldn't have the baby . . . '

He treated her. It was painful, he said he would have preferred to send her to hospital, but she gladly endured the fierce burning of the scraping of infected tissue. He went out while she dressed, and he came back with a bundle of medicine. 'I thought it better if I got these myself,' he said, nodding back towards the waiting room and the small dispensary. 'Come back and see me next Tuesday. You've been very lucky. If infection had really set in, there would be nothing we could do. I hope you've learned your lesson. You're not out of the wood yet. I'll need to keep an eye on you.'

She had recovered, physically, at least in the short term. With the drugs and other treatment the infection had cleared, but she did not know what long-term damage had been caused. She had started her periods again, but they were far more painful, and heavier. The mental scars were different. The guilt, the weight of shame and sin, never really left her. She thought it was God's cruel joke that she should fall prey to such weakness at the very time when her absent husband seemed to have found, so late, that he truly loved her.

Then there was the fear — like at this minute, with her mother-in-law and Iris asking such probing questions, and, worst of all, Julia's crackling presence — that she would be found out, that that would be God's final judgement, and everyone, including Teddy and little Teddie, would know just how sinful she was. She thought that if that happened, she would kill herself. She was not being melodramatic. She did not think she could live with their knowledge of her wickedness.

'You need building up, my girl,' May told her firmly. 'Why don't you come and stay with us for a bit? A good long rest. We'd be over the moon to have you and Teddie — '

'Aye. Living in the lap of luxury, eh, kidder?' Julia grinned savagely. 'Hardly know there's a war on, out there with the country folk!'

'Julia and Dora are looking after me fine!' Marian said desperately, her eyes pleading for May not to take offence. 'And you're always bringing us loads of stuff.' It was true. May and Iris never failed to bring a box piled with all kinds of extra goods, and gifts for both her and Teddie. 'I just wish they'd get on with it, and get this blinking war over!'

Everyone was waiting now for news of the second front. There were stories of the south of England being choked with hordes of troops, Americans everywhere, and half the south coast sealed off from the public. But everyone was cautious about predicting a quick success. The bitter fighting which had gone on all through the Italian campaign had proved that a toehold in Europe would not be easy to maintain.

'He'll be all right, Marian,' May said, as firmly as she had spoken before. 'The camp's out in the countryside. Well away from the cities. They'll be safe enough there.' The newspapers were full of the thousand bomber raids taking place daily and nightly over Germany.

'Like you lot, eh?' Julia sneered.

'I haven't noticed any thousand pounders dropping round Birtley, either!' May shot back, reddening. In fact, there had been few air raids anywhere in Britain over the past months. People had got used to sleeping undisturbed in their beds once more, instead of the nightly treks to the shelters.

'Oh — don't!' All three women turned in surprise at the heart-felt cry that came from Marian. Their astonishment made her already blushing face even redder. 'I mean,' she went on, twisting in embarrassment, 'don't squabble, you two. There's enough fighting going on,' she ended feebly, shocked herself at her outburst.

'Quite right!' Iris affirmed heartily, to cover for Marian's confusion.

'Oh, ye don't want to take any notice of us, lass!' Julia declared wickedly. 'Our May and me have always rubbed each other up the wrong way, haven't we? She's always thought she could tell us what to do just cos she's five years older than me. And cos she's done so well for herself and her bairns. Left us all miles behind, I'll give her that!'

May tried to keep her voice light and calm, to stop the tremor she knew could betray her emotion when she was roused. As she invariably was when Julia revealed her envy, or animosity. 'It's not a crime to get on, Julia. And I'm the first to admit I couldn't do it on my own. And didn't.' She looked squarely across at Iris, who coloured up, and managed to look both uncomfortable and pleased at the same time. 'And I haven't left you behind,' she emphasized deliberately. 'I've never been ashamed of my family or where I come from. And I never will be.'

'Good for you!' Julia cried ringingly. 'There speaks the canny lass that used to wipe her bum on 'Titbits' in the back yard netty.'

When May and Iris left in the early evening, Julia refused their offer of a lift, but without the usual cutting remark to accompany it. 'Thanks but I'll hang on. I'll wait and see our Dora. It's the only chance I get to see the young madam these days. She never thinks to drop in on her own home. And I'm used to walking home in the blackout. There never was any street lamps out our way. And it's that fine these nights you don't need your torch. It's smashing to get some decent weather again.'

After they had stood and waved the car off on the doorstep, Julia reached out and put a hand on Marian's turning shoulder. It was an unusual gesture from the hard-faced older woman, and Marian was surprised. Julia's voice, husky at the best of times, rasped as though to compensate for the embarrassment of the sentiment she expressed. 'You don't have to worry, ye know, kidder. About me blabbin' on to anybody. Least of all our May. I haven't even told me own husband, for God's sake!' Her voice grew harder. 'And I've threatened our Dora's life if she breathes a word to a living soul. She can be a selfish little bitch, I know, but she'll not let you down neither.'

Marian was not as good at hiding emotion,

or at denying it, especially since her fall from grace. She felt her throat close, then the tears poured out, and she was clinging on to Julia's scrawny frame, her head resting on the bony shoulder. Julia's hands came up, awkwardly, and patted the heaving shoulders. 'There, pet. Don't upset yourself.'

Marian was still sniffling minutes later, when they sat at the kitchen table, the pot warmed up and two cups of weak tea before them. 'I know I've been wicked. I'm not good enough — but I want the chance to make it up. To Teddy — and to little Teddie. When I think — how bad I've been. I'd never have believed I could have done all that.'

'Listen to me. It's all this bloody war. People getting taken away from one another. It's not right, people being left alone, to cope with the bairns and everything. Your Teddy was no saint. There's many a lass wouldn't have given him the time of day after what he did to you. Running off like that, before little'un was even born.' She held up her hand to still Marian's protest. 'Let me say my piece. It's not like you're some flighty little baggage.' She hesitated. 'And that lad. Jim. He thought a lot about you, you know. It wasn't just — for what he could get off you. You know what I mean. Dora told me — he was real cut up when you chucked him. Did she tell you? He's up and off. Put his notice in and left the works. They reckon he'll get his call-up now.' Marian glanced up at her in fresh dismay, and Julia put her rough hand over hers. 'What I'm saying, love, is that the pair of you weren't just randy little sods. And there's plenty more who are, and don't give a shite, believe you me!'

22

John was surprised to find Lt.-Col. Warren waiting outside the classroom door in the wide corridor of the Technical Institute. 'You want me, sir?'

'Yes, if you're free. Can you spare a minute?' It struck John at once as odd that the senior officer of the Education Centre should be asking him if he could 'spare a minute'. He was, to say the least, a rather distant figure of formal, unbending authority in front of his junior officers.

'Thinks of us as a long-haired, Bolshie set of intellectuals,' Tommy Wilkinson, a fellow lecturer seconded to the Institute from the REME, asserted. 'He's scared stiff of schoolies. He's a regular, you know. He'd have had his pension by now if the war hadn't come along and saved his bacon.'

Together, John and his superior watched the class of new recruits ambling off down the corridor in their ill-fitting new uniforms. One of the first intakes of the Jewish Brigade Group to be fully armed and trained by the British as a front-line unit. 'What do you reckon?' Warren grunted, nodding at the departing figures. 'If you ask me, we're making a rod for our own backs. Teaching the beggars how to stand up against us as soon as the war in Europe's over.'

John decided it would not be politic to point out to him that around 30,000 Jews were already serving in the Allied forces around the world. 'What is it you want me for, sir? Not a rocket, I hope,' he smiled, aware that he was gently pushing his senior. But he sensed that Lt.-Col. Warren was oddly reluctant to broach the subject.

Warren cleared his throat a little noisily. 'Haven't had much chance to get to chat to you, Wright. Don't see enough of you chaps. Everything all right with you? Perhaps we could get together — private talk. Strictest confidence, of course.'

John's brain raced. Then he felt himself prickle with suspicion, and the beginnings of acute embarrassment. Jenny's letter had stunned him, visibly enough to make his carrying on about his normal business a tremendous strain. He had failed to the extent that his colleagues swiftly realized something was badly wrong. For the past two months and more, he had been withdrawn and self-absorbed, to the point where — what? He wondered. Word of his transformation had clearly filtered through to

Lt.-Col. Warren. Just how much was his superior aware of?

This bunch that Jenny had got herself mixed up with, this underground intelligence stuff. MI5, and SOE, and all that crap! It was too unreal for him to take it all in, at first. All he knew when he read and reread the letter, forcing his mind to master it, was the deep wound of Jenny's infidelity, the sick irony of it. Horst Zettel's name came leaping at him from the page, somehow inextricably interwoven with this new name, this stranger's name without a face, that had shattered his world a second time.

I have become involved with someone, a fellow working for military intelligence, Martin Castleton. He took me over when I got mixed up in MI5 work. So much for doing one's duty. In a way none of this matters, except that it's shown me to myself. The fatal flaw in me, if you like, which I knew about all along. Which, as Martin pointed out to me, damn him, Horst had shown me anyway. I told him all about what had happened between Horst and me. I couldn't help it. It somehow just all came out, all the sordid details of it, over the months we worked together. I can't really explain — the intimate relationship Martin and I had. I don't mean my infidelity, and I'm not searching for excuses. As I've said, it's all part of the one thing, that started with Horst. But with Martin — it was strange, being so close. A kind of confessor role that came from the nature of our work. The hours, the places. The enclosed intimacy of it, as I've said.

He saw through me in a way you never have. I hated it. Hated him for it, sometimes, showing me myself so nakedly. The self Horst showed me, the self I've always run away from. I'm not the figure you thought me, John. The figure you made me, and I tried to be for you.

Hell! I'm beating about the bush, aren't I? What I'm trying to tell you, my darling, is that I've let you down. Betrayed you, again, in the worst way. I've been unfaithful to you, with Martin Castleton. This is no excuse — I don't mean it to be, it's even sicker in a way — but it's only happened once, and won't happen again. And it took eight months for me to do it. The important thing is it's happened. And just like before I wish it hadn't, and my skin crawls with disgust at myself. But it doesn't alter the fact of what I've done.

I'm not asking you to forgive me, but I can't stand the thought of our life together *being a lie. I won't do it. If you want to do something, start proceedings against me, I'll understand, and am ready to do whatever you suggest. Or we can leave things the way they are until this is all over and you're home again. I'll wait to hear from you.*

'A talk, sir?' John brought his mind back to the colonel's question. 'We're right in the thick of it now, with this Jewish Brigade and everything. I don't see . . . '

Now Warren was clearly uncomfortable. His eyes moved away from John's gaze, his face assumed its stiffest pose. 'All this is in the strictest confidence, you understand? If there's a crisis of a personal nature. In your domestic situation. One or two people have expressed their concern. The change in your manner. These things happen. I'm not trying to pry, believe me.'

John's tone, his furious expression, was not that adopted by a junior officer to a superior. 'It's a pity people haven't got better things to occupy them than gossiping like a bunch of old women!'

Lt.-Col. Warren's manner reverted to cold correctness. 'Very well. But we're doing an extremely useful and sensitive job here, Wright. We mustn't allow any of our private affairs to interfere with our duty. That's all.'

The rage ebbed from John's face, the tension slackened. He nodded. 'I'm sorry, sir. I didn't mean to be rude.' Warren nodded back, still stiffly. 'I hadn't realized how much I was letting my mood affect me. You're quite right. It *is* a private matter, and I'll make sure it's sorted.'

'I've taken what you've said. As I told you, this is all in strict confidence.' He paused, then added gruffly, 'I have every confidence in you, Wright. I'm sure you'll cope with things. Nuff said, eh?'

'Thank you, sir.' He clicked his heels, came to attention, as Warren nodded for the last time and turned away. John felt the urge to be out of the building, into the brightness of the open air. He was supposed to be back at Torch House after the lecture, to pick up his duties there. There was a mound of paperwork waiting. It could wait. The army could wait. The war could wait.

He stuck his head inside the smoke-filled office by the main entrance, where his driver was lounging with a mug of tea. He made to rise, but John motioned for him to relax. 'Finish your char. Then take the jeep back. I'll make my own way. Got a few things to do. Take your time.'

'Not a bad bloke, old Wrighty!' the lance

corporal offered when John had withdrawn. 'Not like the rest of these poncy gits!'

The high summer heat was fierce, the humidity heavy, so that John was soon sweating inside his light garb, but he didn't mind. He liked the clean cut brilliance of the light, the boldness of this sea port, with the great sweep of its bay and the majestic backdrop of the Carmel range extending its curving length. He found himself threading his way through the busy centre of town, into the narrower, quieter streets of the old German colony clustered at the foot of the mountain, which rose steeply, the rocky scrub marked by the dark growth of taller trees, their foliage standing out against the pale outcrops of rock.

The old Templar houses the German immigrants had built when they came ashore in 1870 were beginning to look a little dilapidated now, many of them standing empty. Local people had taken them over from their original inhabitants. He crossed another road, into a sandy street whose buildings looked in much better repair. The houses were solid, with neat gardens, shady trees behind their walls. Persian Street. Named after yet another influx of immigrants, fleeing from some persecution or other in their native land.

He thought suddenly of Sara Arad, and her contemporaries. So many people had come to this land through the ages, escaping persecution, seeking a better place. They were still doing it. She was settled in her new home, the kibbutz she had told him about when they had first met, a year ago. He had seen her once more. They had spent the weekend together. He fixed up accommodation for her at the NAAFI, they had gone out by bus together to explore the old Arab city of Acre. John had taken advantage of his rather special status as an Intelligence officer to wear civilian clothes for their outing. He had the feeling Sara was relieved, though she had never given any hint of discomfort at being seen on the arm of a British officer.

He had enjoyed it very much, realized how much he missed feminine company, especially when they danced at the Army Garrison Club. And when he kissed her cheek as he put her on the train to return home on Sunday evening. Jenny had teased him about it in her reply to his letter telling her about the weekend.

His teeth clenched, his jaw hardened at the memory. Teased him when she was already far less innocently involved with this bastard Castleton. Though they hadn't done the deed at that time, not the act itself, no doubt he was well on the way to achieving his filthy way with her, their kisses far more than innocent pecks on the cheek. He groaned softly to himself at his powerlessness to stop these blinding sexual rages consuming him. The tormenting images of details, his own intimate knowledge of Jenny's body, of making love to her, visualizing the physical convolutions of her infidelity.

He even wondered sickly if she knew what the effect of her confession would be, if she derived some added, vicarious thrill from knowing his torture. Then he felt ashamed at even thinking for a second she could be that cruel. And yet — the helplessness engulfed him again, this time at his failure to understand her. To understand that side of her nature which drove her, clearly against all her scruples, all that was decent within her, to do such terrible and wounding things against their love.

He was forced in turn to examine himself, far more deeply than he would wish, to face questions he would rather not face. Was it his sexual inadequacy which was the cause of it? Did he fail to satisfy her as a man? He shied away from the thought even as he mocked savagely at himself for his fastidiousness. Had it to do with his upbringing? Brought up with only female example predominant around him — May and Iris, and their cosy genteelness. The Tea Cosy! The very name taunted him.

But there was part of him that also could not deny his abhorrence, his disgust at what Jenny had done. That was what he could not accept, could never comprehend, in spite of her flagrant admission to him: that her sexual instinct should be so base, and so urgent, that it could override all that was decent, could cancel out all the strength of their love for each other.

It frightened him that he genuinely could not understand it. Or her. He knew sexual excitement, arousal. Of course he did. He had felt the secret throbbing of his manhood when he held Sara as they danced, smelt the fragrance of her, her smooth flesh close, her cheek as he kissed her. He could even accept, though it was hard for him to do so, that it was possible for women, too, to feel such primitive urges. But he would never in a million years succumb to that instinctive lust. The very thought filled him with revulsion. And Jenny had. Worse, she knew it for what it was, did not attempt to hide behind the old lie of love. Clearly, she suffered all the torments of conscience after she had committed her sin. Her decency had forced her to admit it, even though she knew the awful risk she took of destroying their lives together. But that was afterwards.

He found that his steps had led him along the leafy shade at the edge of Persian Street to the lower slope of the mountain. The path narrowed, but led on, with a school on his left, and lower, humbler dwellings on his right. Steps had been cut in places where the slope steepened. And he could see, higher up, a straight pathway had been cut, in terraces, the land either side turned into a neat garden, with a formalized layout of flower-beds and shrubs. He could see the grey, rectangular shape of a larger building, with circular windows high in its solid walls, and tall, arched windows beneath.

He had noticed it before. It stood out, such a large edifice, halfway up the slope. Someone had said it was some kind of temple. Clearly not a mosque, there was no minaret or dome; the roof was quite flat. He had never been this close. He moved on, toiling up the dusty road, saw as he drew nearer that there were slender cypress trees, some already venerably tall, around the building, whose solid stone blocks he could make out now. He came to a simple picket fence and a gate. Directly ahead of him, to the left of the temple building, was an attractive-looking stone bungalow, with a balcony that must offer splendid views of the harbour and bay below.

He wondered briefly if he was trespassing, reached out and opened the gate, shut it behind him. He climbed the last flight of narrow stone steps to the levelled grounds, and was startled at the beauty of the gardens that stretched all round him, the neat paths, the orange trees, and beautifully kept grass. All at once he was struck by the peacefulness, the cool of the air. He turned back, gazed down at the sparkling sea, hazy in the distance, the gradual curve of the bay and the shimmering white villages he could see far away, to the north. Nazareth one of them, perhaps?

A short, brown figure appeared from the direction of the house. His olive complexion made John think he was an Arab, though he was dressed in a white shirt and dark trousers. He wore sandals. 'Sala'am aleykhum,' John began, taking off his cap and wiping at his wet brow.

'Good morning, sir. You're very welcome. Would you like to see the Shrine?' The English was good, the foreign accent noticeable but hard to define. The smile, and the dark eyes fixed on John, were strangely calming, and refreshingly candid, with none of the veiled hostility or, worse, obsequiousness, too readily offered to British personnel from the local populace.

John returned the smile. 'Yes. I'm sorry. You must forgive my ignorance. I'm a stranger. What is this place?'

They fell into step along the gravelled path towards the big building. John was impressed by its plain dignity now that he was up close. 'This is the Shrine of the Báb. And of our beloved Master. Abdu'l Bahá.'

John stopped, touched his arm briefly. 'I'm sorry,' he said again. 'You'll have to explain everything to me. I don't know anything. Is this a Muslim shrine?'

The man smiled again, shook his head. 'We are of the Bah'ái Faith,' he answered. 'The Báb was the Holy One who foretold the coming of our Lord, the Blessed Beauty. Bahá'u'lláh. The Manifestation of God, for our age. As were Moses and Jesus Christ and Muhammad. God sends us His Messengers until we heed His word. We believe all religions are one. We work for the unity of all mankind.'

The enormous simplicity of the stranger's statement made John's brain spin. They reached the stone portico, and faced the high doors. 'Please take off your shoes.' The man was already slipping his feet out of his sandals. He held the door open.

John saw a beautifully patterned eastern

carpet, a heavy chandelier suspended from the ceiling. He could see a recess, with a thin, veil-like curtain over it, and on a low plinth a shallow bowl. It was filled with rose petals.

'I'm not a believer,' John said. 'I mean — I'm Christian by . . . '

Again, the warm smile, a slight movement of the head, which dismissed such distinctions. 'Please. Enter. Pray if you wish. God will hear.'

John felt the emotion flow over him. His throat closed, his eyes filled with tears. The carpet was cool and soft on his stockinged feet, the room seemed full of light and space, and a serenity that wrapped itself around him like a child's familiar blanket as he moved into the blessed spot.

23

Teddy had never been able to visualize hellfire. Now it came to life in front of him. The cracked and bubbling roadways were mere corridors, tunnels through the arching flames, pale and tawny red that seemed to roar on both sides and meet overhead. He wasn't even conscious of much smoke. That came later, with the faint ghost of filtered daylight. He was quite sure at one point they would not survive the night. They were racing down what had been a city centre street, one of the narrower side-streets between tall buildings, and suddenly there didn't seem to be any air left. He could feel his hair singeing, the skin on his face stretched, his clothes starting to smoulder.

A woman walked out of the flames, seemingly untouched. She started to walk to them, arms dramatically outstretched, then she appeared to combust before them, to burst into flames which in seconds engulfed her black-clad body. Before they could reach her, she whirled around, the flames fanning, her scream piercing even over the steady thunder roar, and ran back into the maelstrom. Teddy dreamt about it many times, wondered always if it had been real.

In any case, they were running desperately themselves, in a desolation of fire. When they saw the small canal, they plunged into it thoughtlessly, uncaring whether it was bottomless, ducking under the scummy water, feeling as though they sizzled on contact. Only then did they realize the narrow space was full of thrashing, sobbing figures, women out of their depth, floundering, clawing to hold on to the high sides, all mouldering wooden piles, others trying to support terrified children.

They did what they could when they had recovered themselves sufficiently. Nobody noticed their prison garb. They were too black and filthy in this night of terror. Everyone was the same. Dirt-streaked faces, in which the eyes showed, wild and white, and the teeth, and the vivid red of the lips, like wounds in the crusted flesh.

There were half a dozen of them left. They had no idea what had happened to the rest of the squad, or the guards who had been assigned to them. To Teddy, the idea of guards, and prisoners, of German and English, seemed absurd in this elemental horror. The divisions which had made this nightmare possible came back to him later, after the group had floundered and pulled their way along the lee of the high staithes, the non-swimmers clutching desperately to the shoulders of companions, their feet now and then hitting bottom, squelching in the ooze, stumbling over the countless unseen objects that littered the bottom.

He thought bitterly how elated they'd been when they were first detailed for bomb clearance duties. They were like excited school kids going on a trip when they fell in and climbed into the trucks. 'Extra rations!' people told one another. 'Chance of all kinds of perks.'

'Women!' someone chuckled, nudging his neighbour, and everyone laughed. 'Dead right. You know what parties are like. Their old man away at the front. They miss it, same as us. They don't mind where they get it from. One dick's as good as another, eh, lads?'

There had been some fierce argument. Many said it was collaboration, several refused to go and were put in the cooler. 'We should all refuse to budge. Sit down and don't move. We're within our rights.'

Then the British Senior Officer himself came from the officers' camp down the road. The rumour flew about that the Jerry commandant had told him they would shoot any POWs who refused to obey orders. 'This is basically humanitarian work,' he told them uncomfortably. He sensed the cynicism behind the silent stares. 'It's not directly helping the enemy war effort. It's the civilian population who suffer by the disruption to normal life.'

'Yeah, we know!' a voice called out. 'I was in the East End in fuckin' forty!'

'Silence in the ranks!' an NCO dutifully bellowed. The officer flushed, didn't even ask for the miscreant to be located.

However, their initial excitement at passing beyond the confines of the camp seemed a long while ago, in the horror that had engulfed them since. Teddy could not believe that London had endured anything like this four years before. Surely they would never have stood out against Hitler? Surely the Jerries would pack it in now? There had never been raids of the intensity of this one, he was quite certain. The sky must have been full of Allied planes, and German resistance would surely crumble.

The little group made its cautious way along to where the canal flowed into the wide River Elbe, and joined the exhausted fire crews at a makeshift rest area. No more than 200 yards from them, the black, gutted shapes of vast warehouses stood out, theatrically stage-lit by the flames which shone through their wide, windowless openings. Now, as the sky paled to red dawn, the pall of smoke could be seen, the daylight surreally filtered through its opaqueness. Eventually some elderly home guard members took charge of them. Though some resentment was shown when the firemen and ordinary citizens found out they were POWs, most were too weary or shocked to care. The Britons were fallen in, marched back into the ruined chaos. The fires flickered as if they, too, were tired now. Black, charred remnants of timbers burned like old campfires, now and then buildings toppled, falling in on themselves in a whooshing cloud of dust and tumbling brickwork.

They were put to work, mingling with local civilians, piling the still hot rubble on to carts and lorries, even wheelbarrows. The ruins smouldered, their feet were burnt through their boots. All at once, there was some frantic shouting, and Teddy and two others ran as bidden to a building where the ground floor was all that was left of a high block of flats. The rest reared upward in a mountain of destruction.

Teddy quickly understood that there were some people trapped inside, in a basement. A soot-streaked man had forced a tiny aperture, a black hole only inches wide, through the piles of masonry. Everyone was shaking heads, the man sobbing for breath. They were telling him it was too risky to try widening the hole, or passing through, that the building would collapse further if they tried. Then there came, faint but painfully clear, the cry of a woman, and a child's thin scream.

'I'm skinny enough. I can get through there. Let me go.'

'Don't be bloody mad!' one of his countrymen warned him. 'You can't go in there, Teddy. You'll have the lot on your head.'

But he was already gingerly sliding his legs through, wriggling and contorting his body to pass through the narrow gap. 'Hold on to that rope. And don't even sneeze!' The knock of displaced bricks was terrifying as he slithered forward into blackness, then his feet were hanging in space. There was a soft whoosh and he was engulfed in a choking cloud of dust, and the daylight was shut off behind him. He fell forward, the rope burning at his waist, and landed on all fours on a level stone floor, with about four feet of space above him. The roof of this vault consisted of huge slabs of masonry, stone relics of the original foundations, tumbled together, but forming a shaft leading into the interior.

The air was fetid, and full of the stench of

the fire. He crawled forward carefully, feeling ahead of him with his hands, moving the rubble in his path as though it were preciously fragile. 'Hello? Anybody here?' he called, even his voice hushed in fear that he might bring the tons of stonework down on top of him.

'Ja!' The sobbing voice called out, shrill with fear, and hope, and he edged forward. After a few yards there was a filtering of grey light, as though a thick fog had descended. Dust eddied in the faint beams. Light was getting in from somewhere.

There was a wall standing ahead of him, and the space actually increased, the wrecked roof sloping upward towards it. The woman was curled up, facing the wall. Most of the tattered clothing had been stripped from her back. Its scorched ribbons stirred as she tried to move, and he saw through the gaping holes that her skin was black, too, stripped and blistered at her shoulders, and down the thin back, and her thighs above the black stockings. She moaned quietly now, gabbled urgently, again tried to move, to draw back. Beneath her, cradled by her body, right against the wall was a little girl. The toddler's hair showed blonde through the dirt. It looked oddly thatchlike, until Teddy realized that part of it had been burned away, on her right side near her brow. The ends were frizzled, he could even smell them as he bent close to see how badly she was injured.

The little dress was filthy, but in place still, the blackness of her face, arms and legs, thick soot, the skin unblemished. Her mother's body had shielded her from the flash of searing flame that must have shot through the cellar in a brief but terrifying burst. The woman's face was set in a rictus of agony, but she clutched at Teddy's arm with clawing hand. The nauseous smell of her burnt flesh enveloped him, he stared down in fear while she tried to move the child, then gestured fiercely for him to take the infant. Her voice broke harshly.

'I'll get some help,' he answered, but at her tormented cries, he eased the girl carefully from under her and held the whimpering little form to his chest. He shuffled one handed back along the low tunnel, calling out as he did so. He could see the freshly fallen jumble of bricks which marked the place of his entry. Soon, bricks and dust fell again as rescuers worked as delicately as possible to clear the opening. Suddenly, there was a more ominous rumbling and sliding of rubble, then a crash behind him which sent a hot blast of air and a thick, choking cloud to engulf him. 'Quick!' he screamed, and shielded the child from the material that showered on them at the hasty, scrambled efforts of the men digging them out. At last, there was an opening wide enough for hands to reach down and whisk the little body through the gap. More frantic still, hands clawed down, seized Teddy's arms and dragged him over the jagged bricks, tearing his flesh. Then they were tumbling in a crazy slide down the slope of the ruin, and there was a crack like the detonation of another bomb. The whole building shuddered, caved in yet again.

Teddy lay sobbing on his back, coughing at the noxious brown whorls of dust all around them. He knew that the girl's mother would never emerge alive, and if he had not heeded her desperate warning all three of them would have been entombed.

★ ★ ★

Tony Ellis could feel the sweat clinging to him inside his clothing. He wiped at his face, tried to stop the fierce trembling. He felt like crying. 'I was bloody terrible!' he said. His red head shook in despair. 'I told you! I knew I would be.'

'Nonsense!' Frank's hand fell with possessive heaviness on his shoulder, the fingers dug into his thin frame. 'It was so — authentic.

Wasn't it, *liebchen*?' He appealed to Lucy Stratford, who nodded enthusiastically.

'You were good,' she smiled, and Tony blushed, wanting to believe her. 'Frank's right. It was real. They would know it wasn't an actor reading some script. It sounded absolutely genuine. I thought it was splendid. Honestly.'

He gazed gratefully up at her. Only now, weak-kneed and sweat-soaked with relief that it was over, did the reality of his treachery strike him. He clung for comfort to Frank's murmured words in the privacy of the bed last night. 'This is not for any political cause, my sweet, but for humanity's sake. Your bombers are killing thousands of innocent victims. The women and the children. For four nights now. You know it, you have seen it with your own eyes. Go outside, look at the city. They kill more in these four nights than we have killed English in the entire war.'

Tony thought about the latest weapon launched by Germany. The pilotless planes that would bring the Allies to their knees. There were British women and kids being killed at this very minute. Weren't they innocent, too? It was the same on both sides. Old Winston and his 'fight 'em on the beaches', and the Führer with his 'New Order'. The bombs never seemed to get to them. He was wise enough not to voice his thoughts, though. He had already learnt how mercurial his lover and master could be, the changes of mood that could presage a storm. Survival was the game, as Lucy was always reminding him.

Her gentle urging had been a powerful addition to Frank's encouragement. And the steady look from those candid blue eyes of hers, the touch of her hand on his arm. 'Anything that brings this madness to an end even a day sooner is worth it. Do it. It's right, what they say. This bombing is an outrage. Wholesale slaughter. Mothers and babies don't deserve to die like this.'

It was true. He had been terrified himself. Even though they spent the raids deep in a fortified shelter, they could feel the tremors, hear the crump of the tons of explosives. So, now he had done it, his voice had gone stumblingly over the air waves. Lucy was right, they would know it wasn't an actor all right. He had listened to the recorded playback. Like a kid blundering through a reading list.

Never mind. It was over. He was surviving. And like many others, he suspected, he wasn't pinning any hopes on Hitler's secret weapon changing the course of events. And he had a feeling he'd be in trouble whichever side won. But his new master was laying plans, had already laid them, he wouldn't mind betting. Lieutenant Lipman was also a survivor. And Tony was his darling. For now. He must make sure it stayed that way.

24

The blows which came thick and fast after the major disaster of her unfaithfulness and subsequent confession reduced Jenny to a dazed apathy almost. She had anticipated them, and told herself she was past caring after her torturous letter to John. Even so, she wilted before the blast of fury from Martin Castleton. 'You've told him?' His voice cracked with disbelief. 'You sick little idiot! What for? To get him going, poor sod? To give you a cheap thrill? For Christ's sake!'

His disgust was absolutely genuine. She shared it, but for a different reason. He stormed at her. 'All right. So we were a one-off fling! Fair enough! Conscience makes cowards of us all, as they say. But to go blabbing to your husband about it afterwards! It's pathetic! I thought better of you, Jenny, I really did! And you think it makes him feel better, telling him you've had your bit on the side? Or is this some new, liberated female idea, eh? We can sleep around just like the blokes. Is that it?'

'It made *me* feel better, telling him!' she hissed at him, her face paper white. 'Even if

I've lost him, it's better than lying.'

'This isn't some true confessions story. We're fighting a bloody war. We don't play by the book. We can't afford to. We've got to win. Rules go out of the window. All kinds of rules, private and public. We get through somehow. What bloody harm could our little affair have done John? Ignorance is bliss. But no. You have to screech it from the roof tops. All the way to bloody Haifa! 'Look at me! What a wicked bitch I am! I've had it off with another man!' ' He bellowed with rage and flung his arms wide in the air.

His brutality towards her helped, in a way. The fact of their sleeping together seemed to be forgotten in the fury of the aftermath. Within a week, she received orders that she was being posted to London, to offices in the City, in a building on the second floor over a department store. Banished from the Rome project, she became a member of a typing pool and was bullied constantly by an ATS sergeant for her poor performance, and for the fact that she was the only Wren in the entire section. It was part of the counter-espionage department in which Martin Castleton served, and she was there, as she well knew, so that they could keep close tabs on her — perhaps out of concern, perhaps as a punishment.

She lived like a recluse outside her hours of duty, in gloomy lodgings that housed six of her work mates. In her devastated mood, she had little social contact, and they soon left her alone. 'Bloody miserable little sod!' was the unfeeling epithet which eventually one of them flung at her, but it scarcely mattered. She was so low that the constant attacks of the 'flying bombs', which had begun just before her move, and continued throughout the following months, seemed almost a fitting addendum to her private misery. They struck in daylight as well as the hours of darkness. Even she grew aware that the old, never-say-die spirit of the Blitz of 1940 was sadly lacking. The strain told on the nerves of a people worn by more than four years of danger and deprivation, who had looked forward desperately to a quick victory after the invasion of Normandy. To be faced only a week later by this new and dreadful weapon of mass destruction stretched fortitude in many cases to breaking point.

In her darkest moments, Jenny assured herself she would almost welcome oblivion. Until one evening just before the sixth blacked-out Christmas of the war, one dropped sufficiently near to her lodging house to shake the building noticeably and to blast out the downstairs windows at the back.

Lamps swung and dust showered down, while fresh cracks spidered all over the flaking ceilings and she stumbled and slipped down the stairs on her bottom to the cellar she had scorned, sobbing and praying frantically all the while to be spared. It helped to get her thoughts on a slightly more even keel, where despair mellowed from profoundest black to the grey of despond.

But when she received, after an agonizing interval of more than two weeks, John's wounded, extremely curt reply, which made no reference whatsoever to her admission except to say that he 'needed time to think', and saying that he would or could do nothing at present, she felt that to carry on in her present task, to continue this almost non-existence in the cold anonymity of this military dead-end of a job, was too intolerable to contemplate.

There seemed little hope of her private crisis being resolved in the near future. The euphoria of the second front had rapidly waned. The Allies seemed set to face a prolonged and costly struggle to liberate continental Europe, and her enthusiasm to contribute to their cause had run dry. John's negative response, with no suggestion of a speedy resolution, told her far more elo-quently than any outburst of passionate vituperation how much she had hurt him. He was right. There was nothing either of them could do about it. No words on paper could mend or finally destroy them. They had to face one another in the flesh.

This state of limbo was added torment. She spent painful hours wondering if there was any way they could resurrect their relationship. Did she really want to? She loved John, of course she did, but could she bear the nobility of his forgiveness of her? And how could she forgive herself? Her face and body burned as she pictured their making love again, and, every time, the spectre of two other men's bodies, their passions, lying between them.

When she found out the possibility of securing an early release, she had no real hope that anything would come of it. However, she *was* a trained teacher, and just last year the Ministry of Education had finally waived the regulation about married women not being eligible to carry on in the profession. She had to resist the urge to fling herself at the stuffy figure of the officer who called her in to tell her that her request had been granted. The prospect of her escape from her present suspended state was like a lifeline.

Martin was away, to fresh fields of intrigue

in Eastern Europe somewhere. Not that she had any wish to set eyes on him again. There had been no climactic finale to the affair. Such scenes were definitely not his cup of tea. Nor hers, she assured herself hotly, though with perhaps a shade less certainty. She still suffered when she thought of their briefly tempestuous climax to the long and tortuous relationship. But the physical desire that still disturbed her was indissolubly linked with the shame.

As it was with the memory of Horst Zettel. It hurt her more to face that additional pain. It also made her even less sure that she could ever contemplate a resumption of her marriage, even though she knew that John was, and would be, the abiding love of her life. The hardest pain of all was her knowledge of this, and her betrayal of it, twice, and for such sordid reasons. No amount of self-deception could serve to disguise that fact. The weight of it pressed upon her, making her present existence even less bearable.

John had written twice, short and neutrally cool notes, suggesting yet again that they leave things 'for the time being', until he could get home. There seemed little chance of early release in his case. The situation in

Palestine was fraught with disturbing possibilities. The most recent event had been the hanging of two Palestinian Jews, members of the Stern Gang, for the murder last November of the British resident-minister in Cairo, Lord Moyne.

The actual procedures for escaping from military life were complex. She was transferred to the barracks at Portsmouth, and promptly dismissed on two weeks' end-of-service leave. It no longer struck her as incongruous that she should be sent off for two weeks, and then brought back to be told to go away for good. She drew her pay and travel warrant and set off on the long journey home.

John had told her he would give no hint in his letters home, and advised her to say nothing. Now, the sense of taint, both recent and of long standing, drove her to take a bold and unexpected decision. It seemed that circumstances were dictating her course for her. The route to her home at Keswick had by chance proved a circuitous one, an LNER train up to Newcastle, where she would take a connection across to Carlisle. She determined to break her journey, to visit Hexham and tell May Wright the unpalatable truth.

Even as she made up her mind, she could feel her insides hollowing with fear. Perhaps she was turning herself into a masochist; no longer content with her own self-loathing, she was now seeking confirmation of it by calling down the scourge of others' contempt. She hardly knew what drove her. Desperation? A need for this revilement she knew she merited? Her revelation would hurt May beyond measure. But then, she reflected, would it, really?

She had never felt at ease with May, from the very beginning. John's mother had been against their engagement. In the long interval when John and Jenny had separated, Jenny had often imagined how secretly relieved May must have been, however carefully she hid it from her son. True, John had told her how his mother had urged him to go to Keswick before he reported for military service. And it was that visit which had brought them so dramatically together again.

But May's reaction to the *fait accompli* of the wedding had been mixed. Of course, like her own mother, she had been hurt by their secrecy. But was it more than that? Was it the very fact of the marriage that had disturbed her, despite her good wishes for them? Bitterest of all, Jenny reflected, was that these subsequent events had disastrously proved her to be right in her doubts.

By the time Jenny had changed trains at

Newcastle Central, and journeyed out to the neat little station at Hexham, she was quaking at the task she had set herself. Her courage kept failing. She almost succumbed to the temptation to stay on the platform, to take a train out again and leave it for another day. But some obstinate spark of foolhardiness made her carry on, in spite of her wavering resolve. She walked quickly through the busy town, her bag bumping against her hip, nodding at the ready smiles and greetings for the trim figure in the King's uniform.

Her heart felt as though it had broken loose at the familiar sight of the cottage, the signs of budding spring in the neat garden, reflection of the ordered lives of its owners. She almost giggled hysterically when the door on which she tremblingly knocked was opened by the domestic help, Ruby. 'Why, hinny! Howay in! They've gone over to Teddy's lass at Low Fell. The' should be back any minute. Ah'll put the kettle on. Sit yeself down in the front room there. The'll be over the moon when they see ye!'

Jenny's hands were shaking when she heard the car draw up. They were also wet with perspiration, and she wiped her palms on her skirt as she stood tensely, then made for the door. She was beaten by Ruby, who cried in triumph, 'Look who's come to see ye then!'

and May and Iris yelped with pleasure. She was engulfed in their hugs and kisses. She did not know whether to be dismayed or relieved when she saw Marian and her little girl clambering from the rear of the small car. Even in her distraction, Jenny noticed how much slimmer Marian was. Her face was almost gaunt compared with the round youthfulness she remembered. It suited her. She looked altogether more mature, her beauty more sophisticated.

The delight of May and Iris in seeing her made Jenny ashamed of her earlier thoughts about her mother-in-law, and about her decision to tell the truth. What good would it do? And May would be deeply hurt, if only at the knowledge of how much pain had been caused to her son. But Jenny also felt guilty at her relief that Marian's presence made a confession impossible, at least for the moment. Everything was so complex, Jenny thought wearily.

She took the chance when it came of accompanying Teddy's wife and little Teddie on a walk before tea time. The youngster wanted to go down by the river. 'We'll soon have to stop calling you little Teddie,' Jenny smiled, as the child tugged impatiently at her mother's hand, ready to dash off along the meadow once they had crossed the main

347

road. 'How old are you now?'

'She'll be nine soon, won't you, love?' Marian answered for her. Teddie nodded, raced away. Jenny suddenly realized how much she had missed the company of children, and her work with them. She would be so glad to get back into teaching. She was anxious to do so, before the floods of newly demobilized men poured back on to the work scene. There was talk of emergency training schemes to bring in new teachers — and priority would doubtless be given to the menfolk. Jenny recalled Iris waxing eloquent about the 'last time', when women who had worked, as May did for a while, in factories and elsewhere, doing vital jobs, had been expected to return meekly to home and hearth and surrender their new-won independence.

But her thoughts would not keep from the preoccupation which had seized her on the train journey from London. She realized just how lonely and isolated she had felt these past months, surrounded by girls and yet totally cut off from them in her misery. She suddenly discovered how far from self-sufficient she really was. The urge for a friend, and a confessor, was all at once overpowering. And somehow, she felt different about the quiet figure walking at her side.

Marian no longer seemed the vapid doormat of those long ago pre-war days.

Impulsively, she linked her arm through that of her companion as they strolled in the breezy afternoon. 'Listen,' she said, leaning towards her. 'I've got something to tell you. Something pretty bad, I'm afraid.'

Only later did she recall the look of fear which swept across Marian's face, the instinctive flinching, almost as though she knew already what was coming. That she did not was evident by the round-eyed dismay when Jenny, striving to remain calm, told her tale. It was a bald account, but she left nothing out, save any excuses. She blinked back the tears, stared out over the river to the fields and the distant road beyond to hide them. 'I don't really know why it happened. It wasn't as though I hadn't known him — we'd been meeting together for months.'

Jenny was surprised that the fact of her adultery was not such an earth-shattering revelation to the blonde girl. What seemed to shake Marian more was the news that Jenny had come to Hexham thoroughly determined to make full confession to May. 'My God! You're going to tell her? You can't do that! She'll be totally flabbergasted. You mustn't! Why not wait — and see? You and John — mebbe you'll — be able to sort things out between you. It's over — with this feller, isn't it? You'd never . . . '

The grip on Jenny's arm tightened convulsively. 'Don't tell her!' Marian pleaded, her eyes moist, her features marking how agitated she was. 'Please! Not yet! Leave it to John. It's up to him. If he doesn't want her to know . . . ' Her voice faded unsteadily, she was close to tears.

She stopped, forcing Jenny to a halt. Her grip tightened even further. All at once, her face was white, with two pink spots standing out on her cheeks like badly applied rouge. 'We've all done things. Things we're ashamed of. You're not the only one, Jenny.'

And in the fresh afternoon, in the shadow-dappled grass and the fresh green, tossing trees, Marian told her own sad story, in a low voice haunted with grief.

25

It was difficult for Teddy at first, after the initial euphoria of freedom. The chaos of the last days at the camp, when the guards finally fled, and the groups of ragged, half-starved prisoners stood anxiously at the open gates by the deserted guard hut, listening to the distant rumbles of gunfire, was unreal. They scanned the road to the west, screamed and waved their arms and danced every time the American fighters roared low over them, waiting in hope, and in terror that something even now might go wrong. Some braver or more rash individuals wanted to head out themselves, go to meet the advancing Allies, but most offered caution. 'Stay where y'are, man. Ye never know what ye might run into.'

Then the first Jeeps and armoured cars came in a cloud of dust, and all was a delirium of gorging and drinking and bathing, the dream going on and on, until, one day, Teddy was back in England, in his too-large demob suit and carrying a cheap suitcase of new clothes, nervously heading northward.

It was less of a strain being with his ma and

Aunt I. He clung to them, sought excuses to keep them all together, either at Hexham or at his own home in Low Fell. It was easier to cope with Marian's presence while they were there, and with his daughter, too, for little Teddie, with her long, thin legs, and that unnerving, sombre, dark-eyed stare ('she's got her grandma's eyes, haven't you, love?' Marian repeated with embarrassing fervour, in adulation of his mother), was a complex, nine-year-old stranger.

The three of them had moved shyly into their new life together. 'You're so thin!' Marian had cried, touching the prominent bones of his shoulders when she saw him for the first time without his shirt, reaching out instinctively, then blushing furiously at the contact.

'So are you,' he said. She told him she'd been ill last year. Complicated women's complaints, lasting all through the summer.

'I'm fine now,' she smiled tremulously. 'Now that you're back home again. I can't believe it. I'm so happy!'

But there were disturbing times during those first weeks when he wondered whether that were true. She was different. Not just in her looks. There was something about her, a quietness that seemed to him a sort of wariness, something secret she held back from him. Then all at once, with a rush of guilt, he deduced that she was frightened of him. Frightened of what had happened before, of his desertion of her, his restless dissatisfaction with their life together. It made him feel sick with dismay, and with pity for her. And filled him with a determination to make her understand those days were over.

It was a feeling he had become familiar with over the long years of his captivity. He had tried more than once to tell her of his remorse in letters. Now, both of them appeared choked with mutual embarrassment. He could only hope desperately that she would be reassured, and convinced, with the passing of time that, in being absent from her, he had at last learned truly to love her.

The sexual problem had not helped with the tension of reunion. To his consternation, on their first night in their own bed, in spite of his quivering excitement he had found when he moved to her that he was suddenly impotent. Anxiety only exacerbated the problem, soon gave way to wounded shame. Oddly, he had a sense that Marian was more relieved than anything at his failure. She held him close, his head touching her breast, stroking his hair, telling him how little it mattered. 'It's only natural, isn't it?' she said, while his raging mind screamed with mocking laughter at her choice of word. 'It's been so long. For both of us. Don't worry.'

But he did. For the next few nights he didn't even try, so afraid was he of his inadequacy. He wondered if she was afraid as he was. He lay stiffly at her side, their bodies lightly touching, trying to appear relaxed, and tormented by his thoughts. As he had done during so many lonely nights in the sighing, creaking darkness of the prison hut, he probed relentlessly at the nature of his sexuality. He went over again that strange intimacy he had shared with Tony. Thought of the narrow, expressive face, those long, curling, deep-chestnut lashes, the slender whiteness of the long throat.

Was he then a secret homo? A pansy? Tony had aroused him, physically excited him. How could he deny it? But though he flung the crude, accusatory epithets at himself, equally he could not ignore the compensatory truth. Deprived totally of female presence, of the gentleness of femininity, and in the brutalized institution of the POW camp, his aberration was both explicable and excusable.

He recalled the insidious change in Tony himself; Andy Macaulay's earlier warnings against the constant barrage of jokes and innuendo directed at the youngster by his fellow inmates. Teddy himself had been guilty of it. The transition from a figure of fun a substitute for all the frustrated physical desires the prisoners suffered, to an object of real desire, had taken place without most people realizing it.

Teddy remembered the Christmas concert, the shockingly thrilling transformation, its stunning effect. The air was thick with real lust, the roars of encouragement dangerous, the atmosphere rawly sexual. Any attraction on Teddy's part had been shared by scores of his fellow inmates. And he had sternly resisted, thrust the embryonic temptation away. He had even felt bad about the harsh way he had reacted towards Tony, to let him see how thoroughly he rejected any such notion of deviancy. The hurt expression on the youthful face was another smart to Teddy's tender conscience.

If he really *did* have homosexual leanings, he could surely have found ways to indulge them. With Tony, or with others. There were those who did. The 'beefers' were known, and tolerated, too. Most of them made no secret of it, camped it up far more outrageously than Tony did. Tony's one fatal sin was not his sexual inversion. It was his refusal to take sides. His fraternization with the enemy.

As though seeking further mitigation, Teddy's solitary musings led him to earlier but equally painful and tender memories. The vision of another slim, pale body returned, and one as delicately youthful, almost boyish. Except that, vitally it wasn't — it was sweetly, achingly feminine, and he had not resisted, had been helpless against his impulse and his hunger. The fierce joy of consummation with Rosie Connors returned now to haunt him again, and to fling down the gauntlet of his infidelity in challenge at his feet.

Small wonder then that Marian, after all this time, should seem so distant, be so quiet and ill at ease with him. Innocent as she was, the great burden of his unfaithfulness must surely cast its own aura about them. He was frightened, but more afraid that he would be unable to prove his love to her, and do his penance. He wanted nothing less.

That night in bed he reached for her, moved by the widening of her gaze, her look of tension. 'Listen, love. I know I've let you down badly in the past. I was never a good husband to you. But I want you to know how much I love you. How proud I am of the way you've brought up Teddie, all on your own. How you've managed. I'm happy here. I just want to be with you. I'll never want anything else, Marian. That's God's honest truth.'

He was startled at the depth of passion in the cry she gave, and the frantic way she came into his arms. Her head pressed on his bare chest, she sobbed as he had never heard her cry before. Great, gulping, tearing sobs that shook her, shook them both, while he held her in stunned silence, her tears soaking his chest.

★   ★   ★

When the desperate summons came, in Tony's childish, square writing, for him to visit him in the military detention quarters, it seemed to Teddy that Nemesis was at work. Awkwardly, he explained the urgency of the long and difficult trip to Marian, who accepted it so readily he felt inwardly angry at the further guilt her compliance caused. 'He was only a kid,' he told her gruffly. 'He didn't know what he was doing. The Jerries took advantage of him, that's all.'

The first Teddy had heard of it had been some time after he had been repatriated and sent home for a long leave, before his final demobilization. He had been summoned to make a statement concerning Tony. For a while, he was afraid he might be called to give evidence at the court martial, but he heard nothing further until Tony's own plea had dropped through the letter box. A plea Teddy could not refuse, in spite of his deepest reluctance. It required enormous effort to answer it.

* * *

Teddy set his face in a bright grin, to hide his shock as he stared at the figure seated opposite him through the wire mesh. 'What do you reckon? Not too bad, eh? Free gratis, you know. My demob suit.' At least it didn't hang quite so badly on him, he was filling it a bit better since he had begun to put the weight on again. Six months ago, when he had received it at the centre in south London, he had appeared even more shrunken inside its generous cut.

Tony Ellis looked dangerously close to the breaking point beyond which would lie the refuge of mumbling insanity. His eyes, inside their rings of almost theatrical darkness, flickered incessantly around the bleak visiting-room, darted to Teddy's features as though pleading for help, then flicked away again, aware that there was no hope in the false brightness of Teddy's grin. The auburn hair had been shaved to a stubble which emphasized the thinness of the face and frame beneath — a frame whose muscles seemed to jerk convulsively of their own accord every now and then. He shifted continually in the hard chair to disguise these spasms. The pale, bleached tone of the prison fatigues added to the air of hopelessness.

The surroundings of the detention centre completed the sense of desolation closing about him. Teddy had already visualized something of the nightmare of life here in the military prison at Colchester, apart from the legendary tales of horror he had heard in the years since he had joined the army. The MP corporal who had searched him and led him to the room divided down its middle like a cage had smiled sadistically. 'Little Nazi poofter'll love it in a civvy nick. Benders like him always make out all right. Mind you, some of the boys in here have given him a run for his money. Silly little nancy tried to do 'isself in a couple of months back. That was after he got sentenced to the chop.' He made a sound of disgust deep in his throat. 'I still say they should top the bastard, alongside his boss, old Joyce. Save the expense of keeping him alive.' Lord Haw-Haw had been hanged three days into the new year.

Tony had indeed been sentenced to death by the military court, but his sentence had swiftly been commuted to detention inside a civilian prison, 'at His Majesty's pleasure'. They had picked him up around the time of the final collapse of the Reich, waiting with a bunch of mixed nationalities who had worked as underlings of the propaganda machine. Lucy Stratford had surrendered herself also, and been given a lesser sentence. Her Irish lover had not been found.

Nor was there any trace of Lieutenant Lipman. The mess of reality brought no cleanly satisfying confrontations with justice. Though of course, he might well be unearthed months from now. In the chaos of defeated Germany, all kinds of criminal scum were lying low. He could be hiding under an assumed identity in any ruined city or town, or in one of the packed camps for the thousands of displaced persons. He might be long dead and rotting somewhere, and please let it be so. Chances were they would never know.

Teddy had wanted to stand up for Tony, but there was little he could say. The impersonal bureaucracy of official just deserts wasn't interested in his opinion. 'Was he to your knowledge carrying on homosexual relationships with German military personnel while he was in the camp?' the young Intelligence Corps sergeant who looked like a schoolmaster pursued, and pursed his lips in disapproval when Teddy stubbornly answered,

'No. Not to *my* knowledge.'

In spite of all the evidence, the death sentence stunned everyone, including those who had more readily supported the prosecution than Teddy. He had to wait further weeks, over the first peacetime Christmas, and the first with his loved ones for six years, before permission came through for this visit. And now Teddy felt helpless at the minutes seeping, wasted, away, marked by the black hands of the large wall clock and its resounding tick.

'What's all this about you trying to do yourself in?' he said, with desperate aggression. 'Christ! They just let you off the hook and you go and do something like that. You've got to stick it out, man. While there's life, eh?'

The body jerked, his shoulders dipped as Tony twisted once more, swung back and forth in his seat. 'I had to get out of here. Any way. Feet first if I had to. It didn't matter.' The starkness of his reply sickened Teddy. 'They're animals in here!' the low, tormented voice continued. 'Even for a fruit like me there's limits!'

'You'll be out of here soon. You've got my address. Let me know where they send you. I'll write. And visit.'

'Will you? Promise?' The gaze held Teddy, made his heart ache with compassion. Tony shuddered, his voice came closer to breaking than it had all through their meeting. 'I'll be an old codger before I meet that missus and daughter of yours.'

'No, course you won't. Keep your nose clean. Give it a year or two, when everybody's calmed down. They can shorten your sentence. Parole you. Anything.' If only you hadn't made that stupid bloody broadcast, Teddy thought, as the dreaded moment of parting approached. That's why they threw the book at you, you poor little sod. Already the guard was bellowing, the prisoners springing up to attention like automatons behind the cage.

'Bye, Teddy. Say hello to your family for me. You'll probably have another six kids before I see them.'

Teddy was relieved that the ordeal was over, and a little daunted by the prospect of the long evening and night's travel in the raw January weather. His heart filled with gratitude at the thought of going home. There were problems still to be faced there, he knew well enough. But he was going back home. To Marian and Teddie.

26

'Come on. Sit down. Let's eat first. Before we talk, I mean!' Jenny said. John smiled, and sat opposite her. She gestured at the quick meal she had prepared. 'Is it all right? I mean — there's no special rules — about what you can eat? I don't know — you don't look any different, except you're very brown.' She shrugged helplessly. 'I thought you might be wearing a long nightshirt and a turban, or something.' He laughed, a genuine chuckle of amusement, and she relaxed a little. She knew she was sounding shrill and twittery, but she couldn't help it.

His letters over the past ten months had not prepared her for this meeting. By mutual consent, they had not discussed their personal crisis. He had written regularly, but not often, perhaps once a month — far less than she would have wished. Several times she had sat at her table and written passionately, heart-searchingly, of her guilt and love, her tears streaming down her face. But always she had torn up the pages, cast them aside, and waited until she could reply to his correspondence, in the same neutral tone.

She told him of her decision not to head back home after her demob, and of her post at a school in Raynes Park, and her glorified bedsit — a kitchenette with just enough room for an ancient stove and a sink, and a shared bathroom down a flight of stairs. He had answered that he could quite understand her need to be distanced from family, to make a fresh start in a completely new environment.

His letters were cool, detached — and utterly strange to her. Especially when he wrote more and more about this strange religious sect he had become involved with, of whom she had never heard. The Bahá'í Faith. Even the name sounded mystically eastern and alien. It didn't help her to feel any more at ease with it. It only served to emphasize the great gulf that had opened between them, the shattering that had started with her infidelity and its confession. This new religion he had found was another frightening example of the barrier, the separateness which had arisen between them. She had no part in it, even resented it, bitterly, though she could understand all too well the illogicality of her feeling. After all, what right had she to share anything with him now?

When, at last, he had written telling her of

his departure from Palestine, by troopship, and the date of his arrival at Southampton, she had felt panic. Then a desperate relief that the state of limbo would soon be over. I'll be there to meet you, she wrote, wondering if she had any right, if he might even refuse her.

It was a new, but not exactly happy world he was returning to. The day his ship docked, bread rationing began in Britain, and in the land he had left behind terrorists blew up a wing of the King David Hotel, killing ninety-one, many of them key administrators of the troubled territory. The events in both places mirrored the private turbulence which gripped both the strained figures who sought each other out. It was a year since hostilities had ceased. There were no longer thumping bands and guards of honour and flying streamers, but troopship arrivals were still a regular occurrence, and a sizeable crowd of waving, laughing, weeping relatives stood on the quayside.

Her fair hair caught the sun. She was bareheaded, and her hair blew across her face, longer than he remembered it. Her arm was raised, she had seen him. It was a tentative moment.

Two hours later, they clutched at each other, instinctively, obliviously, and his body ached with love when he felt her slenderness against him, her trembling, the rack of her sobs. Her face glistened, smeared with tears, her mascara in dark runnels like blood from her eyes. 'I wasn't going to do any of this — I'm sorry — I shouldn't.'

In the train, and then in the small apartment, the new awkwardness, the gentle, nervous consideration, had set in. 'We'll talk later. After we've eaten.' Neither of them seemed willing, or able, to find the courage. Again, she seized on the subject of his new religion, grateful now to use it as a delaying tactic. He had told her a lot about it in his letters, its tenets, its strange history.

He laughed at her speculative ignorance. 'No funny robes, or hats. Not many prohibitions, as far as food goes. No booze, though.' He held up the cigarette he had just lit. 'They're not keen on this. Or any other drugs, but it's not a case of 'Thou shalt not'.'

She knew already that one of its basic beliefs was that all religions were essentially one. That God had sent His messengers to this world at various stages in humanity's development. Krishna, Moses, Zarathustra, Buddha, Christ, Muhammad — and now, the Holy One for our age, Bahá'u'lláh. And His co-founder, His forerunner, known as the Báb, the Gate, His John the Baptist, who had announced His coming, and met a martyr's death, executed in 1850. Less than a hundred years ago! she had to keep reminding herself, in Persia. And Bahá'u'lláh Himself, exiled by the Turks to the Holy Land, spent forty years in prison, and died only fifty-four years ago, in 1892.

All so strange, and foreign to her. Love mankind, work for its unity. That was the Bahá'í belief. Simple enough, and nothing new. Why should it seem so alien? 'Tell me about it,' she asked again, now, almost desperately, it seemed to John.

He stared at her eyes, the plea he saw there. He gave a little shrug. 'I haven't actually declared,' he said softly. 'That means I haven't officially become a member of the Faith.' His mind went back to that spacious, simply furnished room in the dignified, grey stone house at the foot of Carmel. The Master's House. Abdu'l-Bahá, the Servant of Glory. Bahá'u'lláh's son, who had shared His exile and imprisonment.

He had assumed the mantle of leadership, and been knighted by the British for his humane work in Palestine during the Great War, and died, worn out by his life of sacrifice, at the age of seventy-five, in that house at the foot of the mountain. There were several portraits of him, as an old man, with flowing white beard, calm, serene eyes that told of suffering and of triumph. There was one in the Pilgrim House, near the shrine where his remains lay beside those of the Báb. It hung in the light, airy room whose windows opened out across the wide bay, and looked towards the distant Bhají, and the mansion where stood the shrine of Bahá'u'lláh Himself, the Holiest of all places, which John had visited.

But the portrait on the wall in the Master's House, in that silent room, which he had seen most recently, just before he left Palestine, had affected John deepest. The blue eyes had looked at him, and into him. He had sat there, on the cushioned bench seat which ran along the wall opposite, and gazed until his eyes had filled with water, and then closed in involuntary prayer. It was a feeling so powerful, at once sad and yet immensely peaceful. He had felt it before, disturbing, profound, the first time he had entered the Shrine of the Báb, all those months ago, and the custodian had left him.

The cool of the uneven floor had struck up through his stockinged feet. He had sat, humbly, in one corner of the deserted room, leaned weakly against the plain, whitewashed wall, almost as though he had a sudden urge to sleep, his head back, his eyes closed. And felt the peace and holiness of the spot wash over him, cover him like a blanket of warm familiarity.

He felt it again, as he sat facing the portrait, all alone, yet comforted by the presence of so much goodness. He had met a good many believers in those months since he had stumbled upon the Faith. At first, he had examined his own feelings critically, wondering why these ordinary men, and women, should have such a profound influence on him. You're just feeling vulnerable, he told himself. You've lost Jenny, everything you valued. You're looking for a substitute.

But it wasn't the truth. Their inner strength, the simplicity of their faith and their practice of it, astounded and moved him. Like Hugh Porrit, the army chaplain, waiting like John to be released from military service and from his ordination as an Anglican minister. They spent many hours together, and with other believers, in the Pilgrim House, discussing the Faith, and working in many practical ways to help the widely differing communities that made up Haifa.

'Are you really sure you want to give up the ministry?' John asked him, both doubtful and impressed at his conviction. It seemed a drastic step to take. The priest had impressed him further by his absolute certainty.

It was Hugh who had arranged this final

meeting, at the House of Abdu'l-Bahá, one which, John knew now, he was very privileged to be granted. A meeting with the Master's grandson, Shoghi Effendi, the Guardian of the Faith, who had been appointed in his grandfather's will, to take over the leadership.

They had left John alone, in this room where Abdu'l-Bahá had always received the countless pilgrims who had made their way to the blessed spot, to collect his thoughts — and to absorb the spirituality of such a special place, he realized later. It was an essential, and very precious interval.

The Guardian came and talked for an hour, sitting at one end of the long settee, smilingly telling John that it was the very spot where his grandfather liked to sit when meeting pilgrims. When John awkwardly confessed his still somewhat uncertain views, he was told that the first essential condition of the Faith was that one should seek the truth, independently, and sincerely. 'Look with your own eyes, and not through the eyes of others. Free your heart from prejudice. Be sincere in your search. God will guide you.'

John recalled the unassuming, quiet figure now, and the profound effect of meeting him, the time they had spent. It was later that the real profundity had settled on him, in the long, useful hours of contemplation and review he had undergone during the voyage home. It was with him still, he realized, as he tried now to tell Jenny something of what it all meant.

'It's something — I have to meet some other people here in England. There are some Baha'is up north. I think it's something I need. I can't ignore it.'

He sounded so unsure, his gaze uncertain as he looked at her, that her heart went out to him. With a jolt, she found she had for several moments forgotten the great disaster of their broken marriage, the wreck of their life together. She knew the time had come, the time that she had both longed for, and dreaded.

'It shows how different we've become,' she said tremulously. She looked at him. 'I can't understand it, this new belief. Any of it. And — me. Well, you know what I've done. And I'm sure you can't understand *that*, either.' She shook her head, fought down the threat of weeping. 'I can't understand it myself.' She visibly sagged, worn out by the tension she had been carrying within her all day, and longer. 'I don't know why I did it. Except . . . ' and suddenly the tears were there, she was crying, and she no longer cared. The words poured out of her, words she had not expected or thought to say, an impassioned explanation of the betrayal which she had just told him was inexplicable.

'It was you! I was missing you so much — I was so lonely, and miserable, I couldn't stand it any more. Being alone — wanting you — and sitting with Martin, being so close to him.'

Her wet face was torn with an anguish that tore at him. Her voice broke, it was raw, tearing at him, too, so that he could hardly breathe, could not speak, but listened to the racking sobs. 'I needed you — wanted you — all the time we were apart. I used to touch myself — rouse myself — I couldn't help it. That's what it's like, that's what *I'm* like! Not all hearts and flowers. It's terrible — ' with a cry, she collapsed once more, her body slumped, her head bowed, and he watched the dark honey of her hair spill over her arms, the curve of her shoulders shaking with the cataract of her grief.

He moved without thought, knelt at her side, then his hand hesitated as it reached out towards her. It moved again, but rested lightly on her shoulder, gentle, uncertain. It was she who twisted round, came to him, clung desperately to him, burying herself against him, so that his arms came up, in spite of himself, and held her to him, rocking her softly while they hung swaying on the floor.

27

May lay in the dark, listening to the sounds of the cottage settling itself down to sleep. She could see the starlit paleness of the square of window, the gently stirring flowered curtains. Still, after more than a year now, she felt a surge of relief that the oppressive seal of the blackout drapes were gone. She thought of the sunlike brilliance of the man-made terror which had last year burst in the sky over Japan, heralding a new, perhaps final era in man's powers of destruction. Blackout, gasmasks, buckets of sand and water and stirrup pumps, were like stone age weapons now. That world had gone for good. It should be a dawning of hope. They had crushed the forces of evil that had been let loose on the world — again! she thought, ashamed of her cynicism.

Last time, when war had ended in victory, she had been too numbed, too wrapped in her own despair at Jack's loss, even to notice the hysterical celebration going on all about her. Now, she felt a deep uneasiness inside at so much change. She clung like a fearful child to the comfort of familiar things around her.

She felt Iris stir in her sleep, heard the soft flubber of escaping breath at her half-snoring exhalation. She moved closer against the warm bulk, slipped her arms around her, and pressed her belly into the broad meatiness of the curving buttocks. A wave of emotion swept through her, her facial muscles twitched as she smiled in the darkness. It was a deep pleasure to feel that body against her, to fit herself so snugly round it. Almost a sensual pleasure, she acknowledged, a little guiltily, yet amused at the notion. Perhaps she was sexually attracted after all, as Julia's cruel gibes had hinted on more than one occasion. Perhaps she and Iris could have become lovers, in the physical sense. She squeezed more tightly, as if in defiance, and Iris stirred, grunted, and May eased the pressure, genuinely guilty now at her idiotic thoughts.

Oh, Jack! How long now? Twenty-nine years since you left me. I still remember, and still miss you, my dear. She talked frequently to her dead husband when she was in bed. It was like a substitute for prayer, she often thought. Not that she didn't pray, too, as soon as she was settled with the light out. You don't mind me loving Iris, do you? In every way except sex, she's had to take your place, love.

What would have happened if he had

survived? she wondered. She might have had a whole string of kids. Five or six, like her Mam, all grown up now and getting on with their lives. She might have been gran to a whole host of children, instead of just dear little Teddie. Surely they'd have to get round to calling her Edwina soon? She was turning into a right leggy young madam.

Guilt came again, at her too sombre thoughts. She should be weeping with gratitude. God had spared both her boys, and they were sleeping safe and sound, all under her roof again, either side of her in the cottage they had grown up in, and with their wives beside them, as it should be. How many times had she prayed for that miracle to happen, for them to be spared through all the dangers of the past six years? That was why she was able to cuddle up to Iris's solid body and think her daft thoughts, for they had to 'bunk up together' to make room for them all.

It had been a good 'do', the long awaited celebration and thanksgiving for the return of her sons. Of course, Teddy had been home a year himself, and they had rejoiced at his home-coming, but now John was back, too. And different. Different as they all were. She wondered if she were being hyper-sensitive, overemphasizing the changes. But no. They were too glaring to be dismissed.

Both her sons' marriages disturbed her, made her uneasy, though there was nothing on the surface to cause her anxiety. She tried to tell herself again, with John and Jenny's return to the scene, just as she had numerous times over Teddy and Marian, that the troubled years spent apart were bound to have a deep effect on the young couples. It would have been just the same with her and Jack, if he had survived, and come back to her after those terrible times. It would have been hard for them — but no, really, she couldn't believe it, not for her and Jack. Their love would have been there, they would have been together again, in every way.

Teddy would be all right, she kept on telling herself in the months that he had been back. He was quieter, more self-contained. Not a bad thing. He was no longer the impetuous, volatile boy he had been before the war, making those rash and costly mistakes that had hurt poor Marian so. He was responsible, aware of his duty now; he wouldn't let them down again. It was Marian who worried her more. The girl was so quiet, turned in on herself somehow. Of course, she had always been quiet, wouldn't say boo to a goose, but that had been different. She had been so open then, so naïve, and too willing to please. Now her quietness was different, a wariness, as though she had something locked up inside her. Once or twice, May had suddenly caught a look of disturbing fear in her face — a scared expression which May could find no reason for.

The miscarriage in the spring had been a bitter blow. From the couple's guarded talk, she had assumed there was a strong possibility that Marian might not be able to have any more children. But that surely could not account for her change of character, to this tense withdrawal? They had Teddie, who was growing into a lovely, lively girl. And they were reunited. That should be enough for them.

Her thoughts moved to John. Newly home, her eldest boy, she had wept such tears of thankfulness when she held him for the first time in five years. But already, in the very few days he had been home, she had noticed such deep changes.

This new religion of his — it had worried her when he had written of it. Things were so different, fanatical out there. A melting pot. And one that was going to erupt in renewed violence according to the news. After all the horrors of the past six years, British boys' lives were still being threatened — and taken

— out there. She felt ashamed at her secret hope that, once he had picked up the reins of everyday life back home, this fervour, or whatever, might wear off.

He was different, though, she could tell already. Quieter even than before, with a quiet strength, she acknowledged reluctantly, almost a serenity. He didn't argue, wouldn't have mentioned it probably, had it not been for her probing, and Teddy's down-to-earth scepticism. 'What? You're not allowed to have a drink, for God's sake? That's no good, man!'

She had shushed him, but could not help having a go herself. 'What's wrong with church and chapel?' she had been forced to come out with. 'With Christianity?' She had never been an ardent believer, she would always have some corners of doubt and confusion, but she was no atheist.

'Nothing, Mam,' John had smiled. 'Nothing at all. Like all religions. They're all telling us the same thing. They're all right.'

'Eh? That can't be. Look at the place you've just come from. There's been more fights in the name of religion — '

'That's not the fault of religion. That's what man has done with it.'

He had changed the subject, and she had been glad to let it go. There were other things to worry her more. It had become increasingly obvious, even in the space of a few hours, that, just as May had observed with Teddy and Marian, things were far from right between John and Jenny. And to a far greater degree. Almost too worrying for her to dwell on, though, now, in the silence and solitude of the night, she was helpless to prevent it.

She had joked about how everybody would have to make the best of the crowded accommodation. She wanted them all to stay after the party, to have all her loved ones under one roof, after so long apart. 'You'll just have to squash up and manage in a three-quarter bed,' she chuckled, with a knowing glance at John and Jenny. She was inwardly mortified at the look of naked pain and shame on Jenny's face — the flood of colour which swept over her features, and her start as though a raw nerve had been touched.

'That's fine, Mam,' John answered firmly, after a pause which had lasted less than a second, and seemed like an eternity.

May's brain had raced frantically. Why should the very mention of husband and wife sharing a bed spark off such a reaction? In a panic, she had pushed it away from the forefront of her mind. It returned to disturb her now. She had watched them, with a kind of cold, inner fear, after that.

John was solicitous towards his wife, his gentleness as disquieting as any coldness would have been. And Jenny was so untypically reserved, and silent, so unlike the assured personality which had, in earlier days, sometimes irritated May in its confidence.

Yet again, she stirred against Iris's comforting bulk, and tried to dismiss her gloomy reflections. Come on. The boys are back home. Safe and sound. Things will work out. They have time now to make it so. She recalled all at once Iris's neatly scripted words in little Teddie's autograph book on her last birthday.

All will be well,
And all will be well,
And all manner of things will be well.

Julian of Norwich.

The prayer, or whatever it was, had stuck in her mind. She repeated the words in her head now, and took comfort from them. They will be, she told herself, and snuggled in the warmth of the bed. Everything changed, things *had* to change. Surely she had learned the lesson in her half century of life?

Fifty-two next month, Jack, she said to the darkness. And we've come through this last lot, thank the Lord. We'll cope with what's waiting for us, with help, won't we?

Goodnight, my love.

And she turned, burrowed afresh into the peaceful, warm hump of flesh that lovingly accommodated her even in its unconscious state.

THE END

We do hope that you have enjoyed reading this large print book.

Did you know that all of our titles are available for purchase?

We publish a wide range of high quality large print books including:
Romances, Mysteries, Classics
General Fiction
Non Fiction and Westerns

Special interest titles available in large print are:
The Little Oxford Dictionary
Music Book
Song Book
Hymn Book
Service Book

Also available from us courtesy of Oxford University Press:
Young Readers' Dictionary
(large print edition)
Young Readers' Thesaurus
(large print edition)

For further information or a free brochure, please contact us at:
Ulverscroft Large Print Books Ltd.,
The Green, Bradgate Road, Anstey,
Leicester, LE7 7FU, England.
Tel: (00 44) **0116 236 4325**
Fax: (00 44) **0116 234 0205**

C1553376I1

Please return on or before the latest date above.
You can renew online at www.kent.gov.uk/libs
or by telephone 08458 247 200

WITHDRAWN

0 3 MAR 2020

H.L.S. Round 3
'FA

HCS o/c
2/14

Byline.

- 8 NOV 2016

KENT ME19 4AL
WEST MALLING
KINGS HILL
GIBSON DRIVE
KENT LIBRARIES

HoLDEN

£t.20
£10.3
LS 94
£hc 12.40